in art galleries around the inspirational journey, *Turning the Page*, has touched many lives. She is also the author of *The Divine Light*.

*Delhi: Anything Goes* was Anita's debut novel.

Dividing her time between Delhi, London and New York, Anita took to writing to express the ever-changing canvas of her life.

ANITA KUMAR is a trained calligrapher and an artist. She has held exhibitions on calligraphed Ganeshas and 'Oms' in art galleries around the world. Her

# CAPPUCCINO
# CONFESSIONS

Anita Kumar

**Om Books International**

First published in 2017 by

## Om Books International

**Corporate & Editorial Office**
A-12, Sector 64, Noida 201 301
Uttar Pradesh, India
Phone: +91 120 477 4100
Email: editorial@ombooks.com
Website: www.ombooksinternational.com

**Sales Office**
107, Ansari Road, Darya Ganj,
New Delhi 110 002, India
Phone: +91 11 4000 9000
Fax: +91 11 2327 8091
Email: sales@ombooks.com
Website: www.ombooks.com

Text copyright © Anita Kumar, 2017

ALL RIGHTS RESERVED. No part of this book may be reproduced or
transmitted in any form by any means, electronic or mechanical, including
photocopying and recording, or by any information storage and retrieval
system, except as may be expressly permitted in writing by the publisher.

ISBN: 978-93-5276-121-0

Printed in India

10 9 8 7 6 5 4 3 2 1

Dedicated to my mother,
my strength, courage and inspiration.

*Each progressive spirit is opposed by a thousand mediocre minds appointed to guard the past.*

Maurice Maeterlinck

Here's to all the men and women who have been separated from their innate dignity and have been denied their birthright to honour their instincts. May they not only believe in who they are but also act on who they are with utmost pride and dignity, without a grain of guilt. They are amazing, just the way they are.

# PROLOGUE

Mom,

I began writing this book on your bed when you were seriously sick.

And then you were gone.

I still wait for you to call out my name and ask me to take you out for coffee, which I did, practically on a daily basis. I remember the excitement in your eyes to dress up in one of your favourite suits. You wore your lipstick gracefully and always carried a bag that matched the colour of your suit and shoes.

You were loved so dearly mom, and I miss you still as I recall those priceless moments when I watched you so closely. In a sense, I feel you through me. On many occasions, I do and say as you would have—you are my inspiration.

This book is exclusively for you because you are the one who insisted that I don't stop writing even when you were on your deathbed, suffering beyond belief.

Thank you for being my mom in this lifetime and thank you for believing in me.

I hope we do meet again, preferably with you as my mom once more, but until then, enjoy your onward journey.

# 1

"Hold your breath, Ma!" I said, calmly outwardly, but inwardly, I was turbulent like the Worli Seaface in Mumbai. There were waves of anxiety and panic whirling through me as I tried desperately, but most ineffectively, to hold on to my breath while attempting to utter the words considered most abhorrent by every 'Indian'. Indians all across the world would've found my expression offensive and off limits and in addition, I would be criticised, cold-shouldered and at best, branded. Simply being Indian meant shirking these words like a deadly disease!

Prior to the confrontation with Ma, I had rehearsed my lines recurrently in front of the mirror and memorised them to my memory. I dropped my shoulders back, drew deep breaths and recited the words like a verse from a kindergarten poem, except I was reasonably convinced the lyrics wouldn't be as poetic to Ma's ears, and would definitely not make her soul dance. Nonetheless, I had come prepared with the same confidence and poise Ma had always presented herself with.

Ma was draped in an orange cotton sari with red paisley designs splashed over it. A tilak—a perfectly round dot of red powder—ornamented the centre of her glowing and almost creaseless forehead, endorsing her marital status. It also worked wonders when it came to evading men from giving her the lustfully glad eye. She was comely, my

Ma—with an aura that oozed a detached sophistication. She wore her grace and beauty even more intuitively as she advanced in years. Her outer composure mirrored her inner self, and I deeply admired her effortless lean figure and excellent mannerisms that reflected her elite upbringing. Her demeanour was appreciated by everyone who interacted with her, and her broad smile that occasionally broke into a slight chuckle always left a pleasant impression on people. She was perfectly polished and poised, and sometimes, I wished her uncompromising elegance had brushed off on me.

At this heart-wrenching moment, however, I quietly mused if she would be able to remember and retain everything she had coached herself to befit Mumbai high society. Savage situations potentially bring out our latent hostility and often, we aren't aware of its presence within us, until our values are brutally challenged. With the benefit of hindsight, we often regret our unruly behaviour, but during such fiery moments, the inner demons surface to sabotage the layers of civility consciously constructed over the years. Most of us know first-hand how ridiculously simple it is to break something in an instance—the same thing that we build and preserve over years of sweat and sacrifice.

Ma was usually calm in situations. That was not surprising, given she had conformed, all her life, to societal norms whilst flattering others' endless expectations. She was not just conditioned to be a respectable and dutiful housewife, but also a daughter-in-law, aunt, and sister-in-law—the numerous roles she adeptly adapted herself to, overnight. She slept with a complete stranger—who was later to be my father—without a moment's hesitation, and on waking up the following morning after the proverbial suhaag raat, she was handed a script, enabling her to enact her innumerable roles with utmost finesse and flair. This obviously required her to forgo her own desires and dreams that she had presumably modelled in her teenage head until she reached adulthood.

She never got to the chance to edit her script or re-write it; she simply did what was expected, not giving the slightest thought to what she herself aspired for. Ma skilfully abandoned the faculty where her own private pleasures and intimate imaginations resided. A woman was innately programmed to adjust, no matter how unjust the situation was. It was one of life's contests very few women shied away from. They believed it to be their foremost 'duty', as natural to them as giving birth, or breathing. Ma was a conformist and that is precisely how my three elder sisters, my younger brother and I were nurtured—taught to conform to conventions without questions. No one had dared to swim against the current. Even when they momentarily risked stepping out of line, or be different from the herd, they were dragged back in their place and calmness was restored—at least in Ma's life. We had learned to convert gloom to bloom within our limits, besides the rebel in me, as I had inherited Papa's genes.

Papa conveniently left the family dealings to Ma, so he had minimal awareness of the events unfolding in our private lives. Along with time, he neither had the fondness nor the forbearance to be involved, so he had convinced Ma she was significantly superior at nurturing the children and cultivating their interests. He was barely and rarely able to call out the exact names of the maids and the only two names that rolled smoothly off his tongue were Ramu, his personal servant and Suraj, his chauffeur. I was somewhat convinced he had lent these names to them for his own convenience, since these were easy to memorise. Both the men exceeded 25 years of subservience and had silently endured Papa's unpredictable behaviour that could turn the blue skies melancholic.

Monetarily, he gave Ma and all his children with everything, provided Ma bailed him out of our emotional issues. He didn't have the time to apprehend the female hormones, so he preferred to involve himself only with my brother's upbringing. When my brother was born, Papa celebrated with family and friends for an entire week. Unable to contain his joy or his bank balance, he showered on Ma with uncut diamond sets and ornate gold bangles, enough to set up her very own jewellery store. Ma was evidently elated as she planned on passing on the exquisite sets as part of our trousseau. I rejected them at once because I found them outrageously outdated. Also, my sisters had drawn out the most exclusive ones for themselves. They tactfully suggested to her that retaining the remaining ones for my marriage would be a good idea, as they would "sit well around my neck." Truthfully, they weren't even decent enough to strangulate my sisters with.

Ma raised four girls with identical values, and she blatantly refused to revise her rulebook with time. The same severity in conduct was infused in all of us, with no regard to the fact that I was the youngest and by my time, the Indian mindset had turned considerably liberal. But no matter what, Ma remained consistent in her principles and practice, and neither of the daughters could soft soap her into bending to our whims. She could never understand we were all born to times in which we naturally fit and she couldn't coerce time to befit our values.

The softness in her rarely revealed itself, except the times she most enthusiastically bathed the idols of her Gods at the crack of dawn. Once she had bathed herself, she would sit reverently before each idol—to bathe, dress and ornament them with genuine 21-carat gold trinkets. As a child, I was subjected to her conversations with her innumerable Gods. I would be compelled to rise at still-not-alive o'clock just so she could assume the satisfaction of instilling these rituals in me, with the hope that someday my own children would be willing participants. To a two-year old, they made as much sense as algebra, but I was far too young back then to oppose. She would hand me some rose petals and would instruct me to offer them to each of the anticipating Gods, after which I would bow my drowsy, blasé head to them. My London-returned teddy would faithfully sit on my lap to ascertain the same mundane practices every morning, but two years later, the poor chap was buried deep in some trash bin and probably burnt to ashes. The rituals clearly didn't serve him in any capacity and I earnestly ask myself today if I am likely to end up with the same fate someday.

If that wasn't enough, Ma would then shove a sugar-laden saffron ball down my throat, nauseating my palate at the unearthly hour. It was meant to cure me of my 'past lives' ill deeds' and invite prosperity into my adult life.

Now that I had entered that phase, I questioned if the same rituals contained the potency to cure Ma of her narrow-mindedness and most impractical beliefs that had no relevance in today's world. On second thoughts, the sugar-laden saffron balls were not completely irrelevant—they did contribute to Ma's diabetes.

Nevertheless, that was the giving side of her disposition, and her forgiving side was yet to be witnessed once I tendered a new script I had dared to draft. I speculated how relentlessly my words would disturb her even-temperedness and the time it would take for her to come to terms with my new reality. I understood the repercussions could be harsh, but I was clueless about the intensity of the explosion. How could I possibly predict the reaction to what I was about to recount when neither of my siblings had ever pronounced the four repugnant words before her?

She was preoccupied as usual—both her professional and social calendars more crammed than mine ever had been. She usually scribbled a note near her landline as a reminder for either an elite social gathering or a charity event in the city, besides her office meetings. She was old-fashioned and preferred the passé pen on paper reminders over feeding significant appointments in her mobile phone. It was sufficient that she answered her phone and was capable of calling other people. She vehemently voiced her opinion on the 'appalling nature' of our desires for the latest gadgets. In addition to that, she often talked about the detriments of social media that encouraged people to seek a quick fix to their limp marriages, causing a rise in the divorce rate across the world. She was concerned about the attention deficiency in youth who, according to her, was compulsively obsessed with social media sites such as Facebook and Instagram. Snapchat was another such app she had made her acquaintance with through her grandchildren, but was evidently uninspired. These good-for-nothing elements, according to her, gave complete strangers a window into others' lives, only making them vulnerable. Children, it seemed, preferred the machine-driven friends to the emotion-driven ones.

She often sat her grandchildren down to challenge its wider benefits and they in turn, would go the extra mile to convince her that sans technology, they couldn't accomplish much. They questioned their grandma if she preferred them to lag behind in their respective schools and colleges, as it was impossible to complete their assignments without technology. Perhaps, they advised tenderly, she needed to update her worldview while they proceeded to update their statuses on Facebook, Instagram, WhatsApp, and whatever else there was.

"I don't understand their incessant need to upload photos every day. It's ludicrous," she commented often. She always felt the need to squeeze the last word in and her grandchildren eventually succumbed, only to silence her. Their nod was neither affirmative, or otherwise, but was instead a silent 'whatever!' After all, grandma was nowhere close to being as 'awesome' or as 'sick' as the next cutting edge gadget.

They knew no different, having been born into gadgets; quite literally. Their mothers—after their birth—regardless of how exhausted they were from the labour, had rushed to update their Facebook status as soon as the umbilical cord was severed. On delivering my own son, the nurses were still wiping him when I had logged in on Facebook to post his pictures. I still remember the happiness of receiving 196 likes and 55 comments.

There was a void in every generation, but then, there will always be something missing. After all, the relentlessness of one's addictions and cravings is in direct proportion to the gravity of the vacuum in their lives.

"Ma, I really insist on having a chat with you regarding a pressing matter. May I have your complete attention, *please*?" I said, calmly but urgently. I pursed my lips and lowered my eyes, so that she would sense the tension on my face and realise there was no room for procrastination. She was usually instinctive about her children's body language and would always pose a question herself, even if we held our tongue in most situations. This time, however, she missed the cue and I was disappointed that I had to address the issue before she noticed anything untoward about me. But then again, denial was indeed one of her tactics—when something didn't suit her, she sourly shrugged it off.

"Yes, beta Shivani, of course, come and sit here. You barely ask anything from your Ma and Papa ever since we married you off. So tell me, what can I do for you?" she responded cheerfully, adjusting her red and orange drape that was encouraged to flow freely down her slender hips. She gracefully sat with her spine erect—the kindness in her eyes and her tender smile intact. It seemed Ma had rehearsed her gentle countenance over the years, only to master it, and now, she always appeared beautiful and happy; content with her life and the various roles she enacted in it. If there were scars beneath the façade, they had either healed with the balm of time or she had become adept at masking them with her well-practised smile. I had yet to see her perturbed, except for the one time when Shiv announced his decision to marry a white girl. That day, Ma's colour transformed so drastically and dangerously, it stirred all the seven heavens. Shiv had deliberately chosen that day since Papa was travelling on business and was expected to be absent from home for a couple of nights. The entire household, including the staff and the servants, froze in their place in trepidation. She had turned whiter than the white girl in question and right now, I wasn't sure if her face would blanch or blush. I was sure though, that my words would trigger an adrenaline rush, making her voice rise notches higher than normal. But I had rehearsed my calmness and come prepared, or so I believed.

"How dare you even entertain the idea of bringing home a white girl? We have our traditions and this sort of behaviour goes against everything we have built over generations; do you hear? Generations!" she reiterated, shaking her hands vigorously. Her face was an ugly picture of fury and frustration. "You need to get rid of her before daylight because I have already promised the Khannas that you will marry their daughter. They are an eminent family, and you will settle down wonderfully with their daughter, who might I add, is attractive and Stanford-educated. She is an invaluable asset and you must not let this opportunity slip through your slithering, lovesick fingers. Get over your boyish crush that dare crush everything your great-grandpa, grandpa, Papa and I have built over the years; for you, all for you, damn it! Does your insolent mind even understand your own worth?" enquired Ma with eyes that pierced through my brother, sharper than the knife our cook employed to slice fruits in the kitchen.

Her eyes froze on him, anxiously anticipating for him to nod in agreement, but he didn't. He stood before her with his head lowered and a hint of disenchantment on his youthful face. His heart was brimming with hope, as he believed that he had found the love of his life. Love, no doubt, gave birth to courage and at that age in life, he didn't understand the transient nature of romantic love. Ma's reaction had shattered his heart and his idealistic world. His body was shaking in response to her rage, but his heart was determined to not be moved by the storm he believed would eventually pass. He supposed it would, after all, he was the blue-eyed baby of the house—the only boy amongst four sisters. He would wait for Papa to return, as since the time he had been conceived, he was never denied *anything*. While Ma was five months pregnant, his gender had been confirmed. After that, grandma left no stone unturned to give him every privilege, which included taking him to the topmost toy shops in Mumbai to buy toys enough for the next five years. Hamley's newest toys were flown in for him, filling at least three rooms of the palatial home. Ma had to bear the brunt of grandma's idiosyncrasies, which involved favouring Shiv on many accounts, while I primarily received the hand-me-downs of my sisters. The baby clothes I wore and the few dolls I had befriended were their leftovers. Even the scraps were not many, as Ma lived in the perennial hope of having a son, and had discarded most of my sisters' toys.

"Whatever you do, don't bring this affliction on your father, he suffers from life-threatening asthma attacks and this will destroy him. Be practical, Shiv, we have a standing in society and you cannot possibly mar it by marrying a girl that has nothing to bring to the table. Don't be an emotional fool. A lifelong marriage will benefit our already well-known family's reputation. You will marry the Khanna girl; Roheen is her name. She will bear a child, preferably a son and before you know it, the white girl will be out of your frivolous fantasies," she continued, while she struggled to lower her voice, lending tenderness to it. She loved her only son and wanted the best for him—the family enterprise and a good word in society, of course. The latter, it seemed, was always more important—an 'Indian' syndrome, where most were plagued with the views and judgements of others.

I only had an opaque idea of what was more important for Ma then; keeping others happy at the cost of Shiv's happiness. Time, our greatest ally, was expected to enable him and the world to turn oblivious to the so-called blunders he had made in his youth, as *all* of us do.

Ma had been consistent in her behaviour and having signed up for a full-time occupation of hounding and hovering over her kids when we were born, she still kept us in her maternal shackles. I recall, most vividly, her urging me to eat, when I had no appetite. I was twelve and wise enough to know I had the option of eating later in case I wanted to, but she firmly instructed Amma ji to force the meal down my throat. If I still resisted, I would be locked in the bathroom, until I agreed to do as I was told. Shiv was still being treated like that twelve-something-year old. However, be it food, the woman he didn't want to marry or taking the family empire to a whole new level, his expression blurted out indifference that day. He clearly didn't agree with Ma and couldn't care less.

I was the only one present out of all our siblings at the time and I listened, without a hint of judgement sweeping my face. But when Ma reported Shiv's 'unbelievable recklessness' to my sisters, it was another story. Clearly, I didn't share my sisters' sensibilities on such matters and neither Ma's, but when it concerned maintaining peace, I was the first to nod my head, vigorously, in assent. Though I must confess at this point, I would've smiled in satisfaction had Shiv managed to break the chains of conformity.

In the end, it was about numbers on the balance sheet more than matters of the heart that mattered to Ma, and being practical was vital to prevent Shiv from sabotaging an empire over a frivolous romance.

On recalling Ma's reaction that day—15 years ago, I began to shudder inside. I earnestly loathed every moment of having placed myself under the spotlight, and longed to be free of it.

# 2

I earnestly loathed the ladies' cloakrooms in the gym, as it was full of blabbermouths and backbiters, particularly when I happened to be under the spotlight. Women spared no one and I couldn't possibly be an exception, given my reputation. They weren't remotely aware of my presence as I stood behind the locker, lugging out my handbag. Their boisterous voices were loud enough to reverberate in the shower cubicles.

"All said and done, she's sick! What's her name again, Richa! I spotted her almost every evening at the fashion week, looking her dashing self. Much to my surprise, she was with the same man who appeared to be her dad at first, but when he began behaving too intimately, I realised he was the sweet-looking sugar daddy everyone's been muttering about. Assumingly, he was the one who brought those new ensembles for her to wear every evening, before ferociously tearing them off her well-sculpted body at night. Yuck! Why him?" enquired one of them, giggling ludicrously after tearing my character apart.

"That's *awesome* man! Imagine, she's had two ridiculously rich husbands—one child from each—and has made heaps of dough from both, enough to afford her the most sumptuous lifestyle. Her limited edition designer bags are the sum total of what she earned from her divorces, besides the hidden savings and jewellery, of course. She has an *awesome* lifestyle and I really envy her, so who cares how ugly the duckling is as long as the perks are super attractive?" insisted the other, shrieking, particularly emphasising on 'awesome'.

"Still man! I don't understand her fetish for Ravi. He is an obscene old man who has two married daughters and a grown-up son. In fact, he may just be a granddad, if not a great one. Dirty old hag! Men in this city have no shame or scruples. They all have a fed-up wife at home and a fired-up mistress outside. Richa is even more shameless, she is with him knowing his one foot is in the grave and that she is nothing more to him than a thrilling ride in an amusement park," said the other, with disdain.

"Yeah, I suppose, but she's totally *awesome!*" replied the other, before adding, "It's cool nowadays to be promiscuous. No one really casts aspersions on other's character, especially, if the individual is associated with an eminent personality. His pocket is full of designer wallets and is brimming with innumerable credit cards after all," she remarked, sarcastically. "We mustn't forget that her first husband, who, by the way, was young and handsome, got her maid pregnant the same time she was expecting her son. Perhaps, she deliberately went for an older man who was bound to have his elderly eyes fixed on her. And don't you know? Hearsay is her second husband turned out to be more interested in men than in women, so even after they had a daughter together, they split. I don't blame her, really. Her lot with younger men hasn't been so bright. She subconsciously gravitated towards a man twice her age, perhaps, to halve her insecurities," she empathised, with a hint of mockery in her voice.

I deliberated on whether to stay frozen in my position or to swiftly stride out of the changing rooms, past the crowded juice bar, down the stairs and to the car parking, into my recently delivered Range Rover. Ravi had purchased it from one of his car dealer friends for my birthday present, in return for being his stunning mistress. He insisted he loved me enough to endow me with every luxury available under the sun. I had reservations about his love, giving minuscule thought to the emotion, as I desired nothing more than a good time espoused with a good wardrobe. As for him, he desired the thrill of being with a woman he escaped to, from his monotonous existence with his wife. To be content with his work and family routine, he sought excitement outside. His neglected and overweight wife confided in one of our common friends that since she couldn't see light at the end of the dismal tunnel, she had accepted her destiny. At this withering phase in life, the verve to protest had disappeared and even though she was dissatisfied, she buried herself in mindless kitty lunches and endless card sessions. Her children had flown their nests decades ago and her grandchildren had extra-curricular activities that choked their days. It drained her merely listening to their packed schedules and so she made sure that her active social life kept her mind sane and satisfied. She was the 'good woman' with a 'good conduct', who deftly turned the other cheek whilst her husband routinely and remorselessly liaised with other women. He had given his wife a sizeable bank account balance, so loyalty wasn't an asset his wife was banking on.

I, too, rebuffed the emotion of guilt, as I wasn't the one to bring the fragile walls of his marriage down. It had existing cracks and I simply became the light that permeated his life through them. I chose to believe that I rescued their marriage in a way as Ravi became more tolerant of his wife after making love to me. I eased his burdens by drawing a smile on his face. He voraciously vocalised how much he needed me in bed, and I had apparently touched a part of him no other woman could. He wasn't very good-looking, but his wealth more than compensated for his lack of physical charm.

It was his fuelled enthusiasm for me that kept me abundantly interested in myself and I spent unending hours and money on my physical upkeep. The greater part of the monetary gifts I received from him, I employed in looking exquisite.

"We must *totally* give her credit for the way she carries herself and I too, have seen her in fashion shows, sitting smugly in the front row. Dahling, everything from head to toe is *totally* paid for, so she need not charge her million men for all her sexual favours. She gets it all lying down; literally. She has the luck, look and a winning outlook," the other said. By now, I couldn't distinguish one from the other as their intonation was too similar, except one of them overused the word *awesome* and the other, I think, *totally*. By the end of the conversation, I could gather one thing—for them, my entire being was *awesome*, and as for me, I was *totally* ready to bounce!

They broke into giggles like a couple of schoolgirls, before one of them commented, "She's always in here working out and yet, she has boundless energy to be out there, looking amazing."

"Yeah! She works her ass off before working on her men with her *awesome* ass. She's figured out her formula and it works wonders for her. Maybe you and I should get our *assets* cosmetically corrected, so we can live like Miss Universe."

"*Totally* babes, but for that, I need to dupe a stinking rich sugar daddy first!" the other said, only to break into a roaring laughter.

If not affection, I had become the object of their attention. They spoke about me as if they were acquainted with me, even though we hadn't as much as exchanged a glance. They made it their right to judge me. They knew nothing about me, besides hearsay, and yet, they rattled on mindlessly. They were unacceptably malicious and I resented myself for not gathering the courage to put a stop to this. I felt a strong adrenaline rush and I was prepared to shout, insult and even threaten them with the kind of aggression they would live to remember. Little did they know that the owner of the gym had been my man three years ago, and now he granted me an unpaid one-year membership that was favourably renewed each year. I could have them barred from entering the gym if I wanted.

"I *totally* wish I had her face and her sexy body. We are in our early twenties and our bodies are not half as toned as hers. She has all the right curves to summon the right kind of men in her life. Beauty is an asset in today's cosmetic world, babes. Beauty may be skin deep, but outer beauty helps women dig deeper into men's' pockets. The average man gravitates towards beauty, preferring it over brains, except Richa *totally* seems to possess both."

Finally, they redeemed themselves and although my indignation would've been perfectly justifiable, I was instantly pacified as they shifted their focus from men and my character to my well-sculpted, 'with a brain' body. One thing they had still gotten wrong was that I wasn't forty yet, but I let that misunderstanding be as I was only months away from the turn of another decade.

The gossip girls were accurate—I was superbly attractive for my age. But it was only because I spent hours grooming myself in the gym. There wasn't a single day I missed unless I was under the weather, or with an ache of some kind. I ran five kilometres on the treadmill like a cheetah every day and went for regular massages. Along with that, I was also gifted with an attractive face and an appealing body that hadn't demanded invasive surgery till now. Perhaps, it was the promiscuity that kept me youthful.

"But seriously, don't you think she has regular Botox and that lipo stuff done? I mean, is it even possible to have that kind of body at that age?"

"That surgeon must be *awesome!*" the other said, screaming in exaggerated delight.

Just when I assumed they had redeemed themselves, they were getting under my skin again. If I stepped out at this moment, they were bound to see me and realise I had heard every word, making it immeasurably awkward for all of us. I was about to step out and yell at them when Ravi's call broke my chain of thoughts. When I chose not to answer it, he immediately messaged me.

*Baby, see you at the hotel in an hour. Wear the sexy red lingerie I bought for you and please don't delay. Can't wait. Love you xxx.*

I needed to hurry home and hastily change into the red lingerie, under my jeans and t-shirt. He was pleading with me to wear it ever since he bought it from Brussels, on one of his business trips. He had purchased three; black, hot pink—which I wore last week, arousing endless excitement in him—while the red one remained. I couldn't imagine how it appeared, a man in his mid-sixties walking into a boutique in Europe, buying lacy lingerie for his mistress. He had exquisite taste and I cherished all his presents as the silk caressed my skin more dotingly than any man ever could.

He was sometimes undesirably demanding, I mused as my mind shifted from the insolent brats to this insecure man who needed a response immediately, before he assumed I was making out with someone else. He didn't trust me and called me incessantly through the day to monitor my whereabouts. On more than one occasion, he had his peon follow me the entire day, which he owned up to later with an innocent expression. He was convinced I'd be flattered, but alas, it only made me realise he was an insecure jerk, puffed up with chauvinistic pride. I had then, very impolitely, dissuaded him from repeating such a humiliating exercise.

For now, I texted back.

*Just getting ready for you, babes. See you soon. Can't wait! Xxx*

Dishonesty was the only policy I abided by with him, as he seldom believed me. I had, therefore, learnt the skill of uttering words that were only music to his hard of hearing ears.

It was several minutes later that the voices vanished, as did the gossip girls. I popped my head around to see if they were still there, but they had made their exit. One day, I'd want to explain myself, I thought. Quick second thoughts, my best friend taught me to be the best version of myself and not worry needlessly about the opinions of others. I sent my message, grabbed my bag and sprinted out as quickly as my feet carried me. My head was lowered and my eyes followed my feet till I was in my car, and that was when I finally released an exasperated breath.

# 3

I caught myself holding onto my breath as Ma casually searched into my eyes, but clearly couldn't figure out what was wrong. After an uncomfortable silence, she stared at me, adjusted her sari with her well-manicured fingers—coated red to match her attire—and finally, rested her moist delicate hands on her lap. She then straightened her spine, and looked at me, unblinkingly. Her seven-carat solitaire sparkled bright on her marital finger as the sunlight soaked her private quarters with its heavenly warmth. She tenderly tilted her head and emitted a faint smile, thus beckoning me to spill out my woes she knew she'd resolve in a heartbeat. I observed the glare of certainty and confidence on her face that expressed, 'Shivani, share your problem and I'll give you the solution in a flash. After all, life's experiences are the mother of wisdom and being your mother, I will lend you answers. Only I know what is best for you.'

'Mother!' I exclaimed in my disturbed and deluded head. Until now, I had allowed her to disentangle my life's riddles, primarily because I didn't dare to defy her and also because Ma preferred to believe that she was in-charge of our destinies from the time we became embryos. She drafted our scripts and ensured we enacted them as finely as she herself had been expected to. Until now, she had addressed every apprehension of mine, resolving it easily and earnestly through her voice, smile and glance. I hoped this too would not be an insurmountable challenge for her. I should've had faith in her, but something was making me hesitate. No matter how much I wanted her attitude to have altered with the times, I was afraid that was as unrealistic as making strawberry jam out of oranges. Her attitude was as inflexible as the rocks embedded in the Mumbai sea.

"Shivani, unless you open up the secret chasm of your heart to me, I cannot advise you. You know that I'm there for you in a heartbeat, my child. There is nothing in God's name I cannot afford as our family has earned enough, so why must you not acquire a slice of the legacy? Ask and it shall be given without a hint of hesitation. Tell me the amount that will make you smile; just say the figure. If not so much in words, just lift your fingers; I know you're shy to ask. Every woman is."

She stated, breaking into a slight giggle, "I'm aware that Sameer takes good care of you, but at times, a woman's needs are greater than her man's heart. How much do you want?" she repeated, haughtily. A large advantage such as money had made her conceited whilst a small disadvantage—a knocked ego, would dishevel her entire being. I didn't want to hurt her ego any more than I wanted her money.

In all likelihood, that's the reason I married the wrong guy in the first place, 15 years ago, I mused. I was made to believe he'd keep me happy because he was from a 'good' family, which basically meant he was 'rich.' 'Good' generally translated into either 'wealthy' or 'influential' or both, and the moral and cultural stance of the family was swept under the carpet as wealth concealed all vices. So to answer Ma's question, except only in my head as I didn't have the courage to voice my opinion to her, I didn't need her money.

I had enough of my own. In fact, I needed something money couldn't possibly buy.

"I don't need the money, Ma! It's something more pressing," I said, this time out loud, but so inaudibly that I doubted she had heard me at all. My tone invariably softened around her, but now it was ridiculously alien, even to my own ears—so pathetically puny it was almost a whisper melting in the air.

Her eyes were now observing me attentively, examining my every facial feature as though my predicament was inscribed on some part of my face. I closed my eyes to shut her and the world out, but the pleasure of doing so lasted momentarily. I felt my tears sting the edges of my eyes and then it happened—they flowed profusely down my cheeks as I sobbed and sniffled, partly out of fear and grief, but mainly out of relief that I could finally express what I should have many years ago. At this precise moment, I ached for my Ma to play out an angelically maternal role by encompassing me in her protective arms and reassuring me that it would be all right in the end because *she* would make sure that life bent *my* way. I wanted her to reach out and place my pale face gently on her bosom, while she patted my head, throbbing with a stream of non-conclusive routes to a future I longed for.

While I had rehearsed my sentences before my cloakroom mirror to ensure every syllable came out effectively, I found myself shuddering with anxiety. I needed to be the woman I always aspired to be. By mustering courage to stand up for myself, I needed to set the tone for the coming generations of women to enjoy a healthy self-esteem. Removed from my own worth, I was acquainted only with the value of serving others. I had been choking on my emotions for too long and they were in dire need of a volcanic release.

As I'd desperately yearned, my Ma was empathetic as she placed her inviting arms around me and began to soothe my wounds like a salve, "Let it all out, Shivani. Crying is more curative than most of us are aware of, so cry buckets if you need to. I'm here for you at every step of the way. We are all guilty of filthy feelings that cage us and at some point, they need to be thrown out to liberate ourselves.

"Don't worry, Shivani, I empathise with a woman's heart and her struggles, but it's all a phase and releasing the pain is imperative," she said calmly—she was unperturbed by my tears. She then returned to caress the top of my head while I cried ceaselessly. She said softly, while pressing the call button, "Let me call for tea and coffee for both of us as *it is* my tea time. My mother used to give me green tea during times of stress while I was growing up, particularly during that uncomfortable time of the month. Perhaps, beta, you too are going through PMS or maybe you are pre-menopausal. Women nowadays are rushing into menopause; you know? Everything is happening too fast. Oh! What women have to endure with their fly-by-night hormones—they take a toll on their minds and bodies! Most of us vent out on our spouses, but I'm sure you are too much of an angel to do that. Anyway, we are natural warriors—much stronger than men—so don't let a few erratic hormones dominate your life, beta. I had no idea you cry like this; so heart-wrenchingly! Perhaps you ought to meet a good gynaecologist for some hormonal remedy. I will call Roheen's if you like. She is still undertaking treatment to induce pregnancy—IVF or whatever it's called. All these new-age treatments are so above my rationale. In our time, getting pregnant was easy but now women spend lakhs on fancy treatments to conceive. It's become a commercial world that offers these extortionate procedures. For me, it was as natural as relieving myself in the morning. I simply turn to God in times like this and this is what most people have forgotten to do nowadays. I'm telling you, that is the cause of the increasing distress in their lives. I do pray that Shiv has a son soon; God knows it's about time for Roheen to prove that my son is a real Mehra man. Your Papa, on the other hand, didn't know when to stop. It was I who took a call after Shiv was born. After all, I'm not a machine. Cry, baby, let every drop flow. I'd like to join you, but my tears have dried up over the years. You're still relatively young, so cry your pumping lungs out if you have to. I won't judge!" she reassured with sublime serenity stitched on her face while her fingers continued to caress my hair, upsetting its style in the same manner my heart had been.

She called out to Amma ji, who I refused to refer to as the housemaid, as she was the endearing lady who was to be given credit for rearing me from the moment I was born. She was my second mother who gauged my every motion and emotion as she watched me blossom into an adult. She served my meals, cleaned my room and laundered my clothes to perfection. She had lent her patient ears as I had wept my woes to her, during my growing years. There had constantly been disturbing issues since I was the youngest of the sisters and neglected by virtue of being the undesired one. My paternal grandma most indelicately owned up to me that she had hoped for a boy when my mother was pregnant with me. She told me she had regularly fed the impoverished in the local Mumbai suburbs throughout Ma's pregnancy in the perennial hope of her giving birth to a baby boy, but then, much to her shock and disgust, I came along instead.

Understandably, she justified, she resented me at first sight and despised Ma as if she alone had determined the gender of the baby. She counselled Papa on how critical it was for the family empire to be run by a son, and that he needed to remarry since she believed Ma was incapable of reproducing a baby boy. Papa reprimanded her and she stormed out of the hospital without seeing Ma or me until Ma conceived again, after only a few months.

Amma ji had been more than a mother to me as she cushioned me from the chauvinistic comments that were blatantly brushed against my gender as well as the vile vibes I was subjected to. I became the most lovable one for her and she never shied from expressing her feelings to my siblings. She insisted that according to Hindu beliefs, I was a boon from Goddess Laxmi, the giver of wealth, and I had indeed enriched her heart, if not anyone else's. As an expression of love, she braided my hair every morning—while singing a tune from the '60s in her melodic voice—before sending me to school. After I returned from school, she bathed and fed me. She then sat beside me as I engaged myself in my schoolwork. Ma barely involved herself in my routines, as she was too preoccupied with Shiv and his meticulous princely nurturing. She had a tender spot for him; it was gender that mattered and it became a wall between Ma and me.

On getting married, I negotiated to take Amma ji with me as part of my trousseau, but Shiv needed her more. Amma ji was competent, so Ma decided she must stay for her one and only son, who'd inevitably have a family of his own someday. After Shiv got married, Ma offered sacrifices to God in exchange for Him to endow a handsome son to her only daughter-in-law—who she prayed wouldn't admit defeat whilst trying to conceive, even if it meant her spending millions to make it happen. It had been years since and if grandma were still around, she would've evicted Roheen in a heartbeat and replaced her with another bride, who probably would have undergone a fertility test before Shiv slipped a 12-carat ring on her finger. Her rejection towards me had travelled deep in my subconscious mind and each time she was mentioned, I felt a rush of sadness settle in the pit of my stomach. Thank goodness, times were changing—though attitudes about many important issues in this household still remained immutable.

As Amma ji turned the corner into old age and Roheen failed to display any signs of motherhood, she supervised the younger maids to fulfil their duties around the house. Though she delegated well, Ma still insisted on calling to her out of sheer comfort and familiarity. While the other maids served the green tea and coffee in silverware, she stood with hands crossed, delicately resting on her torso. Ma never treated her like an ordinary maid, she respected her, most often, enough to involve her in matters of personal enquiries.

Amma ji now stared at me as Meera, the new maid steadily poured tea and coffee for both of us. She then handed the cups—to Ma first, and then, to me, as she proceeded to offer us the options of brown sugar or an artificial sweetener in a silver bowl. Amma ji continued to watch me. My pain was more palpable to her than to my own mother. I was troubled by her appearance that had become unacceptably frail over the past several months; the years had not been as benign to her as they had been to Ma. There was no doubt these were her declining years as for the first time, I noticed a slight hunchback and hands that were significantly more wrinkled.

I stretched my lips slightly to smile at her, but I realised she was in no mood for courtesy. She refused to return my smile and instead, continued to stare even after Ma ordered them both to leave the room. I noticed deep creases form in the centre of her forehead, before she turned her head away. I sensed she was troubled by her exclusion in my private issues, now that she was in the winter of her life and absent from my routine. But I intended to break the news to her after speaking to Ma, gaining her confidence as well as her consent. It seemed Ma had warmed up to me in the past several minutes and now I ought to, without delay, communicate confidently what was on my mind.

"Ma!" I began again, taking a sip of the cappuccino that warmed my dry throat and my wounded heart. Papa had also recounted to me on several occasions how a warm beverage was like a magic potion that healed an emotionally battered heart. He always said, "Shivani, it is like a hug in a mug, warm and embracing." Papa warmed up to me after Shiv was born, partially because his own mother's indifference towards me stung him. He developed a special connection with me after he began noticing the resemblance I bore with him in both looks and personality. I was not only the prettiest, but I had also inherited many of his individualistic traits. He called me his 'brightest spark' and always asked about my being. He avoided hugging me, as any physical contact between him and his daughters was not part of our nurturing or his conditioning. But he had become more approachable as old age approached him. He became close, emotionally, particularly to my children as his prime years ebbed away and he himself began slipping into his second childhood. Most men mellowed with time, and he was no exception.

"Ma! I want. I mean, I need. Ma, I…" I stumbled on my words as I placed the cup down. I looked at my Ma—she sat there angelically as I struggled to spill out the words as calmly as I could.

"Ma! I need a divorce."

There it was—the four obnoxious words that my friend Rajni's husband had dropped on her last year, translating into an acrimonious legal battle. Then there was Sonia, who, after having lived in a childless marriage for five years, asked her husband one day if it seemed worth continuing and he amicably agreed to separate. She now had two adorable children she had adopted. Life gave her two beautiful reasons to rejoice. I had never seen her happier. I found that encouraging while pronouncing the very same words with deliberate emphasis on each syllable.

"I need a d-i-v-o-r-c-e," I repeated, as if by uttering it with meticulous emphasis, it would be granted to me without protest. I hoped that Ma recognised its urgency and without much ado, called upon her lawyer who was likely to grant it in a flash.

I had been staring at the floor when I announced my decision and then, I lifted my head towards Ma who was rapidly placing her cup of green tea on the table. Before I could read her expression, she slapped me hard across my face, leaving me stunned. My reflexes placed my shaking hand on my cheek to soothe the sting and I froze, just like her enraged eyes on me.

"I had to slap you hard to snap you out of your foolishness and I will do it again till you wake up from your stupor," she yelled, trying desperately to regain her composure. She neatened her sari and tried to command her lips to smile while she tucked a few strands of her recently dyed hair behind her ear, revealing her glittering seven-carat diamond studs. She then broke the silence, drawing in rapid breaths as if she was undergoing a heart attack, but of course, she wasn't. Ma was the iron lady in our lives, just like Margaret Thatcher was for her country. She governed for 11 years whereas Ma would continue ruling our lives from the cradle till her grave.

"I expect you will not play this prank on me again and after this moment, we will forget that we ever had this conversation," she said dismissively and then fell silent, as if trying to find a quick fix to the problem. "I am willing to forgive you this one time and from tomorrow, you must come and join me at my office. I assure you, Shiv will not mind you learning about our family business. After all, it is not for profit that you will work with me, but to keep your mind healthy and to maintain a safe distance from bad company; company that encourages you to think in this warped manner. This kind of twisted thinking has created a disruption in our society which will further lead to more divorces than marriages someday. Your generation foolishly insists on manoeuvring themselves away from God's natural settings and that is the reason you are so restless," she yelled, immediately composing herself after.

"What you really need, Shivani, is a legitimate separation from your divorced friends. You must detach yourself from such 'free-thinking' people who try and break the very fabric of our society. I object to such company that turns to divorce as a quick fix to whenever a light bulb goes off in their homes. Appliances break, paint wears off and floors crack, but that doesn't mean you change your home? You simply repair the broken and carry on. Change your company instead, because they are a bad influence. I need you to slash all ties with them, particularly that Richa friend of yours—she is an accident waiting to happen. She has made too many irreparable mistakes in her life and she is no match to you in either conduct or reputation. If you hang around her any longer, you will become like her because we all end up being the people we spend our maximum time with. Choose your friends well, Shivani, or you will be in irresolvable trouble.

"As the Mehra daughter, you will behave differently; better than the rest of your generation. For generations before us, we have been alien to the word 'divorce', and intend to remain so. We are not cowards and when we commit to a relationship, we see it through till the very end. When a light bulb fuses, you change the bulb—not your entire home. As an Indian woman, after you walk into your marital home, you adjust within six months of being there and the only one time you abandon them is when you take your final breath. Do you understand me?" she asked, harshly, as I placed my shaking hand down on my lap. The slap had immobilised me physically, just like my marriage had numbed me emotionally. I had clearly not been able to switch the light on and now it seemed, I was doomed to darkness.

"I must head back to work now as I have more pressing issues to address. Sign up to a productive life, it'll release you from such counter-productive ideas. Come to office tomorrow and be there no later than 10 am," Ma concluded, frostily.

# 4

He didn't bat an eyelid while I awkwardly sat on top of him and made love in my red lingerie. The lingerie didn't just turn him on, it transformed him into a ravenous beast as we made out for what felt like hours, in different positions, in different parts of the room—including the window that overlooked the hotel pool. We were on the thirteenth floor. It was his favourite room and he insisted on renting the same room every single time—considering it lucky—despite its number, 1313.

"You are the hottest babe in town and I consider myself the luckiest man," he stated with lust in his eyes after making out. He tossed his head back on the pillow and stretched his oversized body on the bed. Extending his arm to the side table, he grabbed his Davidoff cigarette pack. He lit it, and offered it to me in a state so breathless, it was bronchial.

"No thanks babes, I don't smoke, remember?" I responded with a determined effort to not sound irritated by his inability to satisfy me. He was burnt out, and we both now lay languidly on the bed. The last thing he needed was for me to break into a quarrel.

He either didn't listen when I spoke to him or his memory was like a sieve, because every time he had offered me a smoke in the past, I had declined, reminding him that I chose not to indulge in smoking—primarily, because my father was a chain-smoker and had succumbed to lung cancer before I turned ten and more recently, I was employing every means to escape premature ageing. I invested heavily to keep my youthful looks in a tight grip, so, naturally chose not to act against my better judgement. God knows, it was tiresome enough trying to keep it all together.

"Richa, baby!" he began, as he released a mushroom of smoke from his mouth. "I'm flying to Malaysia on business next weekend and you are joining me; only first class for my Jennifer Lopez. You will sit beside me, before you sit on top of me in the washroom once the lights are out." He giggled as his inflated stomach rocked up and down violently, as if encountering an earthquake—a tummy tremor!

Before I could voice my objection about the washroom, he quickly added, "Oh, also dahling, pack light as we will be away only for three nights. During the day, you can pamper yourself in the hotel spa while I attend my meetings, and we will engage in endless excitement all night long," he said, again exhaling smoke on my face. I turned away, dismayed and disgusted. In fact, I was questioning if I liked being with him anymore as just the mere sight of him naked was physically revolting.

There were many dashing men at the gym who regularly hit on me and invited me on dates, but because I was committed, I turned them down. Some attempted to lure me into one-night stands, but a fling was no longer my thing, so I politely declined. Once, when my blast from the past walked in, we did nothing more than exchange pleasantries, as Ravi, who chose to keep a tab on me was likely to find out if I ever lied. The gym, unlike for many, wasn't a pick-up joint for me. It was my space to get an adrenaline rush, while others would search for people to rush to bed with. However, despite my best efforts to disregard their advances, I had innumerable men leering at me. But being ridiculously high maintenance, I was out of their league. Settling merely for dinners, dances and frivolous romance wasn't a part of my contract. I had my prodigal needs and this stodgy guy had what it took to float my boat as I inflated his ego. We both revelled in the string less relationship, until time forced us to cut all cords.

He gave me his credit card every time we travelled together and he splurged on me with whatever I wanted—even the things I accidentally touched. In addition, he had lived up to his promise of providing my brother Business Class tickets to Europe once a year, and that was after he gifted him a locally manufactured car, almost at the onset of our relationship. My brother was thrilled, as my mother didn't encourage him to be extravagant. She was a single parent and had saved up for a day when he might actually need it.

Initially, my brother, Ashish, frowned upon all my choices in men, but on realising the size of their pockets, he always turned a blind eye. He had despised Ravi's appearances in the beginning, but later warmed up to his 'chubbiness', reassuring me that there was more to life than just good looks. Money had eclipsed the one noble thought he might have entertained about protecting me from this disastrous love affair. Before he received the car, he insisted I deserved better, and after he drove it, he commented on how incredible I looked with Ravi. It's astonishing how poor values or unappealing appearances are overlooked in the shadow of wealth and power. Ravi's large heart measured up to his other vital parts and because of that, I ignored his whopping belly still bobbing up and down and with it, so was my exhausted head!

After he stubbed out his cigarette, he rolled towards me to hold me by my slender naked waist. He kissed my lips vulgarly, and climbed on top of me, licking every millimetre of my neck. Before I realised it, he was inside me and we were at it once again.

"Gosh! You're a ball of energy who has now depleted me of mine," I gasped, while trying desperately to be in the moment. I'm sure he was on some stimulant, my guess was the one that began with the letter V. Even my much younger boyfriend a couple of years back didn't penetrate more than once at a time—twice had been his best, and that too, after a break. I should have felt flattered that Ravi had an insatiable appetite for me. The man had the stamina of an athlete and it was a wonder that with all the humping and pumping that he did, he had not dramatically dropped his excess weight—not that he seemed to care. Having all the money in the world afforded him the confidence he needed to draw women, a dime a dozen, in his life. They, too, didn't care about appearances as long as their bank balance prospered.

Once we were done and he finally wore a satisfied expression for the day, I darted into the plush bathroom for a cold shower, and it was there that I drew a breath of relief. I reflected under the running cold water, it enlivened all my senses. Momentarily, I entered a space of blankness where no thought accompanied me. I had felt bliss only for a split second, when I heard his movement in the bedroom. I knew that this relationship was approaching its conclusion as my eyes began to reveal feigned love. I ached for a relationship with an individual who shared my sensibilities and who satisfied me the way I had dared fantasise. This time-worn man hadn't pleased me since the very first time we made out.

I touched myself, only to discover that my own hand excited me more than his.

A voice inside me elbowed me, advising me to give him the news once we returned from Malaysia. Perhaps, I'd be breaking his vulnerable heart, but it was anyway doomed to collapse from a cardiac arrest. I tied the soft white robe that caressed my skin lovingly and slipped my feet into the snow-white slippers before entering the room where he was clumsily buttoning up his shirt and zipping his tailor-made trousers. He smiled at me and I obediently reciprocated, after which he hurried towards me to hold me in his strong, but unsteady arms. He whispered in my ears, "You're my favourite drug; an addiction that keeps me intoxicated. You're better than marijuana, my darling." He assured me that if it weren't for the family wedding he was hurrying to; he would've spent the night with me. He must have sensed my aloofness, but I still pretended to be sorry that he was leaving by holding him loosely around his jelly-like belly.

With a weak smile and a hesitant nod, I requested him to extend my stay in the room for a while to recuperate from the exertion of a long afternoon. He laughed proudly and agreed. "You can keep the room as long as you need, provided you don't have another man visiting you!" he warned, giving me a suspicious look. Due to my experiences, I had realised there was always an undercurrent of mistrust in every man-woman relationship. "Do you really suppose I'd liaise with other men when I'm committed to you, babes?" I asked innocently as I pulled myself away from him to draw the curtains.

He smirked and said nothing, so I said instead, "You'll probably always perceive me the way you yourself are! I hope you know that, Mr. Sceptical! Kindly leave me to my nap and go home to your unsuspecting wife." I blurted as he left the room. I locked the door with a sign of relief, and lay myself down on my back, exhaling long and hard. I stared dreamily at the dome ceiling—it had cupids and angels painted, like Michelangelo's images in the Sistine Chapel at the Vatican City. I wondered if angels were a myth; I had never met anyone remotely close to one on earth—besides my beautiful best friend. I beamed as I thought of her and instantly felt my soul lighten up. After some blissful moments, I felt life draw from my body, compelling my eyes to close. My eyelids were heavy and my vision blurred, and it was then that I saw the most radiant angel before me. My heart expanded with gratitude to have her in my life and I instantly fell asleep under the crispy clean blanket.

# 5

An impenetrable blanket of clouds spread across the August sky, and it seemed like it was about to cave in on me. I was a dark silhouette against the misty sky but whenever it turned black, I camouflaged with it, fading into deep insignificance. Some lives were like that and no one really cared about mine, least of all, my Ma—that heart-wrenching thought brought tears to my eyes.

The greyness continued to permeate every cell of my body as I gazed up from the terrace of Ma's magnificent penthouse in Breach Candy, where she often stood, looking down on people. I tried in earnest to dismiss her face which had been a portrait of anger, not too long ago. The visuals of that dreaded moment when she slapped me bruised every thread of my being. Time had the ability to erase the painful memory of spoken words, but images could never be entirely forgotten. They were like the colourful pictures in storybooks we read as children, but are still able to recall in our subconscious mind.

Her stern voice echoed in my head as I stared down at the passers-by who were ravenously relishing meals prepared by the street food vendors. Some were families, eating together from different hawkers, who were diligently serving people all day and virtually, all night long. It was incredible to observe the verve with which these vendors served people for a livelihood that scarcely fed their families. There was a soundtrack of people—chitchatting and cheering on the side streets—as the cars on the roads honked and hooted all the way to their destination. The landscape was something I usually marvelled at and pleasingly soaked in, but today the bunch of people was a blur, just like everything else in my life. The all-consuming sadness robbed me of the power to be in the present. I wasn't even tempted to eat, despite having inhaled the distinctive aroma of the food. Normally I would ask one of the servants to run down and get pao bhaji for me—a deliciously prepared potato dish with unmeasured amounts of butter and masala, served with rounds of warm bread buns. It was dangerously delectable, laden with cholesterol, but I always consumed it without an inch of remorse—even if that meant skipping dinner.

I ordinarily delighted in observing the panoramic Mumbai sights and sounds as they enabled me to momentarily forget my own burdens, except today, I struggled. Nothing about my life seemed normal and I feared that I would remain frozen in that hopeless state for as long as my heart was destined to beat. Pain, it seemed, was stitched to me in the same manner as the families down below—stitched together to eat and to celebrate life's humble pleasures. Some lives were simple, while others were simply complicated.

There was only one person in this warped world I considered calling at this grim moment and that was Richa, my bosom friend and my alter ego who understood and loved me as much as Ma detested her. She may have been divorced twice, but at least she was practical and liberal, living her life according to her own rule book. Her worldview was neither moderate nor modest, but she somehow managed to maintain a balance between her lovers, her children and her personal grooming. I didn't judge her life decisions as each individual had their own story. Somewhere in the depths of my heart, I envied her for the ease with which she lived her life, while I simmered on in mine.

Sangeeta, the eldest daughter in our family was believed to be the Goddess of abundant wealth and good fortune when she was born. The family had celebrated her birth with equal pomp and show—just like a grand Indian wedding—and they had stacked boxes of photo albums as keepsake. Ma was pampered with the most exquisite diamond sets and the most expensive saris, gift wrapped and adorned with her favourite perfumes and flowers. On the subsequent births of daughters, however, no one in the family rejoiced anymore as each of the daughters had impoverished them emotionally. So, I, being the fourth had no hope of bringing a smile to anyone's disappointed face, let alone stumble across a single photo of my birth or childhood.

My Ma never empathised with me, perhaps she felt weighed down with so many of us to take care of. After four daughters, Ma had tirelessly fasted for years to Lord Shiva, asking for only one thing—a baby boy. She believed it would save her from grandma's relentless taunts and tantrums. God, eventually, revealed His good nature, making grandma's soul smile. A baby boy was born—the first son.

Papa too radiated joy after a long time. He stared long and hard at the baby's crotch to assure himself that he had been blessed with a boy. He kissed him there, and on his forehead—in delirious delight—tossing him up in the air and then catching him in his hands to embrace him like a prize he had just won. His masculinity had been rewarded and his inability to have achieved it earlier was now overlooked by those who had questioned it in the first place.

I needed to connect with Richa before I drowned myself deeper in self-loathing. I tried hard to push the ugly vision aside, but it kept gnawing at me. I knew she'd rescue me from myself. As my closest friend, she was the only one who understood the struggles I had been encountering in my marriage, particularly in the past few years. She lent me her patient ear at the drop of a hat and was usually beside me without a moment's hesitation. I punched in her number, but she didn't respond, so I decided to leave a message in her voice mail. I was aware of her affair with a persistent old man who was overly possessive of her. Perhaps, she was with him right now, bringing the spring back into his life.

Meanwhile, I lifted my phone to contact Shiv, who I assumed would be occupied with either his work or his wife. We were in touch, but not nearly as much as I preferred to be. But then again, with the other siblings, I chose to meet only when there was a crisis or a family obligation to be addressed. I considered our bond the strongest of all our siblings as we were also the youngest of the clan.

He surprised me by responding immediately. I felt a lump settle in my throat and with a strained voice, I spoke, "Hi Shiv."

"Hey sis, how's it going? In which corner of the continent have you been hiding yourself? Ma told me she met you the other day and she looked unusually perturbed. Before I could press the issue further, she got a phone call and I didn't get another chance to ask," he said, and he hastily switched from one call to another. He was in his office. "Hold that call!" he told his secretary, while he returned to me.

"Sorry sis, it's just so hectic at work and then there's Roheen who needs her getaways every six to eight weeks. Besides my own business trips, there are just far too many leisure escapes. I'm finding it really hard to keep my feet on the ground. Anyway, let me stop rambling about myself. How's Sameer jija and my beloved nephew and niece, Shashwat and Shriya? Hope they are as naughty as ever! When are you sending them for a sleepover again? God knows how much we want children around us. Ma, I'm sure, has it covered while she negotiates with the sleepy man above. Do you know, nowadays, she makes me sit throughout her persistent prayers and puja? Where there is Ma, there is undying hope! Sorry, I'm rambling again, I shall pause and reiterate the question, how are you?"

"All is well, Shiv, but if you ask me honestly, then no, not really. I'm at Ma's place, on the terrace, and I can't speak openly in case someone's eavesdropping. Kids are fine and I'll send them across soon. I need to chat with you in person. I've thought about whom to confide in and I know you will listen without tearing me to shreds like Ma did. Her feelings for me clearly haven't tamed over the years," my trembling voice trailed off, and I began sobbing.

"Hey sis, stop crying. Hey! Leave the hysteria to me! I'm the one who needs to be crying with Miss Control-freak beside me at work every day!" he said, jovially. "Listen, today I'm jammed, but let's meet tomorrow afternoon at Taj. Do you fancy brunch, coffee or high tea? I have a relatively easy day so you take a call, and I'll be there!"

"Yes sure, Shiv, coffee is good and please don't inform Ma about our meeting or else she'll advise you to nudge me against everything I'm about to disclose to you. You know how it works. Also, Richa may join us, depending on her calendar. I hope you don't mind."

"Absolutely not, especially since she's such a visual treat. You know me, I never mind a cute face. Don't fret, we will fix your life sooner than you dare to believe. See you at the coffee shop at 5 pm sharp. I'm there, sis, in whatever capacity you need me. I just hope you're not pregnant!" he said, amused. "The kids are too old to have a baby sibling in the house! Or you can have one and then most benevolently gift him or her to me. That way, Roheen will get busy and save the money she spends on all the mindless travelling we do. She's losing hope now after having tried to conceive for years and IVF seems to have let us down too. The baby just isn't willing to enter our dysfunctional home. Perhaps, the thought of having Ma as a grandma is scaring the living daylights out of the baby," he commented in jest, making me chuckle.

"Hey, at least I've made you smile. Lighten up, sis, and look at me. Life doesn't always deal a winning hand, especially when Ma manipulates the game. But my measure of success is drawn simply from coping with her controlling nature. I like to view myself as a winner, no matter what, because the only failure in life is the failure to try. Papa always taught me that and I'm still trying hard to get on the right side of Ma."

"I know Shiv, but it's heart-breaking and I'm feeling extremely low," I said, controlling my tears this time.

"Hang in there, sis, because together, we'll cross the rough patches and sail smoothly. Last night, Roheen and I watched *Mary Kom* on Netflix. If she can do it, coming from a disadvantaged background, remember you are infinitely more blessed and sky's the limit for you. Let me be your agony aunt tomorrow, along with the ravishing Richa, who I'm already fantasising about."

"Behave!" I chuckled.

"Oh my God, she makes me weak in the knees. I hope I can focus on building you up instead of crumbling in front of her!" he giggled, as I joined in.

"Sorry, I genuinely love you, Shivani and I will do what it takes. After all, you and I are the only two people who make any sense in our convoluted family," he concluded.

"I know, Shiv! Bless you for being so remarkably patient with life and for an unflagging sense of humour, despite everything. I have a lesson or two to learn from you. I love you and I can barely wait to spend meaningful time with you. By the way, just so you know, I pray to the invisible man up there, who always appears to leave the receiver off the hook during our rough patches. I pray to Him to bless Roheen with a baby, and I hope that along with being invisible, the supreme fellow is not hard of hearing, because you deserve a cricket team of crazy children flying all over the place— wrecking every piece of furniture and ornament that Ma has placed so meticulously over the years," I responded, while realising how fortunate I was to have two of my own. The image of my far from angelic children alleviated the heaviness in my heart.

I had reason to believe he'd be supportive because he had hit the end of the road with Ma many times before, sometimes to the extent of threatening to quit the family business if her interference didn't cease to continue. Being under Ma's insufferable thumb forced Shiv to stay within his boundaries all the time. As far as I was concerned, she had become increasingly pompous, almost shallow. She was oblivious to the delicacies of the human heart and the pain it often carried. But Shiv had a way of drawing a compromise from her.

I often wondered if Ma was born with the dictatorial gene in her and if I had the docile one. She was perhaps born to seek, whilst I was destined to hide. I had settled in that category, comfortably, because I was never encouraged to shine in my own light. Even though Papa had seen a side of me that resembled his, I wasn't rendered the confidence to achieve goals that made him or Ma proud. Getting married to an affluent industrialist and bearing his children was, in their eyes, my greatest triumph.

After keeping the phone, I began musing on the conversation I had with Shiv and how his gesture to meet me had temporarily relieved my anxiety. His voice soothed my injury like only a brother could.

I mused, on the other hand, on how his own life had only partially worked out for him. The decision of not marrying the girl he loved and most reluctantly settling for the one that was 'socially' better for him may have stabilised him, but had left his life incomplete, without children running around and filling a space in Ma's life too. She knitted endlessly in her quiet evenings and carefully stored the finished products in the hope, that one day, she'd gift them all to Shiv's babies. Hope never failed to give birth to enthusiasm.

Despite all this, he appeared to be settled in life, and secretly bent the rules to suit his own whims—at least the rules he could bend. Despite his lack of academic prowess, he had once harboured ambitions to be a lawyer, artist, sportsman, actor and model—at different phases of his life—just like I had dreamt of becoming a singer at fourteen, a dancer at seventeen, and an actor at eighteen. Both Ma and Papa succeeded in gently manoeuvring him towards the family enterprise, while they convinced me that after marriage, I could sing, dance and act. As it turned out, I did end up engaging myself in all these activities, except not professionally, but metaphorically. In all fairness; they hadn't completely stifled my natural flair!

Ma's path crossed Roheen's predominantly at breakfast because after that, she had a jam-packed day with her gym, ladies' social clubs, and social events like art and fashion shows, along with the elite charity events she and Shiv had been supporting. We all secretly hoped that by giving something to society, the universe would be gratified enough to return the obligation and reward us with the object of our desire; in their case, a bouncy baby.

Her activities played centre-stage and she had minimal interaction with Ma, even though, they lived under the same roof. But Ma hardly took offence to her daughter-in-law not giving her time in the day. Her only concern was that she and Shiv were still sleeping together and that the possibility of them having a child was alive. Ma, too, was busy throughout the day, with morning walks with Papa, followed by visits to the factory and office meetings. She spent her evenings knitting or painting, so she had minimal time to pine or whine. She schooled her children with sound, but strict values and unfailingly drew the respect she needed from them. My sisters were in regular touch as she advised them on their domestic, personal and spiritual issues, but none of them lived in Mumbai, besides Shiv and I. They were married in different cities, into eminent business families, of course. They seemed content with their lot, and in case they weren't, no one cared to probe. No one, including myself, delved too deeply into what made them tick, or if they were, indeed, still ticking. They lived a life I didn't relate to and they too often struggled to relate to me and my opinions.

Since Shiv had managed to calm my fears, I was now rest assured that he'd be my tower of strength, no matter how harrowing it was for him to heroically stand by me, while Ma and my sisters gallantly stood against me. He always fought my case, since we were kids, even if it meant getting into ugly wrangles with Ma.

I glanced at my watch and decided it was time to head back home to my children and to my husband, Sameer. I inhaled the aroma of the fresh street food and climbed into my car, somewhat disappointed that I wasn't feeling hungry. But at the same time, I felt light and appeased by my dear brother's support. I was ready to face my reality once again.

Dreary as it might be, duty called.

# 6

Shivani called, I missed a heartbeat and smiled as I usually did on seeing her number on my call log. I returned the call, but her number was engaged. I'll try again, I decided, after reaching home. I dialled my boyfriend instead, who had advised me to avoid any contact when he was home with his family. But today seemed to be an exception as I saw a missed call from him too.

*Sorry babes, just woke up. You exhausted me this afternoon and I've just left the hotel to head home. How's it going?*

I asked, trying to sound attentive. I felt drained. I longed to return to my sleep for another day and a half, but I had to attend a fashion show, and I was already running late. Pressed for time, I couldn't get my hair blow-dried. I decided to tie it back loosely, hoping it didn't reveal the tiredness on my face.

On my way to the show, he called. He voiced his longing to smell my scented body and ached for me to tell him that I loved him, while his wife was out at the parlour, getting herself groomed for some wedding reception that night. He told me how raunchy he felt whenever he thought of me and couldn't wait to make love to me again. He suggested I went shopping with his credit card, as he fantasised about me in purple lingerie.

Before hanging up, I hastily uttered the three words he desperately desired to hear, but I no longer found his neediness an attractive quality. I wanted to give him some time to allow his stimulant to kick in—for optimum performance, of course—but he insisted on meeting again soon.

*You stimulate me naturally, baby, and just the sound of your sexy voice gives me a hard on!*

His message came minutes after I kept the phone. It seemed gross to me now. After being with him for well over a year and having reaped the benefits of exotic holiday destinations and unlimited shopping, I felt the bloom had faded fast. Initially, I revelled in the attention because there was certain excitement about being with an older man, already committed. He, on the other hand, felt energised being with a younger woman, contrary to the way he felt with his wife and so, he willingly splurged on me in a way that was distinctly different from the way he indulged his wife. It was strictly out of duty for her and out of pure pleasure for me. I remorselessly enjoyed being the favoured one, without ever wanting him to be wholly mine. Sometimes, there were extremities of emotion. He would flare up or I would become broody, but that was probably part and parcel of any affair.

Recently, while making out with him, I visualised only the monetary benefits I derived for all my sexual favours. For my shallow gains, I was willing to accompany him to Malaysia and had decided that after the lavish shopping, dining, and sightseeing, I would call it off. His dirty talk on the phone and his dirtier messages were now beginning to nauseate me.

*I can't wait to be with you babes! Listen, my brother is calling me! Will chat soon. Love you.*

I found myself cutting him short.

After texting him the final message, I threw my head back on my car seat. Post the fashion show, I had been sitting in my car for more than half an hour—reminiscing. I noticed there was a feeling of remorse creeping inside me and just like I had felt before ending each of my escapades, I was prompted to think how I could've done things differently. How could I have avoided getting myself into shallow relationships, which in the end, only slighted my character? Upon reflection, I saw all my relationships disintegrating and falling apart, only because of one person; me. I had truly lost sight of who I was.

I thought of everything—how I was introduced to Ravi at a prestigious art show, where he arrived alone. He was a large man with an even larger presence. At first, I thought he was an attention-seeker and later, I realised how right I was. I warmed up to him once the host had formally introduced us. His eyes froze into mine and his handshake was gripping and seductive, to the extent that it did the job of inviting me into his bed well before the show had reached its conclusion. In retrospect, I admired the skill with which he had played his game. He played it well enough to evaporate my resistance to be in yet another destructive love affair.

"I'm an ardent art collector and I've a passion for anything that has the ability to captivate my heart. Who, may I ask, arrests your young heart?" he enquired, with a glass of red wine in his hand.

"I'm not entirely sure," I responded sincerely. "I...I do love Gujral and his horses. His paint strokes are as distinct as they are admirable, and the colours..."

"Ahhhh Gujral mon cher ami!" he interjected quickly. "He is fantastic and he's invited me over at his Delhi residence next Friday. He and I are thick as thieves, but the difference between us is that he is a celebrated genius while I'm an ordinary fellow, with no real talent," he confessed modestly. I looked at him with awe and upon sensing it, he asked me, "Care to join us? It's an open house. His heart is as free as his paint strokes. His personality is as magnificent as his art."

"No, I couldn't possibly impose on you or him like this. I don't even know you," I said.

"Impose? I don't even need to mention that I'm getting my new friend with me. He is so charming; he won't mind a bit. Just allow me to add new hues to your life," he said confidently, and I was floored.

Thereafter, I accompanied him to Gujral's home and brought back a masterpiece. I experienced expensive Italian wines, rare delicacies and an engaging conversation with an internationally acclaimed artist.

I was like a fascinated teenager when I brought home one of his rare sculptures. The elation on meeting him was clearly brimming in my eyes and it was at that moment, Ravi whispered in my ears. "This evening onwards, consider your life a canvas on which I intend to paint the most spectacular colours of joy. Will you do me the favour of allowing me to brush on you, all my skilfully acquired strokes?" he asked as he placed his indelicate hand on my thigh and kissed me straight on my lips, as if we had been together for a while. My recklessness eclipsed my good sense, perhaps a 'no' would've saved me another crash landing. Instead, I responded, "My life's canvas is now in your hands and I'm sure the colours you paint on it can be nothing but spectacular."

He boasted of his own collection and summoned me to view it in his lavish apartment, once we returned to Mumbai. "I would be honoured to have you visit my personal gallery that is exclusively for special people like yourself," he said, charismatically. Following that, we spent the evening at the bar in Taj, where he spoke inexhaustibly about his flourishing business, his convoy of luxury cars, and frequent travels to exotic destinations. I succumbed to the entire package as he afforded a lifestyle that was more than I'd asked for in what had been a night out with the girls.

When I entered the relationship, I couldn't afford a single piece of artwork by any of the masters, and now, when it was nearing its end, each of my guests were welcomed with distinguished artworks on every wall of my recently renovated apartment. My friends were thrilled each time they set foot into my home, for there would be an interesting addition to my collection each time. They teased me about Ravi, but once they viewed my art, they understood my reasons for having turned a blind eye to the lack of aesthetic appeal in him.

Much later in the relationship, he confessed he attended the art show—hosted by a close friend of his—in the hope of meeting someone. He had felt lonesome and frantically sought a companion outside the walls of his marriage. He admitted that the moment he set his eyes on me, he knew I was the one for him. He then employed his charm and money to excite me, which he obviously succeeded in doing. Wealth was a prerequisite to any relationship I got myself into, even if it left me emotionally impoverished. It had been an effective aphrodisiac, but now it was wearing off and I was beginning to resent myself for feigning.

Then there was another hidden reason. Owing to my repressed feelings and the undeniable love I had for another individual, I felt I was cheating on Ravi in my head and once caught, may hurt him considerably. No matter which man I ran into and for what duration, I only wanted to be with that one person. I learned with each transient relationship of mine that it wasn't about the men I was involved with, but more about being unable to express my suppressed sentiments.

The only time I was honest about my sexuality was in my reveries as in reality I lacked courage to be the person I was naturally meant to be. I ended each of my relationship in the hope that I'd muster the strength to reach out to that someone who'd fulfil me, even though the idea was socially, and for some, morally forbidden.

Coming back to the present, I gathered myself and drove back home. I unlocked the door to my apartment, switched on the lights, and headed to the kitchen where my espresso machine beckoned my immediate attention. I flicked it on, whisking the milk as I usually did, with urgent fervour. I was preparing a mug of steaming cappuccino for myself. I inhaled its distinct aroma which always soothed me, no matter what the problem was. My mind wandered to my children who were visiting their respective fathers over the weekend. My heart smiled at the memory of how jumpy and jovial they had been while packing, before leaving. They wore the same expression of joy each time and their innocence delighted me. They had inherited my habit of carrying stuff they would never need, but at least they didn't have to pay for excess luggage.

It was my children's weekend getaway and the anticipated time for their fathers and grandparents to pamper them. They usually returned home with new energy and remained charged the entire week. Ravi bought extravagant gifts for them too—usually gadgets. He sent them sporadically through me, as I wasn't comfortable with his direct interaction with them. It didn't seem right and I had my reservations about them accepting him as my boyfriend.

I reflected at my kitchen table, staring blindly into my mug, while sipping on the last drop of my cappuccino. In the stillness of the night, all that I could hear was the Quartz clock, ticking audibly on my feebly lit kitchen wall. It was 9 pm and I gently pulled out my mobile phone from my handbag to return Shivani's call, but her phone was once again, engaged.

# 7

I was engaged to Sameer for six months before I married him and life had a buzz back then. His incessant gifts, endless phone calls and his endearing affection were showered on me unremittingly during those six months and I was giddy with joy. I savoured the abundant attention; it kept my head in the clouds and my heart brimming with love—not that I knew any different or that I was handed a choice. I tied the knot under Ma's authority, with the confidence that she knew what was best for me. Papa insisted that Ma was, as usual, spot-on in her decision and I did nothing to oppose him. After continually being discouraged to unearth my true calling, I was silenced into marriage. I was told dreams were good as long as they didn't interfere in my flexibility to adapt to my husband and to his entire family.

In the initial years, I glowed as luminously as the morning sun that gave the reassurance of happiness and hope. I was warm with contentment and my sisters frequently remarked how radiant I appeared after marriage. They said they envied me as Sameer mollycoddled me and kept me on a pedestal, while their men didn't even pay heed to the efforts they made to please them, let alone pay any compliments. Even though Sameer made me feel like an Egyptian empress back then, I never failed to believe there was more out there for me.

Sameer called me his Cleopatra and each time he touched me, he reiterated that my milky white skin was the object of his desire. He insisted I exuded the aroma of roses, but little did he know that the bloom was bound to wane and along with it, the scent of a woman's love.

I failed to decipher the 'whys' and 'wherefores' of its wither, but we slipped into a state of discomfort where we avoided eye contact, except when we both descended into an uncontrollable rage. I didn't know exactly when our equation altered from being great, to reasonably good, to ridiculously intolerable.

When my internal life changed, I drew from my wisdom the will to understand the cracks in my marriage. As a couple that presumably were on the same page at some point, we were no longer in the same library now, let alone the same chapter.

Richa was my only friend whom I confided in recurrently and she knew chapter and verse about my wrangles with my husband, the situation becoming more revolting by the hour. She lent me a sympathetic ear each time I carried my aching heart to her and often offered to advise him to mend his ways. I, however, cautioned her to steer clear, until I reached a dead end, or he was likely to resent both of us in equal measures— me for exposing him and her, for embarrassing him. But Richa was my rock, and every time we met, we felt at home. Today too, it was no different, after we finally managed to get in touch with each other.

"What is it with you, babe? You resemble a withered rose that is no longer being watered. It obviously isn't getting any better and the tell-tale signs are increasing. It is upsetting to see your usual peaches-and-cream complexion morph into a pale, almost translucent tint. What's more, there is greyness under your eyes that once glistened with life. I suggest you make a decision before the bloom is off you, as it already is in your marriage. As for now, the only quick fix to be considered is retail therapy! If the sex is no longer on fire, then at least burn his money! We will dress you up so ravishingly that he will want to undress you with his gaze," suggested Richa, with a hint of mischief in her voice and then, she reached for my hand and caressed my silky-smooth skin. "When we no longer feel nurtured, our spirit shrinks. You need to feel love, and once you recognise its source, you need to seize it," she stated, looking tenderly into my eyes. "If he can't appreciate you, you need to make that shift. You know, right, that stagnant water is the breeding ground for many diseases, and you, my lovely friend, need to flow."

She called for our customary cappuccino—whipped to submission. It was freshly prepared for us as both of us were fond of coffee, and liked it brewed the same way. The waiters at the place we regularly went to were trained to meet our requirements, even if that meant stretching a mile for us. In that sense, we were fairly strong personalities, only to have been overshadowed by societal norms.

She flung her bouncy and well-conditioned hair behind her, revealing the perfect angles of her delicate face. Throwing herself back into her chair, she appeared casual in her black track pants, crisp white t-shirt and hot pink Nike trainers. She befitted the sporty and spruce look, both in equal proportions. Her carved figure was enviable, even though, she considered mine to be a notch better. Richa never ceased to drown me in alluring compliments. She maintained that I was voluptuous—with all the right curves—and insisted my clear glowing skin was the object of most women's desires. I always accepted her comments in good spirit.

"I spoke to Ma regarding divorce and she slapped me so mercilessly that it left my skin aching all day. A legal separation appears to be a definite no-go area and what's worse is she's convinced that I'm merely having one of my 'mood swings'," I began, while scanning the dark circles under Richa's eyes that seemed newly formed. Perhaps, she usually concealed them with make-up. Her eyes too—usually expressive—lacked lustre.

"You're wondering why I'm looking so darn dreary, right? I'm feeling every ounce of what my face is conveying to you. This old man is burning me out. He's around 205, but as fit as a 25-year-old. His passion for me is insatiable and he refuses to settle after one time. The sex is awkward and somewhat arduous as he's titanic and after making out, my energy sinks and my desire to see him again drowns even more," she chuckled as she sipped on her coffee. She quickly resumed, "He is this sex engine, who, once ignited, doesn't have the power to switch himself off. It's like he needs to prove a point despite my insistence on how satisfied I am after the first time," she stated, simultaneously checking her beeping phone. "Yes, it's him again and I must respond before he gets suspicious. His voracious appetite for me has killed mine. I'm done, Shivani. Done to death," she said, turning her gaze back to me and dropping her shoulders down in defeat. She then laughed at her situation, and hastily gulped down the remnants of her cup.

I broke into a chuckle too as she shared her jovial jaunts with her old pensioner, ready to bury him alive. Her evident excitement at the onset had transformed into resentment, like it usually did with all her men. "I understand what space you're coming from, but I can't help envying you for having a man who finds it impossible to keep his eyes off you," I reassured her.

"My mind is now dejected and my soul, depleted. But then again, I don't mean to sound ungrateful, as he has, after all, refurbished my apartment that my first husband bought me, embellishing it with artworks worth millions. I've travelled the planet with him, doing every superficial thing money can buy. I have had vodka shots while gorgeous semi-naked waiters with gold-painted torsos served us the world's most exotic narcotics in private parties lavishly thrown in his very own yacht," she said, sounding blasé. "Shivani, I've had the craziest time with him. Once, he hired exotic dancers from Paris who performed with professional finesse for us. He had flown in a silver and gold sequinned designer dress from Italy for the occasion, making me feel like an Oscar-winner. At every show he stages, he places me under the spotlight and spoils me rotten. I thank him for the amount of money he has spent on me, but the whole deal feels alien now," she said, looking dejected.

"A woman knows instinctively when the right touch caresses her, you know? He just doesn't do it for me anymore. Each time a man leaves me dismayed, I end up wrapping myself in disappointment that eventually suffocates me and makes me look the way I do right now—sad and sullen. He's a complete misfit—an uncomfortable old coat I need to slip out of. Every man I've been with has been an error that cannot be erased quick enough," she paused, before she lowered her excited voice. "The tide has to turn, babes. I was online last night in search of a cute loving dog, but this time, I was looking for the ones with four legs! They're less complicated and certainly more dedicated!" she said sincerely, without an ounce of regret as she poured more coffee. She gulped one cup after the other, as if she was guzzling shots of vodka—only this time, it wasn't served by gold-painted semi-naked men, but by regular waiters.

I eased into a smile as I searched into her eyes. She didn't seem to care much about her men, in fact, she took her fitness regime much more seriously. She admitted to weighing her men by their wallets and didn't extend her search into their hearts. Yet, she often felt sad at the demise of her relationships. I posed the same question I always did after all her affairs—it was almost a routine now.

"Okay, so here comes the million-dollar question for the trillionth time! Is it love or money? I'm afraid I already know that the latter is the stronger attraction for you, but, I have to ask. Is there any emotion there at all, besides your overwhelming love for the lifestyle it brings you?"

She sat up and without feeling conscious, she responded, "In one word, no! I only love his money, and you can say that I am indeed very emotional towards his lavish lifestyle!" she paused and let out a long-drawn-out yawn, indicating many sleepless nights. "I'm sorry, but even our discussions have become predictable. You ask the same question and my answer never changes. It's in my DNA to sleep with blank cheques and I get a real kick from it. It's my high, except now, I'm darn low. I'm a mess, Shivani, this kind of addiction has no antidote," she said, dramatically throwing her head down on the table.

"Let's order their signature chocolate cake because if we don't, then we haven't really lived, have we?" I interjected to distract her. "We could both do with a sugar fix."

"Yep! And we could both do with a shrink too. You think we can pull him out of the cake?" she joked.

"Look, I'm no one to say, but I know that if you just sit in silence and clear your mind, you will make room for a healthy companionship. He won't make you tick and sick in the same vein. You are worth more and you need to know it," I said, except she didn't seem convinced as she fiddled with her phone.

"Ravi is operating from the space of ego and feeding on it is leaving you starved. You look jaded and when he is, he'll shop elsewhere. He's always window-shopping in any case. You are a woman living her life with no boundaries, being enslaved to your fears doesn't really add up. You're too confident to let anything weigh you down. Sign yourself off from married men who incite you to behave against your better judgement. Break the very shackles that keep you locked in these patterns," I advised and as I did so, I felt like I was advising myself too. The more I chatted with her about her emancipation, the more I wanted it for myself, but just didn't know how.

"I know it's terribly toxic; the whole thing, but then that's the way it is. I need to challenge myself to be out there on my own and perhaps, you, my lovely friend, can write chronicles on my failed relationships. The stories of my infinite involvement with men could save women who are living under false notions of finding their faultless knights in shining armours. No one but themselves can rescue them from their inner demons," she said, almost lethargically.

"I don't know what the answer is, but when I look at Ma, I feel it should be self-acceptance. She looks so comfortable with herself, which you and I seem to be lacking. Getting any relationship right is like climbing the Kilimanjaro. I'm done with Sameer as I am done with Ma, because I don't feel love emanating from either," I said, feeling defeated.

"My book's title will be, 'It just isn't out there, girls!'" I said, as we both broke out in giggles.

"Why do they call them sugar daddies, anyway? Mine are always devoid of any sweetness—once the outer layer of honey is peeled off, I get to see the real deal," she said, looking into the emptiness of her cup. I was quite taken aback by her dismay; it felt as palpable as my own.

"Anyway, the truth is *I* needed him as much as he needed *me,* but I'm beginning to feel different. I aspire to walk into the sunset of my years with the best version of myself, one in which I have learnt to love and respect myself and have eventually become my own best friend—something Louise Hay, the renowned American motivator, taught me through one of the trillion books she's written and a fraction that I've read. She's been my mentor for a few weeks now and I'm warming up to the idea of applying her principles to my journey, without feeling guilty of inconveniencing others. I'm done being at the beck and call of a hefty bank balance; I want to be someone who is brave and beautiful, and as secure as she is suave. We need to feel proud of who we are. We both owe it to ourselves," Richa said with a determined look in her eyes.

"We weren't raised that way, Richa. It was hammered into me to place Sameer and my children before myself and I did it in a heartbeat, like a natural instinct. Unsurprisingly, we hold grudges against those who have robbed us of the freedom to express our aspirations and by the time we unearth our confidence, our vitality has abated," I said, eying the chocolate cake that had just arrived.

"I agree. Admittedly, I regret my past that drove me into this express lane, and I want to shift gears into something more sustaining and sincere," she said, indelicately taking a heaped spoonful of the chocolate cake that I also plunged my spoon into, though more sparingly.

"Hmmm! This is orgasmic, like no man I've ever had." With her mouth full of chocolate, she continued, "I'm giddy with all my senseless life decisions that have brought me here; to a place of utter chaos, but here's my psychoanalysis.

"It was to fill a void, an emptiness that only his wallet filled. I relished the guilt-free pampering in the beginning, but now, he's a chore and I'm this duty-bound whore that refuses to bend over backwards for him. I'm frightfully frivolous," she concluded, giggling.

I watched her uncharacteristically devour the cake and then lean back, while she stared into my eyes, intoxicated. Her glazed look stirred me and I broke into a laughter. She swayed her head up and down like she was drunk and then she stopped and stared at me again. This time, I raised my eyebrows questioningly, before motioning her to speak again.

"I'm flying to Malaysia with him and hopefully, one of our Hindu Gods can bestow upon me a reasonable answer. All my heart knows is I prefer to be here more than anywhere else any day; just you, me and coffee followed by wine and whine. But I need to go right now. I don't want to hurt him further."

"You will be hurting him nonetheless, no matter *when* you break up with him. So, save him a ticket and more memories that you'll be creating in Malaysia. More vitally, spare yourself and utilise that energy in doing something productive," I suggested.

"If I go and gently break it to him there, it will hurt him no more than a prick of a needle and that soothes my conscience too. Things will be different once I return, I promise. I'm already visualising myself in a serene place. I read somewhere that it's the feng shui and the laws of attraction principle. When you want something, start visualising it. In fact, I have a grand idea. Let us both close our eyes and visualise what we really want," she justified.

"And what would that be? So far, Ma decides what I want, so do I ask her what I should visualise?" I enquired, mockingly.

"Whatever! Get serious. Close your eyes and take a few deep breaths. Give yourself a few minutes to get into the zone," she ordered, and immediately opened one of her eyes to check if I was following her instructions—she probably knew I wasn't. Honestly, I found it silly.

"Just close them please; do it for yourself and watch the magic unfold. Move outside your past, your conditioning and your beliefs. Trust me, for God's sake. This is for me as much as it is for you. Please Shivani," she pleaded.

When I closed my eyes, I heard her voice. "Thank you! Now, take a few deep breaths and slowly picture your destination. Be bold with your wishes and visions. Let go of all your fears and enter the space your innermost desires reside," she said hypnotically, and though, I giggled at first, I found myself moving into a space of serenity.

"Cast off your distress like something old and build something extraordinary for yourself. So far, we have built molehills but now, with your unbarred vision, build mountains of dreams. This is your space and you can be anything you want. Create your haven and then see yourself happy with the new script you're writing for yourself."

Then, there was silence.

I found myself in a dream-like state as I exhaled my fears and inhaled confidence. I had stretched my imagination to see myself standing on a stage and being honoured with an award of some kind. I was standing tall and my accomplishment seemed big. There was applause and I revelled in the adulation. I was happy and grateful. I waved out at my children in the audience as they applauded for me. I noticed there was no Sameer. He was missing and suddenly, I skipped a heartbeat and opened my eyes with a start.

I faced a frowning Richa, who had her eyes closed.

"Whatever happened?" I asked, once she opened her eyes and gasped. "I guess I just visualised yet another love story gone terribly sour. It always guarantees satisfaction to begin with, but leaves me insane by the end of it. This was futile. I'm clearly enslaved to my patterns. Anyway, what did you visualise?" she sounded miffed.

"Does it matter? I guess it's useless, like you said. The reality is quite the opposite, so let's get real here. Your truth is Ravi, the woman-junkie who needs you for his daily dose of high and you both are slaves to your vices. My truth is Ma, who has always suppressed my desires, and has kept me chained to her commands. And you know what?" I pressed.

"What?" she asked, forcing a smile, though she appeared more strained after the mind exercise.

"I don't believe it was Ravi in your vision. I don't buy it for a minute. We were both supposed to be bold and honest. You don't have to share if you're not comfortable, but just know that I'm more intelligent than to accept that you were envisioning a fleeting fling."

She looked baffled and started digressing, so I let it be as I needed to rant about Ma myself.

"I'm not insulting your intelligence, Shivani, and the point of this exercise was to make you realise there's more out there for both of us. Although you're going to discuss Ma with me and I, more men—we both need to know that we are more than the lives we lead, with all the drama and dejection. Every imagined vision has the potential to be translated into limitless possibilities. If we can see it, we can be it. It's that simple," she added.

"Well I hope you're right and just seeing it in my mind's eye lent me momentary hope to implement my plan of action. You've had a positive impact on me, Richa, as usual.

"Anyway, back to my reality; I can't overcome Ma's narrow view of the world, even in the 21st century. She's in charge of my life and that sadly is my cold reality," I was bursting with emotions as I began to speak of her. "I'm still recovering from her slap and I'm averse to her playing God all the time; so much so that it makes me cringe.

"To *cure* me, she has arranged a seven-day puja at home that's supposed to bring me to my senses. She even compelled me to wear an ominous looking ring on my marital finger. But after Amma ji recounted the story behind it, I furiously flung it into the sea."

"What's the story?" Richa asked, amused.

"Ma visited this gypsy lady in the suburbs who, apparently, contacts spirits to alter people's situations. That is where she got this godforsaken ring from. It's maddening, Richa; you have no idea what it's like—having a controlling mother who pulls my strings sadistically, like I'm her dancing puppet. She further insults me by asking me to engage in matters that go against my very grain, like sitting for hours with pundits and astrologers to radically alter my mindset. So much for our meditation, Richa, in which I envisaged myself on stage receiving a trophy, because the truth is; it's all a lie. I lack courage to even be the star in my movie, so how can you possibly expect me to direct it? There are too many villains in my life for me to ever be the hero," I sighed hard and felt a rush of sweat on my forehead. Richa poured water into my glass, as I continued crying my woes.

"Her only concern is the estimations other people have of her and their evaluation of our entire family. This is why she hides behind façades of perfection, while keeping the unsavoury secrets under her hat. She has her own notions of what works for us according to her beliefs, her convenience and conventions. That's the way she's raised her daughters—with a servant's heart that wants nothing, but gives unrelentingly. She is biased towards Shiv and discriminates against my gender. Has she forgotten that she, too, is a woman?" I said, with knots of anger gripping my solar plexus.

"You don't resent your Ma, Shivani. She's your mom and she loves you as you love her, but she's in her own prison, like the rest of us. Perhaps, you can make her view life from a different window, you know what I mean? Teach her to be spontaneous. Gift her *Eat Pray Love,* the book by Elizabeth Gilbert. Or better still, give her *50 Shades of Grey* for a liberating experience!" she said, giggling again.

"Very funny, Richa. She's liberated, all right, while drawing pleasure from keeping us in her prison. Her love doesn't come without governance.

"She got me this walker from London when I was nine months old. It was actually meant for Shiv when he was born and till then, I had the privilege of using the fancy-looking thing first. And it was indeed, my very first, as everything else, were hand-me-downs. Anyway, it was to enable me to walk and then become independent of the contraption once I could do so. But you know Richa, I'm still stuck in that walker because it seems like *she* doesn't want to see me walk my path," I had tears in my eyes as I opened my heart out to my friend.

"You have to persevere, Shivani. You can't let her rule you forever, so start visualising your liberation and work arduously towards it. Remember, you will only receive what you believe," she advised.

"I'll try, I promise, but she's clipped my wings and I'm exhausted from banging my head against the wall. Oh, I almost forgot! I've a lunch date with my brother and my agenda is to persuade him to convince Ma that a divorce is justified and that she must bend her principles this one time."

"How can I help? Anything for you; you know that," she offered.

"Can you meet us both to strengthen my case? Can't do this without you, Richa, I really need you, as always," I insisted while guzzling down water, before another thought sprang to mind.

"Also, I know I discouraged you earlier, but please speak to my estranged husband? Dissuade him from living in a fragmented relationship when we can both find happiness once we're out of it. After he assigns me what is rightfully mine, I'll walk away to start afresh. We can come up with some plan to distribute time with our children. My divorced friends are admirably amicable with one other so when Sameer and I part, we can hopefully hold a conversation without having the impulse to throttle each other and risk life imprisonment. We're both serving a life sentence in any case and if I'm subjected to this silent state any longer, I will consider it a death sentence. I really will," I said desperately now, as my breath turned shallow. My sadness encompassed me like a cold chill. I thought of how I hadn't been secure in the marriage since I discovered that fidelity was not Sameer's strong suit, besides the fact that he was indifferent and sometimes, even abusive towards me.

"Your Ma is a tough cookie, and you've been at odds with her since you were an embryo in her womb. Perhaps, Shiv is the only person who can twist her arm, being the apple of her eye. As for Sameer, I hesitate because I need Dutch courage to have a word with him, but I guess, for you, I will truly try. He might listen to my perspective, you never know. I'll call him later and ask him to meet at Taj coffee shop or something," she said, lifting her toast and biting into it ravenously. She then added, "But I will meet with him just this once and only for you. In fact, anything for you, Shivani, you know that."

"Yes, Richa, just this once! I promise I won't subject you to this again," I reassured, moving towards her to express how sincerely I valued our friendship. She immediately moved her eyes away from the toast and tea, gazing most tenderly at me.

She was convinced I was her soulmate and stretching out her hand to interlock with mine, she stated with softness in her voice, "I love you more than you'll ever know and I will do what it takes to get your radiant smile back, but you also need to start taking baby steps. You've held your tongue and swallowed your anger for way too long. But I shall try my best, even though, I am afraid to get too entangled because you know how averse Sameer and your Ma are to our friendship. They just need someone to belittle and blame."

# 8

I blamed him for making out with me and for being so darn reluctant in taking me out afterwards. I belittled him for not taking me shopping during the day and clubbing at night. If it was just the overblown bedroom that he wanted us to be confided in, then we should have met back in Mumbai on his return.

"I fail to grasp why in God's name you brought me to Kuala Lumpur when all you wanted me for was to undo your oversized trousers without you undoing your wallet! You've changed at the speed of lightning and you need to stop taking me for granted. I swear you'll regret it. Where are the surprises that you used to keep up your sleeve for me?" I wailed and wallowed.

I stood up naked from the bed to slip on a gown. "I wanted to shop at the pavilion mall and dress up in a new outfit for a night at the Heli Lounge bar, where there is some prospect of meeting younger people on the same wavelength as myself." I was behaving like a spoilt teenager, but the anger in me was bursting at the seams, probably owing to a deeper repressed issue.

"But baby, I've booked us a plush restaurant tonight where we are to wine and dine for hours. Trust me, I wanted to take you shopping, but my meetings got stretched. I'm so sorry, but let me book you a stone massage and a pedicure and whatever else that'll relax you. We can both go as a couple, I too would benefit hugely from a Thai massage. They are the most effective!" he said, desperately trying to appease me— confused by my overreaction to a situation that could easily still be rectified. He had, after all, handed me his credit card before leaving for his meetings.

"What movie are you living in now, Ravi? I've been alone and frustrated the entire day and trust me, I'm more relaxed than your ass can ever unwind me. Therapy for me is shopping and clubbing, and the latter, I want to do till the wee hours of the morning and not merely while you speedily throw down your pegs of whisky, only to rush back to the room. You always want to do things your way and I'm tired of it," I said, all too hastily.

I found myself searching for excuses to fire him out of my life and hoped my sadistic strategy proved effective. I'd engaged his mind all this time, but then, there were very few individuals who didn't raise youth and beauty on a pedestal, particularly when theirs had faded away. I had many advantages in this affair, but I needed to move into a more meaningful direction before the rose of my youth lost its bloom.

Ravi's life—like a melting candle—was burning out. Currently, he was reliving his youth through me and was in dire need to tighten his grip because if I loosened mine, he'd have to go through the drill of playing the chasing game again. But time, unlike his fortune, wasn't on his side.

Since a teenager, I was gifted with an arresting charm that lured guys to gravitate towards me. Shivani insisted I was like an engaging piece of art that prompted people to stop and scrutinise and on feeling the satisfaction of having viewed something so beautiful, they carried on. I had the most intriguing aura and most people unflinchingly asked me on a date or at the very least, exchanged numbers, after exchanging pleasantries.

I chose to be high maintenance, therefore, the sugar daddies met my material desires whilst I satisfied their erotic obsessions. I learnt to be smart and often, serpentine. I played my cards with skill, considering the hand dealt to me was a compromised one. My experiences with Ravi had kept my excitement alive awhile and now, I wanted to walk into the next phase of my life without grudging him in greater measure than was necessary.

Stemming from my second divorce, my life was thrown into deep disarray and I was embroiled in bleakness. I went from being in the limelight to being thrown into the shadows. No one knew who I was then and I wasn't in the space to hone my individuality. I became an introvert, until I identified my aesthetic attributes that pressed my life's pulse to run again.

Both my husbands were eminent personalities, so initially, it was an arduous task for me to rebuild my portfolio as a single woman. But later, I began to earn my respectability as an individual. Initially, however, I slept mindlessly with anything that looked remotely appealing. Shivani, my most dependable friend under God's sun had the wisdom to point out that anything on the outside of myself was momentary and I needed to get comfortable with myself first. But I continually attracted the wrong man. The polygamy continued as I remained in a deluded place of running into men for the sake of running away from myself.

In addition to my existing struggles, people made sensational claims about the alimony I fought for and attained, along with my unending affairs. It was a front-page headline that never faded away. Some stories have nothing to do with reality, but people end up believing them anyway. Plenty of seasoning is added too, for effect.

Another fallacy about my life was that I fell in love with a man's wealth more than I did with him. Even though that hadn't been intentional in the early days, I fell into a habit of trying to steal a lifestyle. These aspersions did nothing to rectify my behavioural patterns, but it taught me to strengthen my immunity to hearsay as well as prying ears and eyes.

He apologised instantly for not taking my feelings into consideration, bringing me back from my visit to memory lane. "I want to make it up to you. I swear, I'll be a better lover who pleases you with the same intensity as you please me. Tonight, we can go to all the bars in the city; every single one of them. I'll postpone all my meetings. We could postpone our return by a day, two or three. Whatever you say, I'm willing to do. I want to satisfy you in every way because I know I can," he proposed with dire desperation in his voice; he was panting from speaking too fast. He then came sprinting to wrap me in his arms, "I promise to take you for retail therapy. In fact, tomorrow, we will shop till we drop. I had a series of meetings today, but all I wanted was to be with you. You are my oxygen and I know I will suffocate without you," he said, trembling with anticipation. He kissed me hard on my lips, before manoeuvring me back again in bed.

I almost felt as pitiful towards him as I did towards myself and given that we were miles away from home, I softened my blow.

"I'm sorry Ravi, it's just that I've been on the balcony, staring enviably at the guests down there—swimming, sipping vibrant-looking cocktails with their partners and gazing up dreamily at the clear azure skies. The radiance on their faces was a reflection of the joy they shared with each other, while I wore this wretched frown on my face all afternoon as I burned with jealousy. In spite of the landscape being unflawed, I felt it was barren and bleak without your presence. I felt hollow without you, baby, and just needed you to be there for me. I was scared to be alone, that's all."

Gosh, I was being counter-productive now. But my insecurities were spilling out as fast as his urge to make love to me. He was so ravenous that he stopped me from talking by pressing his lips on mine, and in that moment of silence, I heard the sound of his insatiable lust. He was far from an adept lover.

After several dissatisfying minutes, he rolled off me and flopped onto his back, exhausted. He vehemently flaunted his ability to do it once more, but I sank back and closed my eyes to shut him out. He was still in a state of flailing intoxication, but he lit a cigarette on realising my unwillingness and switched on the television to surf the channels. I contemplated standing under a cold shower to cleanse myself of the sweat and hypocrisy, but I ended up taking a nap.

Kuala Lumpur had a distinct flavour and I imagined savouring Malaysian food on the tip of my tongue, while my eyes were still shut. The fact that I was finding thoughts about food more tantalising than his touch was a sign of having lost my appetite for him. As I drifted into light sleep, I heard him confirming a reservation for the most exquisite and expensive place—Latife, a French cuisine-restaurant, that served a six-course meal to their guests. At that moment, I decided not to make a scene by insisting on having Malaysian food that night, as tomorrow I'd stage another outburst to exhaust his patience and force his exit from my life.

"I've arranged a six-course candlelight meal for us and as we enter, they will serve your favourite pink champagne as an aperitif, while an eminent band plays for us in the PDR. The evening has been fine-tuned to whet your appetite, my love," he said, gazing into my elusive eyes that I now opened in response. I wasn't heartless, but as much as I tried being in the moment, I envisaged ending the affair that was already over in my head. In the same vein, I was deeply sympathetic towards him, sensing that his insecurities dug deeper than mine and he seemed lonelier than I was. We both were feeding off each other's misery.

The one noble thought I entertained evaporated as I realised he would switch from being a lover to a husband as effortlessly as he switched channels on the television. He acted in front of his tired wife who in turn was in denial to protect herself from the humiliation. This way, it was probably easier for her to cope and concentrate on more pressing issues than her man's loyalty.

I wasn't forsaking him for another man this time; I was simply quitting this relationship to regain my dignity. I had caged myself into endless lies and now that I was shrinking under them, I longed to set myself free.

Within minutes of surfing the channels, he fell asleep with his mouth wide open. He soon began to snore and one of his hairy legs protruded from the duvet. Next to him on the side table, were his watch, wallet and spectacles. He was dead to the world and I didn't want to nudge him as I slipped out of my thoughts. I gently sat up, straightened my hair, and flung out of the duvet. I took a shower and after slipping into my yellow floral dress and matching sandals, I headed down to sit by the aquamarine sea. I ordered for myself some flower tea and sushi as I was famished after the never-ending poking with him. I punched in Shivani's number, while relishing the most scrumptious sushi and soaking in the most splendid sunset.

Her number was unreachable.

The smoke from the barbeque filled the air with mist, but once it cleared, I viewed the unmistakable beauty of the horizon. I gazed out towards the turquoise sea that had pink and orange colours of the sunset merging into it. I captured its magnificence on my mobile phone's camera and at once posted it on Instagram, with the title, 'Mirrors of the cosmos.' I immersed myself in the rhythmic ripples of the sea, unlike in Mumbai, where it was murky and at times, misty. After an hour, the light began fading and the clouds moved their curvaceous heads to form a pale blue sheet. A female vocalist greeted the evening with a song from the '80s, lifting the air with a mild melancholic magic. I hummed along the song by Bonnie Tyler along with the vocalist, who sang it just as soulfully as the original. A feeling of dread slowly took residence in my gut as I imagined being in that lonely space again where all that escorted me was my eclipsed heart. The skies turned from crimson to purple and as I bit into the final piece of sushi, I looked up to see that it was swiftly turning deep blue.

Stillness had finally settled on the horizon after many colours had danced around on its infinite canvas. Life was like that too. Our lives bathed in different shades during different moments. And then, one day, through it all, there was calmness—a stillness that arrived only after having passed through the changes. The vocalist smiled at me as she concluded her last note and I applauded and requested her to sing one of my favourite tunes from the same era by Cher, 'Believe.'

The tune instilled strength in me and inspired me to believe in the life I deserved. After tonight, I wasn't going to be afraid of ending a chapter, only to begin one that was more meaningful. As much as I was grateful to Ravi for his generosity, I decided to delicately, but diligently, strike him out.

# 9

I needed to strike while the iron was hot and there was an inextinguishable fire in me to speak to Ma, to pursue the pressing matters that had been repressed for too long. I owed her a reasonable explanation and perhaps, now was the time to pour out the years of woe that I had inadvertently allowed myself to be consumed with.

In keen anticipation, Ma was knitting, as she was alone at home that late Sunday afternoon, while Papa was out playing flash with his retired friends. She glanced up at me through her Cartier spectacles that were perched at the tip of her nose, making her look exquisite. I secretly hoped I grew to be as graceful on entering the winter of my life.

"I have arranged our most revered family pundit ji to dissipate all negativity that surrounds you. He will pray ardently that you fall in love with the institution of marriage. I need you to become averse to the concept of divorce and to no longer consider your marriage an ailing limb," Ma began as her calm countenance was swiftly shed to demonstrate a repulsed expression. She spoke in her usual condescending tone, especially employed with me.

When in conversation with Richa, I had been able to recognise her striving for superiority as a complex of some sort. But at this point, when I was in front of her, my finger pointed only towards myself as I felt I was the one causing

Mt. Everest to crumble. To me, she was practically perfect, while I was fundamentally flawed.

She placed her knitting down and stood up, taller than me. All I really ached for was for her to hold me and tell me it was not my fault that I was desperately unhappy. If only she asked me about my life situations, instead of dictating them to me. From the time I was in nursery, I was told what a house, sun and a flower were meant to look like on paper and their shapes were always the same. From school onwards, I was again told the relevance of each subject and my curriculum was decided by the authorities. As an adult too, I was told to get married, have children and to accept whatever life threw at me. I was never asked and when people like myself are relentlessly told what to do, we never find the voice to speak our truth. At almost forty, the realisation that she had chartered my entire life was dawning on me, and even now, I couldn't live on my own terms.

She wasn't smiling, but stood with a stern expression. The compulsive urge to put me down was in her expression, as she pulled her spectacles closer to her eyes to scrutinise me more prudently. I drew a deep breath and mustered the courage to speak before she did.

"Ma, can you please hear me out before engaging in anything so absurd and annoying?" I spoke up, only to be blatantly ignored as if I wasn't audible to her.

"Following the rituals, we will visit the Shiva temple and be seated in a puja that shouldn't exceed two hours. Subsequently, we'll eat the divine food and come back with constructive thoughts that will encourage us to move forward in our lives. Once you understand that your warped thinking is a transient experience, it will lose all power over you. You're better than this, but right now your intelligence is eclipsed, owing to external influences. I'm tenacious about protecting you from spiralling into the depths of divorce, needlessly. Your restlessness will abate once this is done, and everything will look better in the morning," she said, with a face set in righteous determination.

'Everything will look better in the morning? I don't have acne or a rash that will miraculously vanish with the salve of a single prayer,' I found myself wondering.

My understanding was far removed from all this—the temple and its endless rituals, rites and doctrines. I was a pragmatist who believed in being a decent person instead of a hypocrite who sought divine solutions to clean the slate. There were endless disputes out there concerning religion, and such theories stirred commotion in me, as it did in the real world.

After observing Ma's relentless ritualism in childhood, I had ceased to take the notion of God seriously in my adulthood. Particularly after marriage, I didn't know how to connect with Him on a one-to-one basis, without rituals and superstitions creating a barrier between us. In my life, I had been offered many misrepresentations of Him and they only widened the gap between us.

I found myself bearing the brunt of her domineering nature, but something in me was flaring up. Sooner or later, I was bound to explode. For now, I maintained a silent decorum. Besides the rituals, she inculcated abstinence in the form of fasting on a weekly basis to me, which was the most ineffective introduction to the Almighty because from my perspective, it kept me caged in suspicions and starvation. Given my forced beliefs and my resentment towards Him for starving me every week, God mustn't be in a hurry to catch up with me anyway and perhaps, if I did divorce, I'd be deleted from his database altogether.

In one way, my faith grew to be more practical, silently disputing Ma's beliefs. I poured my compassion on those who were less favoured and I was mindful not to harm anyone. I believed that the wheel rotated full circle to land back on us as I had seen karma visiting us time and again, earnestly knocking on our door to awaken us from our dishonest dealings. Ordeals often came to salvage us, but I noticed how conveniently people around me bore the pain of loss as incidental and didn't care to clear their conscience by cleaning up their act. Karma never slept and people, generally, never awakened.

As I silently stood before her, what was becoming increasingly loud was her derogatory behaviour towards me and I was able to attribute it to a very deep insecurity in her. These desperate actions unveiled the dark traits in her and it was frightening to learn the extent she went to, to make life bend to her whims and wants.

The narrow spaces between the wider ones of frustration in me, however, were filled with overwhelming admiration for her indomitable strength to hold the fort while she held herself together. She was extraordinary in many ways and despite my resentment towards her, I found myself giving her the benefit of doubt. I was beginning to acknowledge that I wasn't a leftover scrap and it was important for me to feel the worthiness I had never felt. As Richa and I engaged ever more frequently in creative visualisation, I found myself feeling more positive and less subservient to Ma.

Her myopic understanding of the world could be blamed either on her generation or her family that lived by only one word—sacrifice. To question authority was inconceivable to them, and the authority figures commonly constituted the male members in households in addition to the elderly, and it was my grandma in our family. She had the final word in all family considerations and conclusions while Papa and grandpa voiced their expertise in business matters. Presently, however, Ma had succeeded in all territories as my grandparents had passed on and Papa's health had descended. She controlled everyone, including God it seemed.

"Ma, I know you're acting like I haven't spoken two minutes ago, but I personally feel it's ridiculous to negotiate with your God to alter what I believe in. Can a pundit really play mediator between Him and I to grant me what *you* feel is right for me? Why would He listen to him and not me? I don't even charge!" I said with a tone that sounded assertive to my ears.

"Are you ridiculing my principles and the beliefs of millions of other Hindus held over a trillion years? You will do as I deem fit. In addition, I have asked our family astrologer to give you semi-precious stones to wear in the form of rings to ward off the evil around you," she stated to further tighten the noose around my neck.

She then stared at my finger and noticed the missing ring, "Where is that ring I asked you to wear? It was for your benefit and not the place you've disposed it in, so you must dig deep to find it and wear it at once. I trust you have more sense next time," she said and then, rather agitatedly turned towards the man in a long yellow robe, who had just entered the room we were in. He was waiting with abiding patience for me to sit beside him to soak in his mantras.

She adopted a curt voice and said, "Pundit ji, don't pay heed to this ignorant daughter of mine and do the needful to restore her faith in her marriage and in our religion. Her generation is afflicted with a destructive mind that governs the heart. She, for one, needs good sense to prevail or she will destroy everything I have built for her and for this family. I cannot have her set Mumbai tongues wagging on us because of her so-called 'modern' thinking. Please pray hard for her to fall head over heels in love with her husband again. I am sure he does too!"

She had reached her boiling point and there was no point in fuelling her anger by being more defiant, so I sailed along, except my expression indicated my anger. I felt sympathy for her pundit who was also hired on various occasions to plead with God for Roheen's pregnancy.

There was a dense and almost tangible gloom in the room, and the bleakness of the outside world was a mirror of my inner one. I didn't know Ma any more than I knew her God. Confidence is what she and my husband had robbed me of to convince me that my place on earth was to be submissive and subdued. Her repeated words echoed in my sore head—'I'm looking down at you from a great height; I have the upper hand, seven decades of experience and I know what's best for you so don't argue with my wisdom. One is a very vulnerable number, Shivani, and you won't make it to the shore alone.'

It was not her 'advice', but her reprimands that left me silent, but not subdued—not anymore. I wore an indifferent expression because within, I had already decided to work on my inner strength. Wisdom prevailed in me as right now, I saw no point in refuting her inflamed ego.

Today, I was getting to witness the fragmented part of Ma—hard, volcanic but with a broken spirit. Time had probably done that to her, along with the people she had learned to trust. Those who were meant to love her had betrayed her in many ways. That was my theory and someday, I hoped she would relay her story to me, as I felt there were chapters of pain that caused her to turn steel-like today. Beneath that anger and her troubled heart, her voice had never trembled, except now it did.

"Shivani, I have always believed in giving it my all to my husband and to my children. It's a harsh world out there. A divorced woman is talked down upon and treated as a piece of scrap to be used, abused, and then discarded. I am certain you are not even remotely aware of the perils that await you if you do foolishly decide to obtain a legal separation. Along with the lurking sexual atrocities, you will also be repudiated. Your married friends will divorce you as they will feel insecure about inviting you—a single woman—to their couples' gatherings," she said with bated breath, while I stared at her now, almost with disdain.

"Ma!" I finally intervened impatiently, "I get it, you don't want me to file for a divorce, but can we not get so melodramatic? I think the pundit is waiting for us."

"Melodramatic!" she sighed. "Melodramatic?" she repeated now.

"It'll be melodrama when everything you've been lavishly bestowed with will be taken away from you—the luxuries, the respect and the liberties of spending whenever you want!"

Ma had woven separation and stigma together and I shuddered to think what would happen if I refuted her claims.

I gradually allowed my anger to appease, as I had no urge to go against the current of Ma's turbulent emotions. I decided to distract myself and began staring enviably at the sparkling floor that stretched out before me. 'Why wasn't my floor this clean?' I wondered now if my maids were lying about using proper cleaning and polishing agents. Everyone lied, I concluded as I felt my blood boil and my eyes reveal anger. My maids were not keen on domesticity any more than I was in sitting here and pretending to listen to Ma's lecture. They were drearily doing their duty as I was doing mine; both most resentfully. I knew that on facing my maids, I would vent out on them. I felt pretty hopeless in front of Ma, but at least I had a hold on them.

"What is vitally important, Shivani, is not to overlook under what circumstances you married Sameer. Your father and grandfather were going through a financial crisis and owing to your greatest fortune—your beauty, you received a proposal from his family who then rescued our company. We joined hands and within a year, we became one of the leading Ayurveda companies in the country."

From the floor, my head lifted towards her as she still rambled on; my time clearly didn't matter to her. "Ma, please, can we begin, for God's sake?" I found myself uttering, but she continued as she spoke over me.

"In recent times, our efforts have been collaborative and today we not only have factories and stores, but we export our finished products to the leading countries of the world. I must not fail to add that more than collaboration, it's been co-operation on your in-law's behalf and more recently, there have been talks of them stepping out. They even proposed to sell their share to us. I cannot forget their kindness and I will not allow you to let them down," she said flatly, while her finger wagged up and down at me.

By now, I was exasperated. I interjected with a spill of sarcasm, "Ma, I need to get back home to my children, so can we begin whatever prayers you believe in to purify my contaminated thoughts? I swear, after today, I will never bring up the subject again," I lied.

I hoped she'd back off, but she didn't as she continued barging me with her lecture. She decided not to respond to my plea and so I decided to turn a deaf ear to her.

"Have you thought about what will become of your social calendar that is always full of events? You always get front row seats to every concert, fashion show and theatrical plays. You are a distinguished guest at every social event in town. What about the red carpet treatment that you so take for granted, young lady? You will be reduced to a mere divorcee who will feel the rejection of her married friends and will be subjected to lewd eyes of men in every area of life in Mumbai, including the gym. Is that what you want, to be branded a whore?"

I was repulsed by the way Ma related to my situation that was becoming increasingly insufferable. According to Ma, it was clearly illegal for me to get divorced, but was my fear of her legitimate? My patience was wearing thin, while my anger grew, by the minute, towards my maids at home who definitely lied about using the right polish to clean the floors. I'd polish my own floors after obtaining a plush apartment as part of my alimony. My attention was blurring out on Ma now as I was somewhat confident that Shiv would press all the right buttons. I was already imagining obtaining my freedom and my apartment would be a home to all my friends as I intended to venture into something productive to generate an income—maybe organic juices and energy bars. I was beginning to see the reflection of my blindingly bright future in Ma's luminously clean floors.

"It's blindingly simple, Shivani! You cannot and will not divorce Sameer. Do you understand? Are you even listening to me?" she asked in a hurt tone. I wondered if being difficult was part of her religion. As I sat frozen before her, I drew on every ounce of patience in me and I released a heavy sigh.

"Now let's start the puja and hopefully, when you return to your home tonight, life will become simpler and you will be able to view your situation from a new perspective. Now smile for me Shivani, you are still alive, aren't you?" she asked, without stopping.

"I'd smile for you Ma, if there was a reason. But since, there isn't, let's finally start the puja now that your lecture is over. Oh, but don't worry, I'll be all smiles once your God has blessed me to be the 'good wife'!" I said, finally finding my voice.

I now felt slightly more alive than the nail in her door as she uttered something in response—this time, meekly. I then sat on the floor with her and her pundit ji who wore a naturally severe expression. He appeared to be more upset with God than anyone else in the room. His spectacles were far too loose on him and he kept pushing them up every few seconds while he glared at me, as if I had deeply offended his God. His sombre face had lines etched all over it and his ebony short straight hair that had been oiled for days didn't quite correspond with his haggard expression. It looked like he was wearing a wig and after inspecting him, I closed my eyes to listen to his cryptic chants that were meant to mend my broken destiny. I felt a sudden wave of determination in me that I was previously unacquainted with. As I sat there with a frozen look, I began to feel my fear thaw.

Divorce was now married to stigma, abandonment, loneliness, poverty, rape and more recently, conspiracy and prostitution too!

# 10

Prostitution wasn't what I had signed up for, but had I carried on with my disparaging liaisons with Ravi, I would have been reduced to one. I was beginning to feel responsible for every choice I made. Change often had an insensitive personality as it transformed love to hatred and despite the millions of buttons we had at our fingertips today, there was still no switch that prevented such transformation.

Owing to my impenetrable insecurities, I latched on to people and objects that should've been prevented from entering my life in the first place. Ravi was one such individual and now that my affair with him was laid to rest, I needed to awaken to my truth.

My morning meeting with my mirror was not a very encouraging one. As I had felt tormented by the choices made by me, the angst had taken residence on my face. I noticed fine lines appearing on my forehead, like a permanent frown. Perhaps, it was time for Botox, now that the number forty was gaping at me from around the corner. The two *awesome* young girls at the gym would *totally* savour the gossip. I imagined their faces on discovering that I hadn't, after all, been into any of the men I had liaised with and there was another side to me. Perhaps, I was a latecomer to the idea of waking up to my truth, but then, it was time that aroused real courage.

In spite of breaking up with Ravi, he attempted several times to reignite my interest in him. He continued to whine and whinge till he got accustomed to my absence. The adventure of being with difficult men, locking me in their drama, no longer stimulated my senses. On the other hand, committing to the proverbial good guy with an insufficient income was out of question. It had been hard for me to conform to the norm, so I remained agitated by my secrets. What kept me afloat were my workouts. 'Winners train, while losers complain' was the sign posted at the entrance of the gym and although I didn't feel like a victor, running was the only thing I knew.

I worked out manically, panting on the treadmill to release my emotional and physical toxins. I noticed Ravi calling me relentlessly and his messages slipped into voicemail that I would delete soon after retrieving. As he was a distinguished individual, I had thrashed and bashed his ego, but letting him go had been crucial. Ravi no longer accommodated me in any capacity, despite having gone all out for me, particularly when he gave me the most unexpected surprise as an early fortieth birthday present. We celebrated with pomp and show on the eve of our break-up. He gifted me a figure-hugging designer dress flown in from Milan, and then he walked me through a restaurant which had soft romantic lighting with sensual music. The restaurant was reserved exclusively for us and once we sat down, we were served pink champagne. After we toasted, he gave me the most exquisite 20-carat solitaire that I returned to him the following day, once my conscience awakened.

All my relationships had been epic failures and now I gave myself space to be alone without pining for any individual.

I was still processing it while I continued running—running from my past blunders it seemed or perhaps, towards more, until I broke the cord of fear to act on my natural instincts. I wasn't prepared to partake in any more deception for the sake of avoiding social stigma.

A constructive idea momentarily distracted me from my on-going thoughts. I needed to make the call that could change the course of two lives. He always refused to answer unknown numbers but perhaps, he had saved mine. Despite his apparent prejudices against me, I wanted to be useful to Shivani. Hers was the only friendship that had sustained over the years—practically two decades—and she needed clear navigation. My love for her fuelled my willingness to be there for her and I promised to give it one shot at either resolving or dissolving her marriage. I descended the treadmill and paced towards the juice bar to sit and do the needful. The phone barely rang before he answered in his charismatic voice.

"Hey Richa! Good to hear your lovely voice. How are you doing, sweetheart?"

Mr. Ever-so-charming had saved my number after all. I requested him to meet me at the Taj coffee shop as per his convenience. Without a moment's hesitation, he confirmed to meet me after he returned from his business trip to Delhi. He said he would revert with the exact time and day and as he spoke, I wondered if he really would or was he merely brushing me off. I gave him the benefit of doubt and responded positively.

"I look forward to our coffee, Sameer. Thanks for agreeing to meet me," I concluded as he sounded most gracious and didn't seem to resist seeing me, despite his suspicions on what the meeting might entail. He was too shrewd not to know, but he maintained a composed countenance.

After informing Shivani of our imminent meeting, I spent the evening with my children, along with Shivani's. I had made a pact with her to entertain her kids along with mine as and when my schedule permitted. It kept our children bonded. Shashwat and Shriya bore a strong resemblance to Shivani and she had raised them to be mild-mannered.

We ended up at Crosswords mall where we bowled for over an hour and devoured the most insalubrious junk food, bursting with calories. The boys ordered a margarita pizza with extra cheese, and the girls, a burger each—we shared a large portion of French fries. I could've ordered something sensible for myself, but I was in the mood to blend in with the children. My palate was happy as I also ate an entire cheese burger without a morsel of guilt.

During these blissful moments with the children, I cared two hoots about the impositions placed on my health by doctors, dieticians and adverts. I felt incredibly invigorated, although I knew that at the crack of dawn, I'd be in the gym to retain my carved figure.

I summoned my children to teach me the bowling technique and once they patiently went through the motions with me, I managed my first strike. Shashwat's score was enviably high and my son, Harsh, challenged to beat him in the next game. My daughter, Simran, was competing with her sibling and she hit a spare in most of her shots. Meanwhile, Shriya was not far behind and the game was gaining momentum. In the next game, I managed another strike and there was loud cheering from all four of them as they jumped up and down, most boisterously. The air was dancing to a symphony of laughter, cheer and a triumph of life's small, but significant pleasures. My daughter offered me a high-five and my son gave me a peck on the cheek and as they did, I caught the twinkle in both their eyes.

In the third and final round, I sat back and watched the siblings compete with one another—my two, against Shivani's two. The seriousness on their faces was adorable as each team was determined to win. Shriya reprimanded Shashwat every time the ball toppled into the gutter. I captured each one's expressions on my mobile phone as they played, and I sent the images to Shivani.

In the end, it was I who won—something beyond the measurement of a score. Everything in life wasn't about statistics and the laughter, the cheer and the warmth exuding from the children was more than anything that could be quantified. There was something therapeutic about being in children's company.

If motherhood had a palette, it would be the soft and soothing pastels of Monet or August Renoir. When everything felt futile, I nudged myself to remember the triumph I had attained as a mother. It taught me absolute love and that joy was more tangible than receiving a well-earned trophy.

I may have been down a few games, but I was certainly not out.

# 11

I felt terribly down and out as I sat across Shiv, spilling out the noxious natters I had with Ma in the past several days and her most unacceptable approach to my pitiful state.

Shiv understood that a split-up was necessary in my case, particularly when the situation was clogging the joy in my life. He was willing to lend me his uncompromising support at every level. He was not like the rest of my siblings who immediately reprimanded me, following my heart-wrenching meeting with Ma. They all had a similar opinion and my eldest sister antagonised me with her version of home truths about divorce. She blackmailed me in the same way as Ma had done—they were both employing their face-saving tactics on me. When I expressed my contempt towards them to Shiv, he confirmed that they separately told him what a fool I was to waive the wealth and lifestyle that accompanied my marriage. They reminded me of the society that was bound to hammer me as the object of their gossip. Wagging tongues no longer rattled me as I had more pressing issues to handle.

Shiv had internalised our sisters' beliefs when he was much younger as they had forced them on him, but he no longer respected their impositions. Shiv knew what wearing a noose around one's neck felt like since he worked with Ma on a daily basis, except thankfully, not in the same department.

She was as forensic as she was focused and at the end of each day, she demanded figures and other updates and my brother lived up to her expectations as best as he could.

"She's always been as managerial at home as she is in the office and she's unacceptably self-indulgent about how she runs the show. When it comes to us, however, it's set in stone, Shivani. Nothing can be tweaked, I'm afraid, as her behaviour *is* etched in stone. No one wants to change," sadness was implanted in my eyes as I heard him out because there seemed to be no room for mobility. But in spite of it, I spoke to Shiv in a tone that was sombre, but steadfast. I revealed my strategies for my children and my own future.

On continuing our conversation, I realised how fortunate I was to have him as my brother who never shied away from lending me his patient ear. I loved Shiv's voice—his diction, his intonation and his articulation. He understood the complexities of relationships and yet endeavoured to keep them as simple as he was. He was the first to throw his hands up in the air on any domestic disagreement with Roheen and any dispute in the office with Ma. He chose his peace of mind over his ego. In the real world—outside his home and family—he was preparing himself to enter politics one day and one of the changes he aspired to was to bring women and men on an equal platform. On asking why he wanted to support women, he said he was raised in a female-oriented family and understood their plights and fights. Ma may have been domineering, but she wasn't open to new amendments for women, because she was stuck in a time warp. Shiv was the only one who could open her mind to a woman-oriented world.

"I'm not as driven in the business as Ma wants me to be. But I believe that in politics, I will have my own platform, Shivani. I feel whitewashed by her. Since Papa retired, she has been fiercely active in the office and its affairs, but some of her principles are just traditions that hold no relevance in today's business world," he stated, pausing for a while before carrying on the conversation.

"All said and done though, Shivani, I'm drawn to this dysfunctional sense of responsibility towards her. Sometimes it is wiser to play along, so as to not disturb her equilibrium. She does have redeeming attributes after all, and we are all aware of them. There is something good to be said about traditions too, as averse to them as we may be at times.

"Having said that, I understand how irksome it can be. Whenever trouble brews in our personal lives, she seems to have one universal answer for all of us—pundit ji! It's terribly alienating for those who don't subscribe to such irrationally controlling behaviour," he said, frustrated at first and then easing himself into a relaxed smile.

"You're a guy, Shiv, and because of that, she is biased. She discriminates all the time. It's unfair and I personally feel even Roheen gets the better side of her than I do. I've noticed there's no interference from her in Roheen's affairs," I said, cringing my teeth.

"That also may be out of guilt as she's the one who pushed me into the marriage when all I really wanted at that point was to marry that 'white girl,' and the rest you know," he replied, sinking back into his chair, expanding his well-built chest.

As he exhaled, his eyes penetrated into mine. "Shivani, to be brutally honest, Ma will never grant you her consent for a divorce, no matter how distressed you may be. I'm tactful and I hide behind a mask of caution like you did, but now your bubble has burst. You want her to rearrange your life's order by bending the principles she clings to. That, I am afraid, my dear sis, is a tall order for her."

"Shiv, when have I ever been able to align her to my thinking? She can't relate to me, let alone to my distress. I understand she's old school and can't relate to modern menaces like 'divorce', but do you understand my plight? It's not like it's on a whim that I want my separation, it has been years of silent struggle. My intent is not to sabotage her reputation, but to build a life outside the four walls of heartache."

We both discussed her open hostility towards modern thinking and agreed that she detested Richa for having gone down the road of separation twice.

"Ma is convinced that you don't have a mind of your own, so Richa has cajoled you to divorce Sameer," Shiv said.

"Yep, that's true! I don't have a mind of my own, because Ma has done all the thinking in my life so far! It's clear she can't accept that I do have a mind and I can think without her dictating my decisions. Do you believe Richa's influence over me is really strong in this matter too?" I asked with anger brewing in my voice.

"Of course not, you idiot! Don't let defeat descend in your heart. If you think you're beaten, then you are. Okay, so let's leave Ma out of this equation for now and talk about just you. I agree that the solution to a bad marriage is a good divorce, but then, are you aware that there is no such thing? Just as there is no such concept of a good marriage, a good divorce too is a fallacy."

I rested my chin on my elbow, whilst my curled fingers rested against my lips. The heaviness in my heart must have travelled up to my eyes, for Shiv quickly moved closer to me, and placed his hand on mine.

"Divorce may have become an integral measure of our modern vocabulary and it may appear to be your passport to independence, but it's all very relative. Are you prepared to go through the entire meltdown of emotions, and relationships—including some friendships and most importantly, dividing your children's home into two? Look Shivani, I'm your best friend, but do allow me to play the devil's advocate because if I don't, then you may regret that no one showed you the pitfalls of a separation," he cautioned.

"Carry on, Shiv! I'm all ears!" I said, consentingly.

"I'm going to sound harsh, but I need you to respond to me assertively," he said while joining the palms of his hands to point towards me. "The road ahead isn't without bumps and you're fortunate enough not to be acquainted with life's thuds and thumps. You have, in truth, always dressed in gold and diamonds and for women with your lifestyle it's most favourable to turn the other cheek on your marital issues that disagree with your palate. Redirect your life to either building a career in our family business or engage in whatever most women do to take their minds off their unsavoury issues—kitty lunches, or charity events of some kind."

"Please, Shiv!" I interjected quickly. "Now you're being derogatory and you're insulting my intelligence. I understand you're trying to protect me by expanding my vision to the dark and stark reality of a life after marriage, but please." I pleaded, visibly irked.

"Well, that's because I'm your brother and I do care about you. Perhaps, much more than your mother," he said, with a hint of humour in his voice to lighten the moment.

"I know," I replied sadly and my head turned to the floor in dismay. I was visibly disturbed and was desperate for a respite from my sad situation. I was thinking of what Shiv had said about the aspect of dividing my children's home in two. I was scared of the impact it could have on them and what if I didn't have the courage to build the life they were heavily accustomed to, after the divorce?

"Hey sis!" Shiv said, snapping me out of my chain of judgements. "If you seriously believe in yourself and in the life you really want, then labour hard towards it. Any time you stumble, I vow to be there to hold you up. You have the support, so now, courage is the only ingredient you need to buy from the market to complete your life's recipe."

I felt a touch lighter and I lifted my eyes up to Shiv's boyish gaze that was now trailing Richa as she strode towards us with her blazing beauty. Her footsteps were inaudible like a ballerina's as she came and sat beside me. She made a striking impression and clearly took Shiv's breath away. She appeared more relaxed than I had seen in a while and that's what I admired about her the most—her resilience. As she smiled, she instantly elevated my spirits, enabling me to turn oblivious to my angst.

"How are you beautiful, and what can I get you?" Shiv asked, almost too enthusiastically, clearly intrigued by her loveliness.

"Wine? Vodka? Me?" he added, with a naughty expression on his face. She bounced her lustrous hair back and released a giggle.

"A cappuccino will be lovely, with three spoonfuls of sugar. Don't judge, I never claimed to be perfect," she said, chuckling, slightly embarrassed of her minor vice.

It was all at once a red carpet event when suddenly the cameras zoomed in on the celebrity. She made every head in the restaurant turn and it was not only men who were intrigued, as women equally admired her, seldom voicing their admiration. Beautiful people, it seemed, had an advantage over the rest of humanity, and Richa, worked diligently in being the finest version of herself—both physically and mentally. Living in the present didn't rob her of the small joys of life.

It seemed she had broken free from the cage of rituals and societal norms very early in her life. None of that had been possible for me since Ma denied me a chance to present my argument on every life-changing issue. When I aspired to study fashion post school, she routed me to college to study English honours and my whims to be an actor, singer and dancer at different phases of my life were carefully crushed. Richa continued to be the creator of her own life, while I had remained the reactor of mine.

"You know, you always make it look so easy!" I began quietly, while I settled myself back in the chair, peaceful to be in their company.

"I make what look so easy?" Richa asked, soaking in the atmosphere of the place by gracefully rotating her head on either side, before gently smiling at me.

"Looking so ravishing, amongst your other attributes. You make being beautiful seem as natural as brushing our teeth in the morning. It's a darn effort and even then most of us aren't spot on! It comes to you as effortlessly as breathing, eating and having sex."

"Ah sex! A word that my body is currently alien to as no one around is drawn to me," she sniggered inaudibly, not to be heard by Shiv who was interrupted with a call. "It's my time-out to figure what whets my appetite, before I recklessly plunge into another adventure."

"Adventure is a good word!" intervened Shiv as he got off his mobile. "I don't know what it entails, but I'm in! I love escapes, particularly with stunning women such as yourself, and did I really hear the word sex?"

I frowned, lending Shiv a piercing glare as piping hot cappuccinos were poured into bone china cups with careful expertise. It was served with a selection of afternoon sandwiches, pastries, scones and cakes on a fancy tiered cake stand. I had no appetite, but Richa unhesitatingly grabbed the sweet treats, and said, "No, Shiv! I'm afraid the word was ex!"

"Speaking of which, we both need to resolve my sister's predicament. Would you care for a salad sandwich?" He wasn't planning on giving up.

"No savoury for me, Shiv! I'm gravitating towards sugary foods nowadays. They substitute my appetite for sex!" she laughed before she commented, "I'm a terrible example here, Shiv, and the less said the better, so I opt to listen and offer you guys my silent support. I'm still not composed after all the chaos that I created! I'm a self-confessed mess-maker."

"No, please give us your invaluable input. I insist! This could be interesting. Also, about the sex thing, I could clean up that mess; both yours and mine," Shiv offered, charmingly, with a hint of childlike mischief while biting into his sandwich. It tickled me inside, watching him flirt with my best friend. I felt relieved now after Shiv had drawn the conclusion from our earlier conversation, promising to cover me if I demonstrated enough courage and confidence.

"Well, I seemed to have diverted from the traditional route in life very early on and it was the only choice for me. It's been no easy ride having to deal with society's age-old conventional thinking that's as warped as it is impractical. In my case, I can flaunt the sad record of my relationships and what may be more refreshing to people is that I don't regret most of it. They were all experiences to learn and unlearn from, so I don't kick myself for any of it," she said, finally making me succumb to the carrot cake that was soft and moist, as it had just come out of the oven. The lingering aroma of its sweet spice enhanced its flavour as she plunged the spoon in my mouth.

"Me too!" volunteered Shiv with his mouth open. "You're welcome to feed me," he said, giggling.

"Oh for God's sake. Grow up," I taunted.

"Okay, seriously, women are far more progressive today. I mean look at you, Richa. Your choices were clearly right for you and I agree with your philosophy of living life on your own terms, but what you did, required courage," Shiv remarked, biting into the carrot cake and sipping on his coffee alongside. A pile of biscuits or a slice of something sweet almost always accompanied his hot beverage, and yet, he was very proud of avoiding 'sugar' in his coffee.

He reverted to playing the 'devil's advocate' and even though I knew his intention, I found myself boiling inside. "Okay, guys, what do you suggest I should do, given my lack of strength, courage and archaic upbringing?" I said, stressing the words and giving Shiv the eye. "Your character assassination is demoralising me, Shiv."

Shiv softened his tone as he realised he'd gone too far.

"Shivani, you know I'm on your side and I apologise for sounding condescending," he said with urgency in his eyes. I too softened as he continued.

"Shivani and many like her remain in the grip of the same limitations, caught somewhere between the high walls of standards that were set for women in the 14th century and the shackles of our controlling Ma's conditioning. It's not been a smooth sail, I'm afraid and unless and until you, Shivani are determined, nothing is going to break those shackles of conformity," he said, earnestly now.

"All our mothers seem to have left a deep and lasting impression on the way we conduct ourselves today. I remember so vividly the time when my mother scolded me after I told her I was unable to go down the conventional route in life," she said, enigmatically. "She decided most adamantly that I was incapable of making my own decisions in life. She strongly believed I didn't know what was right for me, so she forced me into one marriage and then another, until I broke the chain," Richa commented, with undertones of sadness, while letting out a nervous laughter.

She then turned towards Shiv and said charmingly, "Shiv, I'm convinced you're not narrow-minded and that your intelligence coupled with your good heart will decide a way out for your sister. It will be a winning situation for everyone, including your Ma. And like you said, Shivani must seek courage to follow her heart, as that's one true attribute that never misguides us." She was sipping on copious cups of coffee and most unexpectedly, polishing off innumerable slices of the red velvet cake too.

"No one has a right to judge the other's choices, but I'm afraid to admit that in this country, hypocrisy exists on a very large scale, so it is tough to come out of the closet with the truth of what we need, what we want and what we are. I don't remember ever being intensely marriage-minded, yet I was never asked for my opinion," she said, emphatically, with frustration in her voice.

"I know it in my heart that you will be fine just as long as you are aware of the perils of throwing away your security blanket," she finally added, to manoeuver me back into the conversation.

"I know it's unbreakable courage that will make my life take a new turn. Anyway, I feel so much better after our meeting, so I'm glad you both took out time for me," I responded.

After a while, we all eased into a lighter conversation as Shiv changed its course. He asked her about her kids and her gym routine as he was enthralled by her well-toned body, despite the pounds of sugar she consumed while sitting and listening to Shiv sweet-talk her. Was she also flirting with him in the same measure as he was with her? The afternoon, generally, went well as they both gave me the strength to find myself and in the end, I realised it was up to me to cut the cords that were stifling me. I knew without a grain of doubt that my two rocks were beside me and with that thought I reached out for the calories now as the other two seemed most satisfied with each other's compliments.

I unwound for the first time in weeks, as Shiv promised to present my case to Ma most effectively. Right now, he embraced the moment as affectionately as he would've wanted to embrace Richa. I lightened up on observing the spark between them, which was likely to extinguish just as we got through, because Shiv was unconventionally loyal to his wife and he wasn't Richa's type in any case.

"Your kids must be as gorgeous as you. Have you considered being a surrogate? With your beauty and my brains, we could reproduce the future Miss and Mr. Universe," Shiv flirted, unabashedly.

"Are you suggesting we get together for the purpose of bringing perfect babies into the world?" Richa said, irresistibly.

"Okay, alright, guys! Time's up. Now, I'm confident that with both your unfettered support, my life will tie up neatly in the end, so seriously, let's call it a day," I suggested immediately, watching Richa's reaction, who was clearly flattered by his compliment. As she lowered her head, I noticed her face flush.

"You're right, Shivani, and you know what? I would always sleep peacefully at night with a brother like you beside me, Shiv!" she said amusingly, while Shiv turned the other way as if she had just insulted him.

Richa and I stepped out to walk across the Worli Seaface as the dancing breeze brushed through us. Above us, there was a pale blue and violet sky with fluffy clouds swaying in their own delight. The sound of the water created gentle ripples of calm within me as my mind floated between my pitiable past to my promising future. I looked across at Richa who appeared to be in sync with nature's timeless melody and a serene smile settled on her soft lips as she inhaled the sea breeze. The purple waves reflected in her eyes that had their own tales to tell. Silence walked beside us as we thought about our own stories.

We must have walked for over an hour, while the glory of the sky kept us wrapped in its embrace. I wondered what it was that made people smile for no apparent reason when they made their connection with nature. Was happiness meant to be an unconditional state, while sadness was an unnatural one?

I was immensely inspired by Richa's perspective on life and her ability to immerse herself in its every colour, regardless of her past that she had brought up in a vague context earlier in the day. She had never spoken about anything besides her broken marriages and the stream of failed relationships she seemed to have healed from. I didn't probe into matters that she herself didn't bring up. In any event, time had its way of unearthing the truth—no matter how deep we tried burying it. The flaunting beauty in and around her always made her stay afloat, as she was smarter than I considered myself to be. Her exquisiteness made me smile on the inside as I watched her pull out a bar of chocolate from her bag to offer it to a poor child. He thanked her and walked on to meet his destiny, leaving us to search for ours.

"Isn't it blissful, Shivani?" she began, with an inspiring smile on her lips. "Beauty is all around us, if only we recognise it and let go of our conditioning. We all have secrets we are made to feel ashamed of, you know. Your Ma isn't the only mother who has succeeded in imposing her beliefs on you; just exhale it all away in this divine moment. I come here for respite and I talk about my woes to the sea and to the sky, and they listen without judgement. Try it some time. It's incredible, Shivani, how nature has a way to uplift and soothe a wounded heart."

# 12

It was difficult to soothe Shivani's wounded heart yesterday, as she spilled out her resentment towards her marriage. Now, I was at the Taj coffee shop—on my laptop, shopping online for a yoga mat. Monday would be my first day with my yoga instructor at home and I needed a good quality mat. Retail therapy didn't always entail colossal shopping malls, as I was quite happy sitting and surfing online.

He walked in, wearing a suave suit and polished shoes, like he was entering a life-changing business meeting. I scanned him admiringly, as I offered him a seat.

"'Hey! Looking good as always! What's up?" he said in a cool and casual tone.

"I know and I'm sorry!" he said, before I could respond. He was looking at his attire, realising just how formal he appeared. "Maybe, I was hoping to get a deal out of this meeting of ours, but hey, if not, then I can turn right back, go home, change and be back in time for dinner, in case you're still here."

He was funny and flirtatious, making me feel comfortable at once. I broke into a giggle while he sat and placed his two mobiles on the table. His gaze didn't leave me and I felt a nervous smile settle on my face. I decided to strike a general conversation, before getting into the real reasons for being there.

"Two mobiles? Double trouble or two timing?" I asked, light-heartedly.

"Neither and yet, both. One is a lonely number and two's company. A single phone won't let me mingle and I will most definitely get caught, while two keep the mystery alive." I searched into his eyes and he stared back into mine and for a split second, I felt a connection. I broke the awkwardness by asking more general questions.

"So, how's work?"

That was the most obvious question to ask.

"Are you serious?" he responded, raising his pitch and shaking his head in disbelief.

"Sorry?" I asked genuinely, not sure what I had said, except for the fact that my enquiry was somewhat bland.

"I said, are you serious? You're really here to ask me about my work? Is there any particular aspect you might be interested in? I need to know the specifics because I don't want to disappoint you. The amount of cheques I've signed recently, my board meetings, mergers, stocks, other investments, business trips, collaborations? What would you like to discuss?" he asked in jest and I was already blown away by his flamboyance.

"You are a funny man, Sameer. Alright, let's not talk about your work because even if we did, I guess it would be a monologue as I wouldn't know how to contribute," I admitted, coyly.

"Oh yes, you would, you're a smart woman! You would nod gracefully as if you've grasped every piece of information. Your social skills are most commendable and I've paid a close heed to them each time our paths have crossed. You are quite something," he said with a glint in his eye.

"You're too kind, but I actually know nothing about business," I added.

"You know nothing about business, dear Richa, and you know nothing about marriages, because you are never really in one long enough to understand its dynamics. The latter I don't mean condescendingly, I promise," Sameer said.

"No, I understand. You're just stating facts and I appreciate it. So, shall we call for coffee? Not that I know anything about what you drink, but tea is also an option. So which one is it?" I tried to change the topic.

"Actually none! I don't do caffeine, as odd as it may sound," he said, jerking his right leg.

"That's rather healthy, I must say," I said, observing his leg jolt up and down.

"So, what's your high?" he continued.

"I have many; some of which I can't get into, given that you're my wife's best friend. One of them, which is legitimate for me to mention, however, is wine. I know it is daytime and you probably don't do alcohol in the afternoon, but a glass won't make you tipsy. It would also keep me company. Oh, by the way, this knee jerks out of bad habit and not because of restlessness, so please excuse me, if you can."

"Gosh, you really are a charmer, I had almost forgotten that about you. About the knee thing, it's *totally* cool," I replied, immediately realising I must have sounded like one of the gossip girls in the gym.

"Thank you, I'm relieved. I'm sure you must have forgotten my charm, it's been too long! I hate to admit, I'm slightly jealous that you are my wife's and partially my children's best friend and today you are here to fight for both," Sameer said, hitting the nail on the head.

I looked over at him, awkwardly, as he swiftly perused the menu and summoned the waiter to get the wine.

"I'm sorry, I should add that it's okay!" he said, reassuringly. "You're a loyal friend to Shivani. I admire that and even though I'm a businessman, I didn't accept your invitation to make any kind of negotiations because I'm afraid at this point, there is no room for any. If I'm to speak the absolute truth, I accepted the invitation as a calling from the universe to spend an afternoon with the most beautiful woman I have ever laid my eyes on, and I don't just mean external beauty. Whatever circumstances have brought you here, I welcome you with open arms."

"Hey, I'm actually here because…," I began, as I soaked in his compliment.

"Because Shivani sent you here and I understand that, but we don't need to ruin our afternoon, mourning," he said, interrupting me, mid-sentence.

"Mourning?" I asked, raising an eyebrow.

"Over a deceased marriage. I don't deny it, but in the same token, there are *incalculable* dead marriages across the globe," he said with a strong emphasis on incalculable. "But that does not mean people go around burying them. They carry on, for different reasons, and mine are as clear as this wine," he said, sniffing it. "This afternoon is not going to be about my life after walking down the aisle with Shivani, but instead, about walking into an amnesic afternoon."

"Amnesic? You mean where we both forget why we are here?" I asked, stupefied.

"Yes, as well as where we have come from. Because in life, what counts is where we are going," he said, bringing his glass towards mine to make a toast.

"Cheers! Mmmm! Good wine. You know what is the most therapeutic thing in the world for me?"

"What?" I asked as I sipped on the wine.

"I don't believe in spas, though I don't mind them in good company, but my most effective therapy is sitting in my home theatre, sipping on red wine and watching *Breakfast at Tiffany's*. I simply adore Audrey Hepburn and if I could turn back the clock, I would do anything to woo her into marrying me. She personifies grace, beauty, goodness and elegance. Don't you think?" he asked and then proceeded to ask me who my heart-throb was, to which I fumbled because I genuinely didn't know. After some more wine and discussion on the gamut of Hollywood stars, he turned somewhat serious.

"I'm genuinely grateful to Shivani for the adorable children she bore and my business that flourished. I'm old school and I will give her credit for bringing lady luck to our family. She has many attributes and so do I, but our marriage has hit a dead end and it's been years since both of us have been back and forth. All our solutions eventually lead us back to that same brick wall."

I sipped on my wine as I listened patiently. His tone was sad and yet, he had the gift of turning it around. His good nature and humour enabled him to deal with the darkness in his life.

"I thought you weren't going to speak about it," I said, once he was done talking about it.

"I owe you something, given you're here. I need you to know there are two sides to every coin. Richa, when you took your marriage vows, did you ever believe you were going to kill your marriage? No, of course you didn't, and I, too, had good intentions at the onset. I liked her and we seemed to be getting along, but then..." he paused.

"But then?" I enquired without sounding too insistent, so as to not push him away.

"One morning, when I went to my bathroom, I stood before my mirror, looked deep into my eyes and guess who I met?" Sameer asked.

"You met someone?' I asked quizzically.

"Yes, I met a very sad person and I didn't like him one bit. He was miserable and he felt like crap. Do you know what that feels like? You feel trapped to the extent you're completely choked."

I felt a tight knot in my stomach the second he used the words 'trapped' and 'choked'. I found myself feeling sorry for him as I related to every word.

"Richa, we can't change people, but we can change ourselves. I needed to change from sad to spirited. I like the last word and I'd use it to describe you—you are spirited, but you, too, are not without demons."

"What do you mean? Demons?" I said, suddenly sitting up defensively. "I don't have any demons, and are we here for me or for you and Shivani?" I said, almost angry.

"You're right, so let's keep the spotlight on me for a while, because your presence is prompting me to speak. Let's just be clear about one thing though, I don't owe you any explanations and I don't even need to be here. But now that I am here, I'm roped into chatting with you. You have this energy that draws people towards you."

"Okay, please Mr. Charming, tell me something about the breakdown of your marriage and your neglect towards my best friend then. She's hurting, but so are you. What's the solution? You cheat on her occasionally, don't you?" I said, steadying my voice. I loved my friend and I didn't want this meeting to roll into a mere joke.

"As I said earlier, Richa, I don't see a way out at this juncture, but I can tell you the time when I faltered. It was a mere kiss and the woman was nothing more than a listening ear. Yet, I felt more alive than being in a dead marriage. Now, I'm generally more energetic about life and I've become emotionally open. In case you're wondering, which I'm sure you are, I'm no longer consumed by guilt and shame. I'm certainly not disappointed when I look at my reflection in the mirror because the man I see now is a happy one and I quite like him. You should get to know him sometime," he said, raising his glass and drinking the wine.

He continued. "Strangely, I'm not anxious over being caught and I certainly don't have any fear of abandonment. It's almost like I take my marriage for granted, as I'm also comfortable with the fact that Shivani and I are tied together for more reasons than just the children. Our families have never entertained the word 'divorce' so there's nowhere for both of us to run. I don't have a woman I love or find remotely worthy of leaving my marriage for and I'm sure she doesn't have anyone either. And to answer your question; am I cheating on her? Does it really matter when both hearts have stopped beating for each other? I've gone into a survival mode and if you want to call that cheating…?"

"Would I be invading your privacy if I dared ask you…?"

Before I could finish the sentence, he interrupted me.

"No, you have crossed that line of formality, and no, I'm not in a relationship. I have friends, but I avoid love at all costs. That's just my motto. I lost my emotional connection with

Shivani, so I sought it and even received it outside. A man instinctively knows when his woman has stopped loving him. She's been emotionally dead for years, and sex has been flung out of the window. Trust me, initially, I was perturbed because I'm not one of those who believes it to be his birthright to be a polygamist," he sighed hard.

He then stated, "Look, I did say at the beginning, right, that I'm not here to negotiate with you for her?"

"Then why are you here, knowing that it would pan out like this?" I asked.

"I don't know, but if you're here to judge me, then I think we should call it a day. In any case, I don't know what you will go back to Shivani with, that she doesn't know already. She is also aware that we both are in a box that's been sealed by our elders."

I sensed genuine hurt and in spite of arriving here with the attitude of being the interrogator, the mediator and whatever it took to resolve their marriage, I felt it was better if I relaxed my stance.

"Men who find love and respect in their marriages don't need to venture. I did so because my home and heart became empty and hey, cheers to my confessions! Can we lighten up, now? I'm going to turn the table for you to speak. You've been awfully quiet and I know from whatever little I know of you that you're a chatty woman. So, now that I've told you I'm not in a relationship, can I ask you if you are?"

"No!" I snapped, abruptly.

"No, I can't ask?" he enquired, looking into my eyes and sending a shiver down my spine.

"No, I'm not and I don't intend to be. I'm a master of disaster in that area. I have such a crying record," I clarified.

"Oh, but you must find another guy in no time to screw things up. I mean, what's life without a little drama? It becomes monotonous," Sameer joked, nonchalantly.

"All right, I throw my hands up in the air! No more about your marriage and I'm sorry if I was offensive at any point," I said, genuinely apologetic.

"You can never be offensive. Thank you for handing the floor over to me. Listen Richa, we don't need to talk about anything here," he said with concern in his voice. "I just want to clarify that I respect you and that is the reason I came out today, not because I wanted to justify my cheating, neglecting my wife or telling you how equally frustrated I am about being raised with values that sometimes don't allow you to follow your heart. Marriage isn't supposed to be this complicated, sometimes Shivani and I can't even have a conversation. There has to be some kind of exchange, but in our case, we glare at each other as though we're strangers and, yes, over time, we have turned into them.

"In a modern family where the mindset would be more lenient, my parents and hers would advise us to part, but here, I think our choices are limited. So, let's not do this anymore. You know I'm in an unhappy situation, now do you want me to validate it? From where I sit, I believe the chapter is closed already."

"No, I get it. So, shall we call it a day? I mean, you need to get back to work and I need to get back to my children."

"I appreciate it, but the wine will be deeply offended if either of us get up and leave so, shall we just play the friend card here? That's my trump card in any case.

"So I have another confession to make. I'm clearly failing in my marriage, and have broken a few hearts outside it as well. Mine is fragmented too. Oh yes, I have a heart, in case you're wondering. You're my wife's best friend, so I do intend to proceed with caution. But I really like you. You don't have to answer right away, but then I guess you do, because the offer is going to expire any second," Sameer said, with the same level of confidence he had exhibited throughout our conversation.

"What? I...I am your friend. Shivani's, your's, your children's," I said, breaking into a nervous smile.

"Hey, lighten up! We don't have to talk about this! But it is not a surprise that I like you, is it? I have always been fond of you. I thought it was obvious.

"Anyway, let me talk about something you're more comfortable with—your motherhood. I have always admired the way you have brought up your kids despite the many hurdles you have faced in your life. It may never be recognised, but I am sure it is fulfilling to see your children grow into good human beings?"

"True!" I sighed. "I love my kids as I love yours. They're good kids and I enjoy spending time with them. It has its rewards and not everything needs to be validated with a trophy or a certificate."

He listened attentively as I noticed his eyes watching my lips, before they travelled back to my eyes, to remain there. He was very handsome, and he was attentive—that's what made me stay. He was interested in what I had to say and that was refreshing.

"I care about the deepest places of their heart—their hurt, fears, struggles and success. I'm their cheerleader, their fan and life coach all rolled in one, but then, I'm no different from any other mom."

"I beg to differ. Motherhood is a god-given ability to nurture, love and feel. It's a gift, a calling and it transcends biological limitations. Simply giving birth to a child doesn't turn you into a good mother. My own mother saw the treasure in me. She was a gift to me as I was to her. I miss her, but then, I know she lives on. I feel her presence at times. For me, she is my God," he said, turning sentimental.

"She's with you all the time. She will always love you," I reassured him, realising he was a sensitive man who was in need of love.

"Are you always this beautiful and buoyant or are you on anti-depressants?" he enquired, suddenly changing the mood of the conversation.

"Hilarious! You're just hilarious and you know what would be even funnier? If I dropped this wine on you. What do you say? You're a real chick-magnet, aren't you?" I threatened him.

"Oops, I think you're drunk. I think it's time for a cappuccino. I remember your love for it!" he suggested, as we both laughed.

"Is this your tactic to keep me here longer?" I asked, flirtatiously.

"Not if this conversation remains as tipsy as you are feeling. Now let's revert to motherhood, without getting sentimental okay?" he said.

I smiled as I felt the comfort of being in his company.

"What is its scent?" he said, now searching deep in my eyes.

"The scent of?" I enquired as I noticed his chiselled face and the dimple on his chin made him look like Kirk Douglas.

"Motherhood, your motherhood. Come on, everything comprises senses—smell, touch, sight, taste and feel. What's yours as a mother?"

"I'm not sure and yet, I think I do. But I never thought about it. Ironically, I thought about its palette. Do you know yours?"

"Yours would be Monet's palette—soft pastille. Mine would be slightly different, because I'm a man. The colours of my fatherhood are more like Van Gogh's—soft, but more defined. Okay, let me help you think out of the box in order to come back to the scent thing. What's the main feature of this place, the coffee shop? What senses would you say are predominant here?" he explained.

"I feel, I see and I touch, but I'm not sure," I said, hesitating, as I was genuinely not sure. "You're something else; so amusing. I didn't know you were so much fun to be with," I confirmed, feeling at home with him.

"I find me fun too! Thank you for not thinking ill of me just because I made some bad choices. Most of us end up living in the grey area when being black-and-white is no longer an option. Okay, so back to my first question. What scent is hatred?" Sameer asked—he was persistent.

"Oh, I'm sorry, are we still playing that game? Well, hatred has no scent," I said, confidently.

"Great! So what is love's scent?" he continued.

"That's really easy. For me, it's Jo Malone'"

"Jo Malone-Roses!"

We practically said it together and then I noticed a sparkle in his eye as he settled his gaze on me, while I felt blood rush to my flustered face.

"Richa, not every relationship is meant to last, but the ones that don't, teach and prepare us for the ones that might," he said, swallowing a lump in his throat.

I quickly looked at my watch—aghast—three hours had gone by, immersed in each other's company. I hated to admit it to myself, but I had thoroughly enjoyed male company for the first time in a very long time. I didn't want to leave, but guilt would gnaw at me if I didn't, so I abruptly stood up.

He looked at me get up and spoke in a tone that was gentle and somewhat inviting, "The coffee's just arrived and I think we should at least wait till it cools. You can have a sip and we can both call it a day—a very good one, I'm afraid," he said, softly. "Please sit down because I refuse to drink two cups of coffee on my own."

I took a deep breath and looked over at him, without sitting, "I don't know, Sameer, but I really think we both should leave. Coffee smells good, but I'm so late for my children."

"They're at my place, aren't they? They always have fun when they're with my children. They all know how to be such good friends. Richa!" he said, offering his hand—manoeuvring me to sit down. "Please stop being in a wrestling match with yourself all the time."

When he said that, my heart skipped a beat and I gazed back at him.

"We are all one small adjustment away from making our lives work and in that, there should be no guilt or shame. We are all, without exception, trying to keep our sanity in these manic times. It takes only one good friendship to make us realise what all the wrong ones were lacking," he said, profoundly.

"That's true," I replied, sitting down. I felt very far away from how I had felt when I had walked into the coffee shop, with an altogether different intention. I just couldn't get over the overwhelming flood of emotions that both of us were feeling.

"If there's a possibility of us becoming good friends, do let me know. I really enjoyed this afternoon. You are potentially good company, but I will only confirm once we've met a few times. So, once you've taken a sip of the coffee, you may answer my question. Here, drink the coffee, it will help you think," he said, smiling. Then he added, "I would love to take you out for a drink some time."

"Very funny, Sameer. And may I ask, would that be a thirst-quenching kind of drink or leading-up-to-something kind of drink?" I asked, almost mischievously, before gathering myself.

"Let the mystery unfold on its own, but first be clear that you want to have a drink with me."

I swallowed hard. With hesitation, I replied, "I'm not sure that would be a possibility. How can it be possible for you and I to be friends?"

He looked at me for some time, before he said, "Possible is a good word and at this point, it's enough for me."

# 13

'If only it was possible to stand up to Ma', I mused as I entered her office, wearing my open wounds under a white indo-western suit, espoused with a red-and-white printed scarf and an elegant pearl-and-diamond set that Ma presented me many years ago. She had generously gifted a Rolex to Sameer and a heavy gold chain to my in-laws too. Even before I married, she had given my 'to-be' in-laws exclusive gifts. In the modern world, dowries are often synonymous with briberies and with so many top designer watches and ultra-luxury accessories, no sane family would've declined the proposal. I was an attractive package for any man and his family.

Her fingers were intertwined as she sat upright on her chesterfield chair. Her eyes stared straight at me with the grace of Gene Kelly, and the resolve of Indira Gandhi. Her tone was unsympathetic as I stepped into her office, with careful strides and a shaky smile. I tried hard to avoid her eyes, but they pierced through me as I swept past her to settle on the sofa opposite her. I couldn't help but notice how well she looked in her cream cotton sari, enhanced with a thick gold-and-silver fringe to lend it an aristocratic edge. A string of south sea pearls hung down to her bosom, enhancing the grace of her ensemble. I made a feeble attempt at being the disciplined daughter she believed she had raised, except that she hadn't. Amma ji was the one who had brought me up, and very often, it was under my maternal grandma's nurturing.

"Hi, Ma, how are you?" I greeted her quietly and immediately realised that my meticulously rehearsed pitch had gone up in smoke as I cleared my croaky throat. I did, however, feel stronger and more positive after the meeting with my brother and my best friend and I was here as a mere formality.

The man standing behind her—with a file in his hand—was impeccably dressed in a charcoal suit, with a pale pink shirt and an accented powder blue tie. He had an average height, with a compelling aura that immediately made me feel short. I needed to maintain a positive disposition, no matter how intimidatingly he and Ma towered over me. I rested my gaze on his youthful face, further boosted with his pepper-and-salt hair. His handshake was firm—almost inviting—bringing a spark to my otherwise dim eyes. I knew I'd end up fantasising about him the way I did about other men, without trying to step out of my boundaries, as I hadn't openly dared to venture down that territory. Not fully, at least. I yearned for a touch that meant something more than a mere marital obligation or habit.

"Hi, Shivani, I'm Ajay, a corporate lawyer by profession, but I have dealt with some exceptional cases of divorce. As your mother's loyal friend and confidant, I have come here to advise you on your rights. So, why don't you get comfortable, and I'll brief you. Would you like a hot drink or chilled mango juice or something?"

"I'm good, Ajay," I said, optimistically, hoping that he had a way out of my redundant marriage, and presumed that Ma summoned him here to seek a solution for me, though

Mrs. Control freak remained tight-lipped. She delicately tucked her long silky mahogany hair behind her ear as she adjusted herself on the sofa and then spoke, "Listen very carefully, Shivani, and then go home and think matters over before mapping out your disarrayed life." She spoke in a tone that was now cautioning me caustically and I swallowed my resentment to maintain an air of confidence.

I hadn't asked Ma to get a lawyer involved at this stage, but she did, all the same. Perhaps, she did care about my happiness and I was just judging her too soon. She needed to be given a chance and although, I had fallen short of her expectations, maybe she was ready to steer us in a new direction now. So, I listened silently and attentively.

"Shivani, unless and until you—the aggrieved party—have ammunition up your sleeve, it is futile to fight a long-drawn battle in court. The law stipulates that you must show that there are legitimate reasons for ending your marriage. I want to begin by clarifying that I sympathise with you. You must believe at the outset that I'm on your side, and therefore, I'm not suggesting that you bear it with a grin; but I must lay the facts out before you first," Ajay reassured, while pacing up and down, taking purposeful strides. He then sat at the edge of the sofa, releasing a deep sigh before pressing his lips hard against each other.

"What kind of ammunition?" I asked, looking at him directly now, as we sat opposite each other. He had a blue file in his hand that he gently placed on the table before him. His presence was beginning to feel like a warm embrace, whilst Ma's felt like a cold shoulder that was perpetually prepared to shrug me off.

"Shivani, you will firstly need to choose a ground for severing the legal tie with your husband, file the case in court, and then prove it with support of evidence and documents. Mutual consent is out of the question, I'm sure, since Sameer isn't interested in divorcing you as per your previous discussions with him. I understand you have brought this matter up with him on several occasions, only for it to be brushed off and to be brutally ignored for over a decade. As I understand it, it's a one-sided argument and you will need to double your efforts to set the wheels in motion to file a lawsuit.

"If it is alimony you want, which naturally you will, then, there is no concept of joint marital property in India, which is why it translates into walking into the war zone for months, and most likely, for years. I'm afraid, our courts are fraught with delays and you will never get a fair alimony; even after a long-haul battle. It's been a raw deal for women since the beginning of time and I'm sorry to admit, but even if you fight tooth and nail in the beginning because I'm sure you'll have the strength to do that right now, you will soon be depleted—both financially and emotionally. Physically, it will take a toll on your health and depending on his resistance, you will be the sufferer, so I dare ask you, is it really worth jeopardising your current status and stature? You belong to a family of high repute, but once you make your exit, will you have an identity or will you pale into insignificance? I'm sorry if I sound derogatory as that I must clarify is not my intention."

"I don't really understand, uh, it's Ajay, right?" I enquired, with creases forming in the centre of my forehead, while knots of anxiety began to take shape within me. "People are divorcing left, right and centre, so how are women surviving if the courts are not granting them their rights? I come across clusters of women in our very own society who have obtained a legal separation and are laughing all the way to the bank."

"They do and they don't, I'm afraid and sometimes, halfway through the proceedings, women change their minds since it's easier to remain in bad marriages than to feed their kids and themselves in the real world, without substantial financial support. As I said, it can take years, unless there is sufficient evidence to support a case of abuse in the marriage. The state of matrimony is ailing here in Mumbai, no doubt. Despite the many tears and tantrums of their marriage, most choose to heal their wounds using denial as an effective salve whilst others have had the wheel of fortune turn towards them. Your small clusters of women friends have been fortunate, but by and large, it's a grim picture.

"The ideals of marriage—be it in the high society or otherwise—are fragmented and fractured, but they survive the beating only if one of the parties completely sacrifices its own desire for happiness and that, I'm afraid, is usually the women. Since the beginning of time, women have been living in denial to get a morsel of peace for themselves in the marriage because outside it, there is slight hope of any. But there are exceptions, of course. However, whether it's 1965 or 2017, I, despite my modern perspective, always advise women to find their true calling within the confines of their marriage. Marriage ought not to be the beginning and end of a woman's life—she should learn to find her light in the darkness."

I noticed Ma nodding from the corner of my eyes and I realised I was wrong about her—she wasn't taking my side. I tried maintaining my decorum, paying marginal attention to her overtly obstinate expression.

"In your individual case, Shivani, putting aside any kind of generalisation, the several rounds of litigation will burn you out and your husband will make sure he leaves you financially destitute. Your mother will come forward to support you for the rest of your life and perhaps, your brother too, but are you willing to give up the lion's share for a slice?" he asked, with unembellished words while turning his gaze towards Ma, either to see if she would agree to grant me anything if I were to be left high and dry or just to gain her approval for the statements he was making—they were probably in accordance with her wishes.

"What if I decided to enter the battlefield and fight till the very end to find the light?" I enquired, without as much as looking at Ma. For a split second, I preferred to be oblivious to her presence. "I mean, what if I can prove his worth somehow—on paper, that is? And then, with those facts, what if I fight hard?" I added.

"Do you even have the remotest idea what your husband's actual earnings are, you ignorant child?" Ma interrupted, impatiently. Her sharpness was trying to ravage the new-found fibres of hope in me, and I at once, felt foolish to think that I would be able to speak to the lawyer without her meddling every few minutes.

"You are being profoundly stupid, so I suggest you zip it and just listen hard. Ajay, regrettably, this insane child of mine is very ill-informed, living in an illusory world of her own making. So please, enlighten her. Divorce is the new rage nowadays and she believes it's like buying the next limited handbag. Undoubtedly, it will limit her access to it, because she will not be able to afford any of the luxuries that she takes for granted. She has a stubbornness to do what is completely wrong and you need to be patient with her on these matters. Entering the battlefield? Who do you think you are—Arjuna, the warrior from Mahabharata? You will lose, you idiot, because you're on the wrong side of the fence."

Ma talked down on me and she ensured that her every word cut like a butcher's knife to induce bleeding, after which Amma ji would dress up my wounds as she had done from infancy to my adulthood. Ajay punctuated the cold war by further 'educating' me on the system that tilted towards favouring the man over the woman.

"Shivani, even if the breakdown of your marriage is irretrievable and you find yourself in court, your alimony will be based on his official income, which is substantially less than what he actually has; usually concealed. And that too, not just in India, but in various parts of the globe," Ajay said, with a tone that was a fraction more urgent now.

"In no way would I like to discourage you from taking such a drastic step that may or may not prove beneficial to you and to your family in the larger scheme of things, and you must consider the consequences of presenting this case in a system that has not yet empowered women. Most women remain in obnoxious situations because the real world can prove to be even nastier. They cannot bear the thought of single-handedly supporting their kids in a country that cannot curtail crimes against women."

I simply nodded, cringing at the lengths my Ma would go to, only to get me to listen to her. This entire information was crafted deliberately, to instil fear in me and to 'keep me in my place.'

"You must tell her the rest too, Ajay—about perpetrators being left off scot-free because the tables are invariably turned to blame women for the crimes committed against them. Victims of rape, for instance, are ruthlessly told that they are responsible for it. She forgets that the mindset against women is still derogatory. If she is divorced, the mindset stoops even lower."

Ajay tried hard to soothe her aggression, "I agree, Shivani, that this is singularly the most repulsive attitude towards women, particularly, since we revere our Hindu Goddesses," he stated, remorsefully.

"Shivani, contrary to your stupid belief of being the neglected one, you were always an equal to Shiv, and you weren't treated as a second-class citizen. Female foeticide is so common in our country, but you were allowed to be born," Ma added.

"I'm aware of the lack of social support to women and I'm also aware that crimes against women are especially highlighted to prevent women like me from taking bold steps towards our emancipation. The continuous crimes against us is meant to crush our confidence and choke our voices. But really, will I be able to live with myself thinking that I am a woman who believes that women empowerment is a mere theory?" I asked, anger rising in the pit of my stomach. I, then, looked directly at Ma, and uttered sarcastically, "Also, thanks Ma! For not killing me 'despite' my gender. That was so noble of you!"

"Theories make an interesting read as it lures people to make a difference, but not a real one—only on paper, in the form of stories or on screens," she retorted, not even acknowledging my sarcastic remark.

"I'm sorry!" Ajay finally concluded, "I was asked to come in today to paint the real picture and not a fanciful one. But if there are any more queries, please do not hesitate to call me any time and thank you for taking out time."

"And thank you, for highlighting only the dark side of divorce and living alone in this 'rape infested' country!" I said, angrily, and then turning towards her, I remarked, "What did you call him here for, besides strengthening your case and leaving me downright dispirited?"

"It's the inconvenient truth that you're angry with, young lady, and not with Ajay, or me. Another truth is that you are ridiculously high-maintenance, dressed in diamonds, pearls and a million-dollar attitude, dear deluded daughter. So, are you still willing to fight tooth whitening and nail art, Your Majesty, while years wane your beauty away?" Ma asked, rhetorically. I resented her for being so abhorrent at this sensitive juncture of my life.

I chose to make her taste her own medicine by giving her the silent treatment as I lowered my eyes to blindly stare at the floor. This time I didn't care much about its gloss as I was consumed with the sadness of having lost the gloss of my own life. My lying maids were no longer an issue for me. I didn't care if they decided to expend their energy on domestic duties or focused on Salman Khan's movies, dancing to his beats instead of mine. I felt my blood rush to my neck, chin and forehead, as I began perspiring with anxiety. Ma's cheerleader lawyer handed me a tissue while she rambled on, "You're not in a strong bargaining position, so my suggestion is you consider other ways to keep your mind off your unsavoury reality."

Ma's eyes were wide as she blushed crimson in anger. She looked terrified; never before had I seen her in this devastated state. The atmosphere in the room wasn't exactly overflowing with friendliness, despite Ajay's best efforts to keep the meeting casual. Ma's energy was clearly impacting his too, as he suddenly appeared uncomfortable in our presence. He constantly ran his fingers through the file that was on the table and then, on the back of his neck.

My heart leapt in my chest as I had never before felt such abject bleakness. But I wasn't going to give her the pleasure of my misery. I intended to gather strength from within.

She leaned forward to talk to me or throttle me, as it appeared, and then she dropped her voice as her anger cut into the momentary silence between us, "I need you to do something for me and don't you dare defy me now as I know what women need to revive their dying hearts. I am exponentially more experienced in the realm of life than you will ever be," she said, with a strange mystery in her voice.

I stared back at her with resentment and this time, it was without any apprehension. She repeated herself. "I need you to do something, do you hear me? I know what's best for you."

I held my tongue as she wagged hers. It felt like she was waging a personal war with me and using the frustration of her past failings as ammunition against me. Perhaps, this was more about her and the women of her generation who didn't have the option of walking away, despite being savagely stripped of their dignity. I released an irritated sigh as I prayed for the next generation to be able to script a new mindset.

"What now, Ma? Yes, please don't hesitate to tell me what's good for me, yet again," I asked, with an obvious tone of frustration and sarcasm. I discovered that my voice was trembling less than it usually did during a confrontation and this led me to believe that I was becoming bolder. I was determined not to render the pleasure of crumbling before her; I had done that once and I had gained no empathy. So now, I decided to hone the gallant gene I had inherited from her. Her own mother was different from her as she was docile and was silenced the minute she attempted to voice her feelings towards a concerned matter in hand.

I was suddenly swept by the memories of Mata ji, my Ma's mother. She always understood and supported me. It was probably because I was very similar to her in my demeanour—quiet and unassuming, but certainly not ineffective from within. I remember her as being very creative and while growing up, I was encouraged to prepare lemon and mango pickles with her. We left them out in large jars in sunlight for days that ran into weeks, until they were preserved. Everyone relished them and she earned her credibility as the pickle practitioner and this tiny triumph gladdened her heart.

She taught me to seek joy in the smallest endeavours—that made a modest difference, but were monumental in keeping us genuinely happy. She insisted that the new-age disease of the mind—depression—was the result of people failing to appreciate the seemingly small things in their lives, often unrelated to monetary benefits. She always told me that this was the reason why our efforts always seemed unrewarded to us, and the only way to keep our self-esteem afloat was to dig deep within ourselves.

She later died of a severe asthma attack after having spent a week in the intensive care. Despite the regular administration of steroid injections, she declined and was unable to hold on to life. As she was passing on, mine were the only eyes she locked her gaze into. She transmitted her love into my soul as I cried inconsolably and ached for her to stay. After she died, I missed her so much that I never prepared or ate pickles again—they didn't taste the same without her tender touch. The people who were supposed to love her all her life suffocated her at every point and eventually, she died of just that—suffocation. We eventually perish pretty much the way we live.

At this point, I was brought back to reality as Ma thanked Ajay for his invaluable time before he excused himself. He curtsied, offered me a reassuring smile before wishing me the best. He left me wondering what I had learnt from the meeting, besides the grim future of women in this country. I was certain it wasn't this dismal for us and many who had flexed their muscles managed to strike a fair alimony and a much fairer life after. With these thoughts, I held on to my growing determination.

"Ma! Seriously, believe it or not, I have a life. It may not be exactly the kind I want, but I need to get back to it, so can you please spill your words out quickly?" I said, no longer attempting to be polite.

The tension in the air was turning denser and it was almost as tangible as my frustration. She drew an extended breath, before speaking.

"Go and have an affair!" she commanded, looking into my deep brown eyes as if hypnotising me.

"W-h-a-t? What is wrong with you, Ma? You have completely lost it, and you think I am the one who gambles with life!" I yelled, in utter disbelief and disgust as I jumped out of my chair and moved towards the rear of the room. My back hit the wall behind me, as I stood there shocked and shaken to the core.

"I've never as much as dared to look at another man while I've been married to Sameer. I've never dared to even fantasise about anyone, but my husband," I lied. "And you want me to cheat on him—my husband who is supposed to be my everything, according to you! Yes, the same guy who you said is the 'supreme power', who keeps the order of my universe and without whose protection, I will get 'raped' or turn into a 'victim' of acid attack? These were your words, weren't they?"

I stood before her in disdain. Was she teasing me, or was she just insane? Ma felt she was losing control and now she was behaving like a senile old woman. Which mother would advise her daughter to seduce a man, outside her marriage? At that moment, Ma seemed like an embittered woman whose once formidable spirit lay in shreds. Was I to consider this sort of advice an unmixed blessing or an unblended curse?

The seams of my heart burst open in one split second. Everything that kept a human heart together—love, relationships, friendships, personal ambitions and desires—each lost their power and the stitches of my heart broke one by one, to tear down its walls. I tried frantically to look past my anger, but its density enveloped me.

"You are driven by the desire to divorce him because you believe you will acquire happiness, so why don't you try seeking happiness while you remain repulsively rich? You can relish a slice of life without any collateral damage and no one, but I, will know about your escapade. A little respite from a bad marriage never did anyone any harm, provided you are shrewd enough to keep it under wraps—metaphorically and literally!'" Ma said, uncharacteristically.

Ma's words had mixed toxicity and I stared at her in disbelief. "Is this the reason why my sisters have remained in their trying marriages? Is it because they're all sleeping with other men?"

What I wouldn't do now to be the fly on the wall of the room where Ma sat and advised my sisters.

"In addition, do you advise them on what positions to try out with these men and how often, while you maintain a diary of my sisters' sex lives and their inch-by-inch progress? Ma, are you for real?" I asked with nervous laughter, forgetting all inhibitions in my shocked stupor.

"Just shut up and listen to me, you impudent child! You are different from your sisters, so the advice I'm giving you is exclusively for you. Your sisters, unlike you, have adjusted to their roles every step of the way, and that too, with utmost finesse and without the fuss. You're the only dark horse of the family! Now, listen hard before you reject my advice without rendering it an intelligent thought," she said, as if hearing the voice in my head.

Anguish gripped me, as I knew, on witnessing Ma's aggravated expression, that I was trapped—stuck in a tight situation that would curb me from living with a morsel of dignity. I at once felt foolish for believing in the beginning of the meeting that the legal man would ensure obtaining a divorce for me in exchange for a legitimate hug.

I slid back into the sofa, urging it to consume me—to make me disappear from this room, my marriage, from this world, and most gravely, from Ma. Ma—who believed to know it all—actually knew nothing; nothing about love, integrity, or just about being human. She was abundantly astute, absurd and aloof in the same beat. She was sure and yet, insecure. She was my mother and yet, more alien than a stranger to me. Her self-indulgence crippled me to the core as she tried yet another face-saving strategy on me.

"An affair is the solution to all your woes and I will do the groundwork for you. Begin by coming to the office well-presented, and your marriage that is doomed will soon be bathed in light. Disengage yourself from him for the time being; mentally and emotionally, I mean. Just pay heed to my sound advice and all will be well, Alice in wonderland! Sometimes it takes three to make a marriage work; Oscar Wilde thought so too."

"Oscar who?" I asked, "and do I really care what Oscar or you think? Ma! I think you're crossing the line and I'm done—seriously and utterly done—with this kind of imbecile advice."

"Speaking of advice, I'd like to offer another one to you. You must be more discerning before teaming up with your brother, Shiv, to conspire against me again. Just remember that between Shiv and I, I am the one who directs your movie. He isn't even the co-director, so don't waste your energy on urging him to twist my arm," Ma said, with an ominous smile on her face.

"Ma! I can't even picture being unfaithful to Sameer in my craziest dreams and you're asking me to cast aside everything I had been conditioned with. Besides, I am extremely reserved, so where on earth would I find a man to love me? I've never been on dating sites, social media and whatever else helps people find 'true love'. And Ma, I spoke to Shiv because he's my brother; I thought he would get through to you as you have made an eternal vow to turn a deaf ear on me. But you know what, Ma? I will never let you or anyone come between Shiv and me, because we are close and he gets me like you never will," I said, surprising myself by finally learning to stand up to her.

"Shut up and listen," Ma began in a frustrated tone again. "I am trying to save your marriage here. An affair will distract you sufficiently from your anxieties. Every woman is unfaithful to her husband in one way or the other. Some go all the way, with other men in their beds whilst others live with different men in their heads. Now, I don't want you to get emotional about this because every woman needs to get in touch with her latent needs, and that, sometimes, only a man outside the walls of her marriage can fulfil. Once you feel sufficiently satisfied, you will learn to appreciate your domestic landscape that currently appears to have lost its bloom. And who on God's dysfunctional earth is talking about love? An affair is what I want you to have—without love—and I'm sure in the process, you will begin viewing your marriage in a new light. Trust your mother on this," she said, with unbridled authority on the subject. "And I do strongly urge you not to be so insolent when I tell you to do something because it is for your own good. You're too much of a lady to let your temper get the better of you and to use unacceptable language. I have a responsibility towards you and you need to accept that."

"Of course you do and I trust your sense of responsibility, just the way I trusted you to espouse me to a man that benefitted you in your business. And the way I trusted you to marry Shiv to a girl who he didn't love, after breaking the heart of the one he did. Now, after all that, I am supposed to trust you to play pimp in my life for some meaningless sexual excitement that is meant to 'liberate' me from my emotional afflictions. You want me to step outside the boundaries of conventions and yet, remain caged within your decided ones."

She walked towards me with her hand raised, as if she was about to slap me once again. She was shaking and her eyes were wide, but after standing uncomfortably close to me, she dropped her arm.

I shuddered, drew a deep breath and moved back. My promiscuity was more acceptable to her than a life of dignity and liberty. Character carried no weight in Ma's material world. Her contradictions confused me, as all my life, I had believed her to be a traditional and dutiful woman who wrote her life's book in one word—sacrifice.

The enraged heat of the sun blazed through her office window, drawing a glow on her triumphant face, while I stood fairly frozen. I stared at her with a disordered mind and she stared back, without flickering an eyelid. I questioned her integrity now and everything she stood for.

Ironically, her idea was meant to protect me, but it further perplexed me. She was adamant about saving my marriage by making sure I swept my personal integrity under the rug, but I suspected there were elements she hadn't thought about. Every cell in my body quivered at the idea of becoming insanely impulsive and ridiculously reckless with my life.

# 14

"I'm insanely impulsive and ridiculously reckless, but not stupid to ever toy with our friendship as it means the universe and beyond. I owe you an apology for not being in touch and I admit that I have nothing to say in my defence," I rambled on, while she adjusted her bag on the empty chair next to us.

Shivani and I met at our customary café after a considerably long interim as we got caught up in life's meaningless undertakings. There was a hammer of rain with a rumble of thunder outside that justified having the piping hot cappuccinos we had ordered, like always.

"Well, it feels great to have you back in circulation. Your men have always robbed you of your time with your friends, but I guess it goes with the territory. Anyway, did you manage to speak to Sameer for me? Didn't you say he set a day and time with you?" Shivani asked, with a hint of irritation in her voice.

"Actually, yes and no! I mean, he cancelled on me several times as was expected, but I'm still persevering. I mean, I'll keep pursuing him!" I said, stumbling on my own words as I began fidgeting. "I've been caught up with my children. I tried him recently though, but his mobile phone was unavailable. As I said, I'm on it and will tell you as soon as I hear from him."

"Are you sure you're okay? You look terribly jumbled," she asked, with disbelief etched on her face. "Is it yet another man gone wrong?"

"Hey, absolutely not! I'm just tired and probably need a break, that's all. You know how it is. As women, we are constantly juggling between our children's needs and our own and before we know it, we're depleted. I'm fine though," I lied, readjusting myself on my chair and flinging my hair away from my face.

"If there's anything I can do to ease things, do let me know. Of course, I understand a woman's challenges. Speaking of which, Sameer and I aren't even on talking terms now and we barely pass each other in the mornings when he's off to work. I don't see him around the house in the evenings and there's this silent contract between us that's given us permission to live our own lives without any prying from the other. Let me know if there's any progress on that front and I will proceed to stand against Ma, even though her stance is firm. I'm feeling more positive, you know Richa, about making a shift in my life."

"I'm glad, Shivani," I said, cautiously adding, "it's high time, if I may say so."

An awkward silence lay between us momentarily and I cringed at the thought of losing her as my closest friend. God forbid, if she opened the can of worms, I'd fail in my attempts to justify myself. It felt like eons since we met and having turned another corner, I found it hard to narrow the gap with a conversation that normally flowed perfectly.

For years, Shivani had wept and whined on my shoulder and now, that part of my anatomy turned cold on her. I wished that I had kicked up an excuse to avoid her today as I felt waves of panic wash through me. I was becoming increasingly uncomfortable and my body language must've made it easy for her to detect that, as she too, became awkward around me.

I knew she was wondering the real reason behind me being withdrawn and wilted, or was it just my imagination? A guilty conscience did much to concoct its own stories simply to ease itself from prickling.

"Are you sure you're not seeing someone new?" she enquired brazenly, to finally break the silence between us. "Is it someone I know and you *just* don't want me to know about it?" she asked instinctively, triggering a sensation that rapidly settled in the pit of my gut.

Her eyes drew towards me penetratingly, as I sat before her, trying hard to be impassive.

"Is he *also* married and you're guilty about it? Something is definitely up, because the air around you has changed considerably," she enquired, shifting slightly in her chair. "If he is married, what's the big fuss? Haven't they all been, anyway?" she enquired, with a trace of sarcasm.

I snapped defensively, "Of course, I'm okay, Shivani. No, I'm not having an affair. Is this how you really perceive me—as a serial slut? I'm sure I have the right to recover from my disappointments and for that, I'm simply taking time out—a sabbatical. I'm not entirely over Mr. Big Ego, who got me accustomed to living in Ravi-land. Nevertheless, I'm cultivating the habit of being alone so that it no longer bites and I don't keep settling for men a quarter of a century older and twice my body weight."

"Hey, chill, Richa. There's no need to be so touchy," she advised, dropping her voice and lifting both her hands before her in defence. "I mean, you're single and it's your prerogative to mingle. I was only taken aback because the notion of you being alone is unexpected. You know, what I mean?" she said, almost sympathetically, before she continued. "But hey, it's healthy to be alone at times and as long as you're not lonely, it's fine. Just stay happy, no matter what! I was concerned because you look whiter than the cloth on this table and I certainly didn't mean to sound derogatory about the married men bit, but the fact is that 'loaded old married men' have become a part of your core portfolio."

"Well, as I stated some time back, I'm blessed with a kind of resilience, so don't stress if you don't see me on top of the world right now. You will, hopefully, very soon. Now, I hand my shoulder over to you, so here, please take it. All yours!" I suggested, pointing to it and trying my utmost to be light-hearted.

"Thanks, because I do have tons to unload and what better shoulder than yours. In fact, *that* is why *I* am irritated with you—you've been so unavailable! Anyway, it's whine o' clock, so let me spill my story first and later, maybe, we can unknot your world by loosening your ties with married men. We need to break this awkward interval between us and glide back into ordinariness," she said and I, too, eased myself into a rhythmic breath.

"Time and distance can convert best friends into strangers if communication between them recedes. So, before I spill my story, I need to wait till my Richa returns from wherever she's flown because the woman sitting before me is certainly not the one I've loved, cherished and opened up my vault of secrets to."

She calmed me at once with her tenderness as I drew a breath to release my angst, before breaking into a nervous giggle. She retreated into her chair, throwing her shoulders down flaccidly. An expression of pristine certainty was stitched on her face—something I had never noticed on her before—and she looked good with it. In fact, she looked confident and that disarmed me.

"I'm sorry, Shivani, I shouldn't have snapped like that, but in my defence, I suffer from chronic loneliness, which is married to waning confidence. I'm learning to appease my internal turbulence and you for one have always encouraged me to scale greater heights, so I'm trying to do just that. Something tells me that along with whine, it's also your wine o'clock. So, let's order a bottle. All things considered, you look dashing and that calls for a toast!" I said, motioning her to begin her endless saga with her Ma.

"Cheers to us! I need you to be rest assured that I'm there for you. I love you *so* much that it irks me when there is this unexplained gap between our coffee and chats. Stay close, and anyway, if one of us floats away, the other will pull them back, right? Before beginning my saucy story in contrast to the usual sad one, I want to say that you too look wonderful, despite your challenges. If I were in your shoes looking as fantastic as you do, my self-esteem would be flying sky-high."

Then, she moved in closer and whispered, "Anyway, what I'm about to tell you is going to shake the ground your pretty feet are on. I never considered in my wildest wettest dreams that I was capable of moving out of my comfort zone and walking confidently into uncharted territory. I wasn't even aware that life could be full of such exciting twists."

"This delicious new development in your life is making me restless, so please get to the point," I urged.

"Oh my God!" she shrieked. "I need two glasses of wine instead of a mere single for courage, but first, let's toast to our most enduring and endearing spirits," she said, gulping down wine like water. She intrigued me as I watched her pour more wine in our glasses and I stared at her blindly, urging her to share her transformative tale.

"What unknown territory are you talking about? Are you getting a divorce?" I enquired excitedly, while placing my glass down.

"No! No!" she responded, nodding her head vigorously. "I think I'm turning into a slut!" she said, so excitedly that her face blazed with the joyfulness of an excited child who had just been introduced to a new toy.

"I think I'm having an affair and oh my God, it feels good to be using that word—*affair!* I never imagined in my craziest fantasies that I'd get close to the forbidden fruit and that it tasted so darn delicious! The meter of my life is running again and I'm finally able to view the light in my otherwise dismal marriage, exactly as Ma predicted. In a few days, she has turned from being governing to a genius. She's filled my mind with renewed hope and excitement. I no longer have the impulse to break my marriage as someone is entering my life to mend it," she said breathlessly.

I practically tumbled over my chair with laughter; she always managed to ease my conscience. The naïve soul who was always subdued would finally break the cardinal rule and she was devastatingly happy for it, whilst I continued feeding on my forbidden fruit which probably wasn't as delectable, but remained my best choice for now.

"I knew there was this air around you that made you look the way you do—all glowing and stuff. So you have finally broken the principal rule of marriage and that too, without a grain of guilt! Who is this divine dude who has miraculously altered the course of your destiny?" I asked, saluting her. I then moved across to kiss her on her forehead and to offer her the tightest hug. A cool shiver rippled down my spine as I embraced her. I harboured immense love for her, as she pulsated with bliss for someone else. With this in my mind, I rapidly returned to my seat with her lingering scent.

"Keep talking, woman and all I want from you is the gospel truth! Is he hot and why on God's crumbling earth have you taken so long to break this vital piece of information? You're oozing with so much love, it is fascinating!" I questioned, narrowing my eyes in deep enquiry.

"Allow me to answer all your enquiries one by one. For the moment, my beautiful friend, it's not at all physical. It's an emotional thing, so there's no real evidence of an affair as such. Owing to its ambiguity, I wasn't sure if I even had anything to report to you. The hot saucy messages haven't begun yet as we are just igniting the flame by exchanging the eager eye at work. I find him attractive, so for me, he's hot and I'm certain that it's mutual because of his body language. I'm so excited and it's all so lunatic because it seems like the only solution for me to turn tolerant towards my marriage. Although I was repulsed by the idea of cheating on Sameer at first, but Ma…"

"Ma?" I asked, shifting in my chair. "What's your Ma got to do with any of this?"

"Well, Richa, it's absurd and it contradicts all Ma's beliefs about a woman's domestic duties and her obligations as a wife, but clearly, she doesn't feel that loyalty is imperative. She's convinced me that an affair can salvage my marital blues and keep me from taking any drastic action. I've clearly failed in my attempt to revive my dead marriage. My decision was a simple divorce, but Ma has come up with the next best solution. You know, she controls the order of the cosmos and with it, my every emotion, motion and now, my sex life too. She's encouraging me to put myself out there and to have an affair. At first, I rejected the idea thinking the advice was fatally flawed. I felt she was adding insult to my injury. But gradually, I was able to envision it and the idea ignited this flame of passion in me. It's an adventure and it's easier than breaking the marriage whose fragments will cut into her morals for as long as her heart beats. It was Ma after all, who commanded me to follow her orders in letter and spirit, so it certainly eases my guilt knowing that she's paved the way for me. I'm getting tied up in knots merely thinking about sleeping with a man outside my marriage. I'm getting goosebumps merely envisioning it," she said, with the anticipation of a teenager attending prom with her date for the first time, knowing that the evening would end with a kiss.

"I must say, your Ma is incredible and I have this newfound respect for her. Anyway, keep talking," I said, with an element of insecurity creeping up in the pit of my stomach. I camouflaged my feelings for her by guzzling down another glass of wine and as it got over, I ordered another bottle. Shivani looked at me questioningly, before swiftly letting it pass as she was consumed by the eagerness to spill her story.

"Prior to this, I was fighting my situation in my head. I was disillusioned with my entire marital saga. My mild depression threatened to sink the very desire to go on, but then I pushed myself hard to work in Ma's office. It was then that I noticed him, noticing me. From that moment, I felt a spark and began looking forward to seeing him every day.

"You know, Richa, I understand now how it feels to be someone's sweetheart—someone outside the four caved walls of marriage, whom I have the power to excite. While walking past me, he looks at me and my heart misses a beat and waits restlessly for the next amorous glance. I feel like a teenager again. When I'm in bed alone at night, my head is preoccupied with his thoughts. I'm ready to take on the world with new vigour," she said with eyes that sparkled with a fresh resolve.

"Wow! I'm listening to a refreshingly new perspective on securing a marriage. Perhaps your Ma could've rescued mine too, that way I wouldn't have had to get married twice!" I said, light-heartedly. "What's his name and what is he doing at the office, besides fervently flirting with you?"

She was rubbing her thumb up and down her marital ring thoughtfully, before she slipped it off with her other hand. She looked up at me with mischief in her eyes and said jovially, "I will continue to wear this thing, but not on this finger or this hand. I don't want to anymore, because it doesn't hold the same significance it used to."

She, then, unexpectedly grabbed both my hands in excitement and whispered, "I'm so blessed to have you and will need to take you into confidence throughout my affair. And you'll be my alibi too! Will you be okay with that? He may call me when I'm at home with Sameer, I can always pretend to be speaking to you. But most importantly, I need tips in bed, since you're the connoisseur," she giggled.

"Shivani! You're seriously getting ahead of yourself, girl!" I said, breaking into an outburst of laughter. Noticing how innocently she was plotting her affair that may never unfold tickled me inside. "I asked you his name and what he does, but you're so consumed constructing a love affair in the air. Why don't we wait till he approaches you and then together, we'll cross the bridge when we actually come to it. Yes?"

"Sorry, Richa, but I'm already planning on crossing all my bridges with him, and if we do encounter any walls, we will break them down together. To answer your question, he's an architect and a damn sexy one at that. His name is even sexier, Raman. Gosh, Richa! Calling out his name is sending another shiver down my spine. I'm all dressed up in love and I'm dying for him to undress me most passionately. Is this natural? We haven't even spoken to each other and yet, I feel I know every inch of him!" Shivani kept on rambling— she was besotted.

I was visibly amused at my friend's naiveté as she was behaving like she was about to lose her virginity. I sniggered, digging my mouth into the wine glass. I couldn't believe that she hadn't even exchanged words with him and already, she was having the most sweltering affair in her lust-filled head.

"He's Ma's architect and he's always in and out of the office. He is currently working on her new block, while simultaneously managing his other projects. He's a really busy man and very soon, he'll become even busier"' she said, with uncontained elation. She had never looked so beautiful and I offered her my unfettered support, along with a deep commitment to be there for her. Besides, I was genuinely happy for her and wanted this to work in her favour.

"Richa, an affair was never on my 'must-have' list but now that it's knocking on my door, I want to open up to a whole new realm of reckless passion. Romance is at my doorstep and I'm not going to turn it away. Do you know why? Because desire feels so darn good!"

"Desire is a callous emotion and it doesn't rest until it has been fed, so yes, I know how you feel. The only downside to this is that once you've tasted blood, it's going to be harder to work on your marriage. I mean, I'm not saying for a second that I'm not glad for you or will not support you, but as your best friend, I must warn you of the possible perils that you may inadvertently be inviting in your life," I warned her, while I played my role as her closest friend, unsuspectingly. I did genuinely care for her, regardless of the spontaneous turn my own life had taken.

A few glasses of wine later, I uttered sloppily, "You know Shivani, catch life before it slips away and be careful not to get hurt. The only rule is that when we cheat, we have to pay a price sooner or later, but then that comes with the territory. Plus, we would die of boredom if we played by the rules."

"Hey, Ma has vowed to take care of every calamity and I know Ma has my back. She's in this as much as I am, so she will make sure I'm covered while Raman uncovers and discovers me! I'm on the fringe of losing my marriage, so why not jump into the ocean and see if I sink, swim or simply stay afloat?" she said with uncontained anticipation. Her dark brown eyes were sparkling, and her bright smile at once diminished the fine lines that had settled on her forehead due to stress and loneliness.

"Well! I have to admit there is something very exciting about being aroused by a man outside marriage. You're right; it's the illicit idea of being seduced by someone unknown that makes you tremble with excitement. Just be careful not to get into it too deep. First love, as they say, is a sweet despair and this is your first, in a sense. Try to keep a lid on your emotions because for women, *that* is the challenge—to be in the moment, without attachment. But hey, it's time to live a little, so once again, cheers!" I responded, enthusiastically.

Outside, we heard thunder and what looked like a bolt of lightning from the window. We continued chatting and I hoped that the affair wouldn't throw the balance out of her life as it usually did with most people, including myself. Her pursuit for happiness might lead to delusion and hurt, but she needed to tread the path to learn its many teachings, triumphs and let-downs—just as I did and still continued to do.

As I leaned back with my gaze etched on her face, Varun—a friend of ours—came strolling towards us. "How are you lovely girls doing? Muah, Muah! By the way, meet my new beau, partner and the love of my life; Rohit. We are leaving for Marbella next week. But once we're back, we're going to catch up properly with you lovely ladies. Is that cool?" he winked and pecked me on the cheek.

"Hey, of course," I responded, while Shivani first smiled and then got distracted with her mobile phone.

"We won't keep you. Love you!" he shook Shivani's hand before walking hand in hand with his beau.

"Gosh, Richa! He is so good-looking, and even dresses with precision. Though his smile is his most flattering accessory. I found him on last month's front cover of GQ and he looked dashing. Now that I'm on the track, I wish he wasn't gay just so I could have a piece of him too," Shivani giggled. "I would love to glide my fingers on his soft skin. Why did he choose to be gay? What was the need when I was *so* available?"

"Shivani, these are not choices; it's not exactly a lifestyle choice for God's sake. He was born that way and I respect people who have the marbles to come out of the closet and carry themselves with their head held high," I felt myself perspiring profusely, while ardently defending the homosexual culture.

"We can rearrange the furniture in our rooms, but we cannot change our sexual orientation. If only we were all bold enough to be the way nature intended. But all said and done, it's simpler for a gay guy to come out of the closet than a gay woman because our society accepts him more readily. No matter how sissified he is, he is eventually embraced. The fact is that they have a tight-knit gay community who support and socialise with each other. It's never this pleasant for a homosexual woman as such solidarity is still missing. I know one who is in her 50s now, divorced and living alone in severe depression. She sits with her psychiatrist regularly to repair the damage that was inflicted on her. When she revealed that she was a lesbian, to her parents, at 19, they made her very own cousins rape her to make her familiar with what it felt to be with a man. And if that was not enough, she was later forced to marry one of those cousins. It's repulsive. She was stripped of the last shred of her dignity, leaving a void in her soul, which she later filled with drugs and alcohol. Her parents wrecked her completely. After she was forced to marry, she returned some years later—bruised and battered. It was then that she isolated herself completely. Even though, she's in the autumn of her years, she is still ensnared in her fear and substance abuse and that's how each one of us is held captive by our own unresolved crap."

"But then hypocrisy is an epidemic that sweeps across our entire nation, Richa. There are many issues that infuriate me too, particularly the issue of staying captive in a terrible marriage. But I can't complain now as I've found my window. Anyway, you were saying?" she said, lightly.

"Well, the same woman has a very close homosexual friend who is more of a brother to her and is openly living with his partner. Although for years, his father was infuriated with him. He relayed to him how ashamed he was and accused him of being 'unmanly'. He was made to feel unworthy for years. He was the only son of his parents, so eventually, he was accepted. His sexuality didn't change, but the times did. Their most earnest and emphatic prayers failed, and the parents surrendered their weapon of manipulation. In a sense, they were freed from the chains of societal conditioning that had distorted their view. His father even went ahead to accept him as one of the partners in their clothing company. Now, he stands equal to his father and represents the company and if he did have a straight brother, he wouldn't be any less successful than him. He didn't change his stance and certainly didn't fall for the controlling tactics played by his parents.

"'Lesbian', on the other hand, is still a terrifying word for many and even the so-called modern people become uncomfortable around one. She told me that once she was talking to a friend in a mall and the friend's mother pulled her away and asked her daughter in front of everyone if she was okay, as she was worried about an 'attack' from my homosexual friend. She was treated like an alien who was carrying a life-threatening disease," I concluded, feeling the blood rush to my face in rage.

"I hate to admit, I feel kind of uneasy myself at the thought of being alone in the same room as a lesbian, but then, I've never been acquainted with one, so I can't really comment. I know in an open space like a mall, I could handle it," Shivani said, with a glazed look in her eyes. It was probably because of too many glasses of wine.

"Are you kidding me? What on God's hope-tearing earth are you saying? Handle what? Do you even know the facts? Most of us are either mostly straight or mostly gay. No one and I mean, no one is completely straight or gay," I screamed, realising later how infuriated I must have sounded.

"Most of us, while growing up, go through a 'transition period' where we explore ourselves—from being straight to bisexual to gay or back to being mostly straight or mostly gay. This process enables people to make a less dramatic shift in their sexual orientation. By a certain age, most people get off the fence and can give themselves a clear sexual identity. When I say most, I mean some are under the lock and key owing to their families, considering homosexuality still remains a social stigma. So, just to clear your apparent ignorance, homosexual people are as *normal* as you are. Being gay or lesbian is *not* and I repeat most emphatically, *not* an abnormality, and you know what Shivani, our sexual orientation doesn't determine the goodness in us. When we are lying in the coffin, it will not be our sexuality, but our goodness that will be remembered.

"Our mothers and that girl's mother who pulled her away, thinking her daughter was under attack, need to be educated. I believe it's not completely unreasonable to anticipate resistance from their generation as they hold a narrow perspective on issues like this, but it can't be expected of us, Shivani! That, to me, is repulsive and this fallaciousness of blaming and shaming has to be cleared. The aspersions cast on a homosexual's character by parents and peers hinder their progress by keeping them locked in the closet and this is the reason most women fade into the background. Fear grips them so forcefully that it compels them to act against their natural instincts," I stormed on, my face flushed.

"Hey babes, please don't get so defensive!" she stated in jest. "I believe in sexual equality myself and I'm about to embark on a territory I'm certain my husband is already too familiar with. It's sad about lesbians for sure, but you need to spare a thought right now for the most sparkling moment of my life. Let me tell you, you are putting a damper on it by talking about something that is so utterly irrelevant. To top it all, you are overreacting, so mellow down, take a deep breath and return once more to me," Shivani gestured with both her hands, fanning them to cool me down. "Focus on me, your friend who is as straight as an iron rod!" Shivani said, eagerly, raising her glass.

I nodded at first in disgust, but after several deep breaths, allowed my irritation to melt. She simply proved that such prejudices had seeped deep in our culture's consciousness and no one gave a second thought before making derogatory remarks about such sensitive issues. I alone couldn't call attention to the ridiculousness of shaming gay culture, so I released a sigh and focused on her instead.

"Yes, Richa, it's time to buy a little joy because fidelity, integrity and all these fancy words are outdated and 'soul-ed' out, so cheers and thank you! It is, after all, your infectious zest for life that I finally caught up with. I can't thank you enough and yes, for all it's worth, I thank my old lady too. Hey, she's proved to be more pragmatic than anyone of us. Maybe she's almost straight or almost gay or whatever. Oh God, I'm tipsy as hell," she said, shaking her head and sloppily letting her shoulders drop. "Richa, I love you and you better make sure you never abandon me because we'll never find friends with the same mental disorder, you know. We are crazy and only we know it," she said, with a clumsy laughter.

I cackled at her renewed energy and humour. She was transformed and I connected to her enthusiasm enormously as it immediately drew a smile to my otherwise glum expression. I raised my glass to toast to the next chapter of her life that promised to bring her a host of erratic experiences.

"Here's to an affair I will love sacredly, secretly, but not silently and you know what?" she concluded, while downing the glass of wine. Tilting her head sideways, she said, "I feel privileged to have this man who will add a new slant to my life," whilst narrowing her eyes seductively.

Despite my acquaintance with the territory, she revived my own memories of the first time I had tasted the forbidden fruit.

"I've always lived in the confines of norms and I'm ready for a rollercoaster ride. I believe everyone deserves to seek their happiness, so my advice to you, my zappy friend, is that as long as you remain 'mostly straight', you must pursue the desires of your heart too."

# 15

My heart's insatiable desire was what I found myself following for the very first time. My vacuous world began to fill and my days started to tick again. I felt the transition take place from gloom to bloom and I understood now that it took more than love, understanding and compromise to save a marriage—it took a torrid love affair.

My ship-shape body brushed against his, tantalisingly, and he glanced at me rapturously. I returned his glance with eyes that were smiling and lips that were longing to kiss him, but were being carefully controlled. This time, he extended his glance to a few split seconds and grinned before he looked away. He then turned around to look at me and now, I was certain that he was interested in me just as much as I was, in him. I felt the churning in my stomach and the urge to walk up to him and kiss him, but I stepped back instead, knowing that the moment had passed. I had seen him enter Ma's office quite frequently in recent weeks, while I began working here and we always acknowledged each other without uttering a single syllable. As days went by, he blatantly flirted with his eyes and this encounter was a step forward for both of us. He was unconventionally handsome—tall, well-built, almost athletic. Despite the tell-tale signs of him not working out, I was floored.

Over the weeks that I began working in close proximity to him, I admired the meticulous manner in which he did things.

His attention to details such as the accessories I wore to work every day—including my handbag and shoes—brought about a certain fondness in me for him. Clearly, he was skilled in wooing women. I granted him permission to enchant me as I savoured every ounce of his attention, after years of neglect from my husband. I wasn't aware of the flirtatious streak in me till Ma thrust me in this direction.

"So, tell me!" I began when we finally stood face-to-face, without a single brick of inhibition between us. I placed my hips seductively on the cabinet next to Ma's desk while she was out, grabbing the opportunity of catching him working.

"How's it going?" I fumbled. "I mean, the latest project you're working on for Ma?"

At first, he sniggered, as he knew all too well that it wasn't the project I was interested in. But then, he played along, as he was equally keen to know me better. "Well, it's a storey with its own alluring story," he began, closing his laptop with an innocent chuckle as his eyes scanned me. "Before I unfold the tedious chapters of my career, allow me to congratulate you on joining hands with your mother and brother at the office. It's good to have you on board, Shivani!"

"Oh! Thank you, Mr. Sharma, isn't it? Yes, it feels good to be on board and it was Ma's idea since she felt that some stimulation would do me a world of good. Anyway, I'd love to hear more about you and your so-called 'tedious chapters' some time, since architecture really does fascinate me," I lied. Flirting was coming as naturally to me as sneezing, swallowing and sleeping.

"I'm glad!" he said with a twinkle in his eye. "My work is my heartbeat and each project is very emotional, and I just called you Shivani because it *feels* good to be on the first name basis, right?" he began, still looking at me fondly and extending his hand forward. "It's Raman! Nice and easy!"

"Hi again, Raman and please clarify because I don't understand. I mean, about you getting emotional about your work. I apologise for my ignorance, but I'm a latecomer to this world and I need to learn from scratch," I responded whilst moving towards him in a pose that accentuated my curves in a figure-hugging electric blue dress. For the first time in years, perhaps decades, I felt comfortable with my body and realised I had what it took to seduce a man. The prospect of sleeping with this man encouraged me to watch my calories, but for now, I wasn't focusing on my day's menu but on how deliciously irresistible I appeared before him as he spoke to me with eagerness in his eyes.

"Oh, I love newcomers, it makes me feel in charge. I can teach you much more than your mind can imagine, so I'm in, if you are! Food for thought!" he commented, flirtatiously. "For now, let me fill you in about my career as an architect, since you've shown a keenness to learn about it. I always begin by making my acquaintance with my client. I read my clients and get to know what makes them tick and then, I relate a very ordinary story with an uncommon twist. I get inspired by my client's personality and make my work consistent with the person's inherent character. I want to know who they are and where they have come from, what they represent and what their company stands for. I link it all together, weaving it with modernity, tradition, innovation and evolution."

I stared at him, and he returned the gaze, not missing a single reaction of mine. His articulate explanation left me breathless and longing for more. He was as charming as he was competent and I was already bursting at the seams with something that felt close to love. Perhaps not love, that was a white lie. At this stage, it was lust—pure impure lust. I felt exhilaration in the pit of my stomach, rendering me the hysterical urge to wrap my entire body around him and to remain there until he tore my clothes and satisfied me like no other man ever had. I snapped out of my sexual reverie and manoeuvred my mind back to the conversation.

"Let me explain it with the help of your mother's example. She has a strong link to her heritage and while she respects tradition, she also aspires to be the future. So, her next office building will comply to that. A decorative chandelier was another talking point, so we've ordered one from Italy for her office. I think it's the offensively opulent Murano she wanted, but otherwise, every room will boast of accent, ambient and general lighting solutions. In her case, I have given her a modern twist, resonant of her values and somewhat contradictory nature."

I beamed a smile at his impressive and accurate assessment of Ma's inherent complex character, but I also listened attentively as I observed his passion for the work he did. I could only imagine how in tune he would be to a woman's needs in bed. It was almost as if he read my mind; his tone of voice softened and he moved closer to me. I felt my heart skip a beat as beads of sweat formed on my forehead. He was too close for comfort and perhaps, I wasn't ready for this, but in the same vein, I knew it in my bones that I was. My breath lost its rhythm while he was calm and controlled. Perhaps, he was accustomed to courting women and I was no more than a number, but who in my deranged world cared? Ma, with her vision, was in this with me, so my insecurity slipped away as easily as I wanted his tongue to slip into my passion-yearning mouth.

"Constructing a room or an entire building is like completing a canvas with its own textures. It's a challenging exercise to base the ideas on the character of the person who the space belongs to, along with coaxing them out of their comfort zone," he said, seducing me with his fluid black eyes. "You never know how exciting a prospect is until you learn to let go of the known. You have to be prepared to walk boldly into unknown realms. The mysterious, Shivani, can be the most seductive," he asserted.

"That's very profound!" I said, swallowing excitement in my throat and attempting to regain the rhythm of my breath. I was convinced now that he was drawn to me as much as I was to him and even though, he was still talking, I was barely listening to him. My head had already begun to imagine us rocking the bed till it threatened to collapse. I watched him talk with his hands and imagined how expressive they must be intimately.

"I either start from scratch or revive spaces that are down and dilapidated. I don't believe in boundaries, Shivani! I tear down walls and build new ones. I'm not immune to trends, but I do like to believe that I'm original. It's a part of my journey to break walls of conventions and build a ground-breaking future. Everything I touch, Shivani, I bring to life and this gives me an incredible high. I have yet to disappoint a client or for that matter, a woman," he said, aware that he had my complete attention. I pursed my lips as he was turning me on more than I cared to admit. I wanted to remain tight-lipped, but instead I took a deep breath and worked on regaining my composure.

"I love your audacious confidence. I've never met anyone so outrageously arrogant," I said, clearly impressed. "Were you born this conceited or did you grow into it?"

He began to laugh in a childlike manner and at the same time, he seemed virile. He leaned against the desk behind him, standing cross-legged. I noticed he was taller than he initially appeared and his body language exuded the kind of confidence that made a woman feel both secure and threatened at the same time.

"Well, arrogance is an integral part of my make-up and as an adept architect, I've earned the right to be supercilious, but not superficial. I'm actually quite proud of my arrogance, but most importantly, I hope it's appealing to you and I wonder if I've engineered the right kind of sweet talk!" he chuckled, as I did too, since I found him refreshingly interesting. He laughed as he continued talking and I watched him, awestruck. "It is the human emotion that inspires me and long after the emotion has passed, owing to its transient nature, it is my construction that remains erect. Shivani, I'm particularly inspired by what drives a woman. Not that I want to seduce you into thinking that I could change your destiny in any way, but I can breathe new life into it," he said, heaving with desire.

I knew at that moment I would let him define and refine me in whichever way he desired. My eyes gave him my consent to build something of our own—transient, but transformative. I trusted his hands and now I wanted his heart, but before that, I burned for his body. His aftershave was awakening the animal in me. I wondered how he planned to alter the contours of my body.

"Shivani, as a child, I revolted against conventions, but now I don't need to. I have reinvented myself. It's probably part of my blueprint to construct people's happiness and to please them in full measure through every resource available to me. You need to try me someday," he said, pulling out a rose from the vase on Ma's desk.

"You can't have the benefit of a rose without being pricked by the thorns. The good and the bad co-exist, but I'm so good that you won't mind the bad in me," he said, piercing into my eyes. I caught onto his every word and action as I grabbed the rose and brought it close to my nose. It exuded the aroma of promise and I inhaled it with lingering joy. The last time Sameer sent me a bouquet was on our first anniversary and after that, it was dinners followed quickly by nothing. But I soon realised that this was not the time to resent my past, but to enjoy the sweet seductive scent of the present.

His razor sharp wit cut deep through me and I was swooned by his suave style. I wished I could've figured out what aftershave he was wearing. Richa, without doubt, would've known immediately. I was still in kindergarten with my wooing skills that would only mature with experience. I pulled out a rose too from the vase and smiling sheepishly, I handed it to him.

"I'm not as good with my words as you are, Raman, but here's my humble offering," I commented awkwardly, as he gently pulled the rose from my hand and stared at me, unblinkingly.

"It's not what you say, Shivani, but what you do that counts. I'm certain you won't regret this," he said, melting my heart with his amorous glance.

As I undid my bag to place the rose in it, a petal fell on the floor and I looked down and smiled. I took this as a sign, my life was taking a turn for something better. Now I felt certain that I longed for his heart as much as he was aching for my body.

# 16

The aching for another heart had come to an end, as I was experiencing comfort for the first time amongst the catalogue of men I'd had an affair with. I knew it wasn't about the quantifiable benefits this time as it was about the companionship, and that was probably the reason it felt right. After pulling the plug with Ravi, my days were dragging me down, but now light had flooded them.

He handed me roses every time we met and I found that refreshing as I assumed men didn't do that anymore. The women of today believed it to be patronising for the man to gift them anything characteristically feminine. I was old school and I felt no shame in being that way, besides the one time Ravi had gifted me a blender for my apartment. I was terribly offended. He later made the situation worse when he said that it was the woman who was manning the kitchen, so where on God's tangled earth had he gone wrong? I told him in my defence that I changed my own light bulb and paid my own bills and I didn't need to be into guns or cars to take an equal stance with men. But his blender had hit below the belt. Subsequently, he made sure he never bought me gifts besides lingerie and in the case of others, he encouraged me to choose my own with his credit card.

But each time this man gave me a fresh bouquet, my heart smiled in delight. He restored my fractured spirit bit by bit as we moved ahead in our relationship. It cut deep that I was yet again involved with a married man and that he was seducing me instead of his wife, but I hadn't strategised any of this. As far as I was concerned, I was walking on the pavement of life in a straight line and he bumped into me. I was about to stumble when he lifted me up with his reassuring hands. I knew that very moment I would never fall again. My disordered life was not just rearranged, it was realigned.

His wife had turned outrageously bitter towards him and had lost the verve to make an effort in their marriage. Her aloofness created a wider rift between them. He had convinced me it was over between them and there was no need to be guilt-ridden. The marriage had been reduced to a mere formality for the benefit of their children and the society they associated themselves with. Although it was always a monumentally bad idea to end up sharing the bed with a married man, it had become an incontrovertible pattern for me.

He was an adept lover and in a woman's eyes, he was the ideal man, with brawn and brain. Every moment with him was perfect and was etched in my memory long after it was over. I often found myself replaying the moments in my head.

I swallowed my guilt of getting involved with him and began relishing every morsel of the illicit affair. He had the knack of inundating a woman with a fullness that couldn't be quantified in words. There were moments when I failed to wipe her out of my head as she stood between us. I often shared my inner struggles with him, while he soothed me with his touch, melting my anxiety each time.

He attempted to ease me of my guilt-ridden conscience as the mere thought of her made me cringe and getting exposed was an unimaginably daunting prospect. Although I had been comfortable in his bed all these months, I had many contradictory thoughts racing through my head, agitating me. I missed my friendship with her, particularly my coffee, laden with sugar and the customary sweet or savoury snack we shared. Lately, she had lost her appetite for food as passion replenished her. The real rewards in our lives were taking small measures to give us pleasure, except now, we were barely in touch. She was immersed in her love as I was in mine—both forbidden.

Today too, he deftly turned me towards himself as he sensed the uneasiness in me. "Let go of your woes, baby, and come back to the present. You have always been my fantasy, Richa. Ever so dazzling and desirable with just the curves needed to straighten my life," he teased, with a boyish giggle that prompted my angst to ebb away, momentarily. My physical yearning eclipsed my mental ache as his hand began to knead the skin on my body in the most sensuous way I had ever experienced. His breath was becoming louder with desire as he glided his body into mine, bringing me back to the present moment, which was in fact, my only reality.

I tensed up as his tantalising tongue moved skilfully from my forehead to my quivering lips, to my breasts to between my legs, whilst I stood limply against the wall with my hands stroking his hair. My eyes were closing and opening intermittently, as I let myself go completely. For several minutes that felt like seconds, there was an explosive wave of pleasure.

He was so skilled that for a split second, I deliberated on the reasons his marriage had reached the end of the road. Had I been his wife, I wouldn't dare permit him to lose interest in me. But then, could anyone remain consistently excitable in any marriage? Most marriages I knew were lonely and Sameer's and Shivani's was no exception. The degrees and intensities varied but it was a compromise for those who had so emphatically promised to fulfil their vows at the onset till the very end. Somewhere along the way, my inner demon reared its head to remind me of the unpalatable truth, sabotaging my potential happiness. I imagined Shivani and Raman making love and just then, Sameer motioned me back to the present.

I felt vulnerable as he raised me on a pedestal, rendering me the ultimate pleasures a man and a woman could experience. His tongue tore through my body and when I couldn't hold on any longer, I let out an ecstatic moan before he stood up and carried me to bed, silently. He stared deep into my eyes as he held me in his warm muscular arms.

"Don't remember the last time I carried a woman to bed! They're already in it most of the time!" he teased.

She was piercing my mind as he continued piercing my body for yet another explosion. Her image was etched on my agitated head and once we were through with making love, I voiced my angst to him. I longed for him to ease my conscience that pricked the very naked body he had just necked.

"Baby, I won't be able to see you for a few days because I'm off to Puducherry for a conference, so lie low until I return and then we'll figure it out," he said, nonchalantly as if I had just told him I needed a pill for a mild headache and he was explaining the way to the local pharmacy. He eased himself into the pillow and I too sank back to stare at the ceiling, before turning my body towards him. A pang of anxiety was welling up in my body. I wondered if he was toying with me or actually going away. He seemed detached and distant.

My insecurities prevailed, perhaps I was merely someone he wanted to use and dispose in the same manner as I had discarded Ravi; without a moment's notice.

"Sure!" was my curt reply as I sank back into the pillow and he instantly detected something was wrong.

He tossed towards me and placed his hand on my navel. He gently began circling his fingers around it. Had I been relaxed, I would have gotten aroused again, but there was turmoil within me now, constantly badgering me. I knew I had set myself up for another heartache that was destined to take me months to recover from. The hole I had dug for myself was too deep to ascend out of and so, I had always permitted myself to remain trapped in the obscurity of my denials.

He then brought his face towards me to press his lips against mine and after some seconds, he moved away, his hand still resting on my toned belly. I held on to my breath, waiting for something to be said to appease me of the fact that we were not transitional lovers. I had experienced that kind of love in abundance during a phase but now that I was approaching my mid-life, I had started thinking differently. If I were married, I'd most likely get divorced, get a boob job, have an affair with an expat 10 years younger than myself, or write a self-help book. That's what people normally did on entering their mid-life, along with taking up golf and practising it in different corners of the globe. The insecurity of losing our youth and entering a phase of dented body parts and tainted spirits pressed us to take new unexplored measures. My mom played bridge every week at my age to preserve her brain. Her generation didn't want to wrestle with nature and neither was it common then to spend obscene amounts of money to rectify the damage our experiences had done. On the other hand, I was prepared to spend gazillions to get a glimpse of what once was and perhaps, better. Bridge wasn't something that could ever float my boat.

With a dismayed look, I pushed his hand off my belly, got up and wore the hotel robe. It was the white robe I was mundanely familiar with and the matching soft towel slippers that escorted me to the shower every time a man shut the door on me. I was often left with my lonesome thoughts that aroused my mother's belligerent voice, prompting me to remain within the conventional boundaries.

*We live in a respectable society; blend with the herd. Don't give me a heart attack by notoriously sticking out like a sore toe.*

Hence, I was never courageous enough to assert my rights. My mother had engendered guilt and revulsion against my own sexual orientation. I was considered evil by my mother if I ever dared walking out of the closet.

"Hey, Richa! Where on God's troubled earth are you going? Stop!" he commanded as I left the bed.

"Don't go! I want you to come back and lie next to me. Now! It's an order from the boss! I need to fine-tune my plan for the next few days with your expertise. For God's sake, *please*, can you stop looking like you've just climbed the Kilimanjaro? Lately, you look so weary and the expression seems to have turned into your permanent facial feature! Can we alter it to a smile because I promise you, it makes you luring and infinitely more loving," he said, urgently, while extending his arm, out from the bed, to grab mine.

"What kind of help do you need from me, boss and why do you want advice from someone who frowns more frequently than she smiles?" I asked, sarcastically, with more than mild irritation in my tone. I was disconcerted. Moreover, I was angry and I wanted him to hear it in my voice.

"Seriously, what is it that you want from me, Sameer?"

He pulled me in towards him and then held me by the waist before speaking, "I'm going to Puducherry for work but I also fancy sight-seeing while I'm out there, and I absolutely refuse to do it alone! You know what I mean, so will you? Will you…? Please?"

"No, actually, I don't know what you mean and will I what? Why don't you try completing your sentence, because I'm waiting," I replied, impatiently.

"Will you take out time to accompany this man who is adrift without you? Only if you think you can tolerate me for a few days. I believe I have the power to take that weary expression off your face and replace it with a more welcoming one. You do know that sadness is ugly, right? I hope you understand I mean well when I highlight the shadows in you," he enquired as he shook my arms gently and looked into my eyes without blinking for even a second.

"So, just to reiterate the question for the benefit of your comprehension, will you put aside everything that matters to you to give priority to this pleading man of yours?" he asked, playfully now.

A faint grin appeared on my face before I stretched my lips to smile. On realising his sincerity, my heart lifted with gladness and the inner tremor stalled as I began to feel foolish for disbelieving him. He began to roll his fingers in the curls of my hair and asked with sparkly eyes, "Will you accompany me, *please*? And then, can you stop playing Einstein? He was a genius and a great thinker, whereas your endless stream of thoughts seems to be more destructive than constructive.

Honour him and use all your time, space, energy and matter on me, allowing the gravity of love to lift you. For God's sake, Richa, now wipe that frown off your face, *please."*

I broke into ripples of laughter. How ridiculously fragile my self-esteem had become. I wasn't proud of it, but in retrospect, it had descended during adolescence when my mother banished it instead of boosting it. I resented her with immense intensity now as I sat amidst a situation that impacted those I loved. I wasn't sure who I loathed more at this point—my mother for moulding my destiny or myself for caging my emotions. In the end, I knew it was up to me to unveil the truth. No one could shape me without my permission, so the scales of loathing tipped towards myself as I allowed my mother's image to melt before me.

He snapped his fingers to beckon me back to the present. He was observing me with profound concern in his eyes and I felt love pour out of my veins as I looked back at him. Of all the men I had liaised with, I was at safe harbour with him, owing to his simplicity, easy-going nature, good humour and most of all, his protectiveness. I felt something more for this man than I had anticipated, hence, my expectations were also raising.

Momentarily, I had an overwhelming urge to release my darkest secret, but then, good sense prevailed as I realised I'd lose him if I did. My mother's words were embedded in my subconsciousness that were resurfacing now.

'If you as much as share your stupid secret to anyone, you will be rejected by the entire world and you will live and die alone. It's a sin and even God will not forgive such transgression. You are doomed to hell, you foolish ignorant girl. I must get you married as soon as I find a match for you and then you will feel normal,' I could hear her in my head.

"Hello? Is anyone home?" he asked, snapping his fingers. "Hey baby, I'm trying hard to salvage the situation but I lost you somewhere in between making love and mentioning Puducherry. Do you have a history there because you've turned as pensive as that grim guy," he said, humorously, pointing towards the print of Vincent Van Gogh's self-portrait on the wall.

"I'm in no way as miserable-looking as him. He severed his own ear and you're biting mine. Hey, and of course, I will accompany you, I've never been to Puducherry, so yes, I'm in!" I screeched, tactlessly, giddy with happiness as I put my mother's cast-iron moral attitude aside. "I really do, but what about my kids' regimented routine, my own rigid routine and my...."

I was glad I had given him a curt response earlier as it had been returned with his enthusiastic one. It was more than I had anticipated and now all my scepticism evaporated. I felt needed again and was eager to accompany him on the trip, but not without being a tad bit difficult.

"Can't routine bend a little and can't the kids be taken care of for a few days, *please*? I really want to visit Puducherry's hot spots with the hottest woman I know." And then, he added, mischievously, "Life and its many inconveniences can surely be cast aside? Real life has a way of interfering with our harmless little fantasies, so we need to find a way of combatting them, *please*?

"Okay, that miserable man on the wall, Van Gogh. Tell me who his best friend was? I'll give you a hint—he was also an eminent artist. If you can answer that correctly, you have a choice as to whether or not you accompany me to Puducherry and if you can't, then I decide for you. Ha! I know you don't know!" he teased me.

"There you go with yet another trivia, along with the most cryptic clue. How do I know who his best friend was and frankly, who cares? I can just about remember the names of a few friends that I have been blessed with."

"Oh, and I was led to believe that you had a fetish for art and artists, including people who visit art galleries!" he commented, mischievously. "Anyway, I will be polite and ask you to join me because you are the most amazing company, despite not being the brightest one."

"How dare you call me dumb? I know about all the Indian artists, so tell me Mr. Know-it-all, who was the artist who got inspired by Francis Bacon and if you don't answer this, then I will call all the shots."

I cherished the sound of his boyish teasing, and his yearning to be with me and it made me cry inside knowing I was with a man whom I had to betray my friend for. I wasn't proud of my deceit but I dismissed the thought as I risked descending into depression. I had, all this while, read his personality through Shivani's narration, but now that the book was in my hand, I internalised it differently. He exuded an honesty I wasn't accustomed to and I was determined not to allow my anxieties to intrude upon our harmony. He was my first real companion, just like Raman was Shivani's first real affair. Maybe I was changing; *changing for the better,* as my own mother would have confirmed. She was convinced that if I pushed myself hard enough in the heterosexual direction, I could overcome what she termed *unnatural* and *dirty*.

I had done well when it came to dis-identifying with my sexual orientation and I would keep persevering with what fit well. Sameer was the first who warmed me from within, like a home-cooked broth that nourished the soul.

He didn't answer, so I nodded affirmatively. As soon as I gave my consent, he breathed a sigh of relief as he brought his body closer to merge into mine, once again. He held me tensely and began to lick my earlobe.

"Can I bite it off? And just for your information, Paul Gauguin was his best friend and possibly the man who cut his earlobe, although that is and will always remain a question mark. The Indian artist you are referring to is Tyeb Mehta, by the way, and Francis Bacon was an Irish-born British artist. Now can I get back to your ear, *please*," he asked, huskily. I was about to explode with passion as I found his knowledge disarming.

"Thanks for accompanying me to Puducherry. I'm super excited to go now," he whispered. "Richa, my favourite quote in the world is by one of my favourite people who advised, 'Develop imagination, throw away routine.' The guy went on to become one of the world's most successful entrepreneurs. Any ideas whose words these are?"

"No!" I responded. I was so jaded that my eyes were quickly shutting as I leaned up to rest my head on his chest.

"Harry Gordon Selfridge! So, let's throw routine away and really enjoy the days ahead. And sleep away, my darling, as I see trivia is clearly not your thing!"

Within seconds, I heard him snore and I too shut him and the world out. Even though, Selfridges was my favourite shopping haunt during my visits to London, I was partially distracted with the pleasures I had just experienced, but mostly, with the guilt that was left behind.

His presence was cathartic—it phased out the angst of my past.

# 17

The angst of my past receded as the present took residence to arouse latent passion in me. Words failed us as he and I climaxed recurrently over the past several hours in different intersections of the room. I had not visited daylight but neither was I craving it, as in the darkness of the room he had rented, he turned into my shimmering light. I was confident that the sky was humming boundlessly with love.

The hotel room was sparsely furnished with straight lines, making it appear sleek and unique. The lighting was pleasantly dim.

"Baby, I chose this room for the most hands-on reasons, it reminds me of you," he said as he gently enclosed me in his brawny arms. The first physical contact with him felt like a dream. I melted immediately in anticipation.

"It seduces me with its sophistication and gentleness that define contemporary simplicity. It is non-conventional and I for one, like that in a woman," he whispered breathlessly in my ear while his hands glided down my body.

"The furniture is bare, without any skirt, trims or tassels. Less has always been more for me and that's the bare truth," he continued, murmuring huskily. He was turning me on like never before, making me tremble with excitement. I had never imagined this kind of foreplay would be such a turn-on, I thought, as I imbibed his whispers of desire. "It's also unruffled like you, but by the time I'm through with you baby, you'll be redefined. I promise, you won't know who you are and that's always a great place to start afresh," he said.

He pressed his lips against my neck and brought them to my breasts, sucking on them vigorously to enliven my senses. Sameer had never made me feel this way, but I instantly blocked him out before the thought of him filled me with bitterness and ruined the moment.

"Oh baby, I can barely contain myself!" I wailed as he peeled off my layers—layers of inhibitions I was held captive in throughout my life. I felt free as I smiled, and cried with pleasure, simultaneously.

He continued to glide his hand down my hips to my inner thigh. An exquisite sensation settled between my thighs as he went down on me and it was the first time a man had ever made me feel so alive. I urged the sensation to last a hundred years but much to my disappointment, he came up after a few exhilarating minutes and kissed me passionately. A coy smile teased his lips and I blushed. I wanted more, but shied. He knew, of course, so he enticingly went down on me again and this time, I began to tremble with erotic excitement.

It was so easy getting addicted to this sort of sensual pleasure and the more I had, the more I craved for it. The only part of my body that was dry was my mouth and before I knew it, he wet my lips with his tongue. Pushing his body against mine, he thrust inside me long and hard.

Sameer had been the only man I had routinely slept with until now and he had failed to behave unselfishly between the sheets. I had known no better hence, I accepted lovemaking as a duty-bound chore; almost like a domestic errand that had to be carried out to keep the system going. Recently, I had been relieved from my duty as Sameer and I barely exchanged a glance, let alone a touch.

Raman then lifted me and carried me to bed and in my head, I questioned why he hadn't likened it to me. Just then, he whispered huskily, "This bed, Shivani, is our retreat that's going to rejuvenate us and that's the effect you have on me. I intend to continue my expedition here all day, focusing on you and only you," he said, urgently.

It felt like my entire life had been a build-up to this moment and now, I harboured no regrets about being the rejected one. Raman had accepted me and that is what made it all worthwhile. No words were exchanged now; only energies of two bodies heaving with insatiable appetites. From the first time he kissed me, I was enslaved to his touch. To get what I just did, I was willing to go to any extent. "That was sensational," I said, opening my eyes dreamily.

He responded with nervous laughter. "Yes, it was!"

As I adjusted my head once again on his chest, I felt my eyelids becoming heavy. I closed my eyes to oblivion and lost all sense of reality. When I woke up after what seemed like several hours of repose, I called out to him in a dreamy daze. I whispered the forbidden words, for which I would have been slaughtered, had Ma heard me. He whispered them back to me as he blew me a kiss from behind the desk, where he sat with a towel wrapped around his torso.

He had been working while I was asleep and as I invited him with my eyes, he rushed back to bed. He lightly tickled my feet and moved up slowly, awakening the desire in me.

"You are one hungry woman. I hope you realise it's our umpteenth time. Normally, I'd be exhausted, but you are too excitable to call it a day," he said, caressing me.

As an embittered woman who had ceased to respond to her husband, I responded enthusiastically to his touch. "When was the last time your husband went down on you?" he whispered as he once again lowered his head.

"I don't recall and frankly, who cares!" I lied, letting go of the resentment I felt towards Sameer as the wave of rapture overpowered all other feelings.

With a voice that was brusque, he said, "I have never felt so good! It was amazing! You're amazing!" he said. "We must resume tomorrow, till forever! You are poetry in motion and I love making love to you."

After steadying my voice, I whispered, with a hint of mischief, "I don't know whether you make it all up as we go along or if you've been down this route a gazillion times, but I'm loving it *so* much that I don't care to read into it. I give you permission to lie to me a gazillion times over."

In his eyes, I viewed a landscape of possibilities and opportunities unlike in Sameer's, where I encountered merely obstacles. I thanked him endlessly for awakening the woman in me and for giving me this emotional high—an act that my husband had failed to do.

I had this uncontrollable urge to smother Ma with kisses for bestowing on me the gift of courage to enter this realm, previously inaccessible to me. My head was thinking way too much and suddenly, Raman broke my chain of thoughts, "I need to leave you now, baby! I have a presentation to give tomorrow and a couple of projects to complete by the end of the week. But see you in office tomorrow and while you're here, I suggest you take some rest. Sleep some hours to replenish your energy for tomorrow," he whispered, kissing my forehead again.

"We will meet after work in case your husband is working overtime."

After he left, I deliberated on how unendurable I would find sleeping with the man I was married to now that I had tasted blood. Presumably, the same as it had been for the longest time—except this time it was because of the spring in my life; Raman. He was my lifeguard who was going to keep me afloat in my marriage. Sameer had compensated for lack of passion in our marriage by smothering me with a sumptuous lifestyle. It was probably his way of counterbalancing the lack of patience in bed, except even that was no longer happening.

I needed to share every microscopic detail of my resurrection with Richa. I let her mobile phone ring persistently before sending her a message to meet me.

# 18

From dawn to dusk, I obsessed over him, and I dismissed her skilfully when I was with him. I thought I had numbed that part of me a while back until I met her again, today.

The enquiries were on the tip of my tongue and I was anxious to know all about her recent escapes. I envisioned her with Raman all too often, but today, I longed for her to indulge me. However, I concealed my sentiments and tried my utmost to appear normal. My breath was irregular as I tried extinguishing the raging storm of guilt inside me.

I was momentarily relieved of my deceit as thoughts of him overshadowed it. My fingers began to circle the stem of my coffee cup as I recalled his touch. My fingers were twitchy and on realising how nervous I was, I pulled my hand back to relax it on my lap. I needed courage to tell her about my affair and to speak about the love I felt. I had to have faith that she would understand because her marriage was technically over in any case. That was my flimsy justification for jumping into his bed—that it had been officially empty and she was blissfully busy warming up someone else's.

I felt my eyes clearing when I thought of the way he pleaded with me when he wanted something—'please!' His boyish behaviour always drew a smile and my cheeks felt the same rush I felt after a good workout. I picked up my mobile phone and sent him a text stating how much he meant to me. He replied.

*Love you to the moon and back. Xoxo*

Then, as always, he challenged my intelligence with another trivia.

*Who was the second man on the moon?*

*I don't know and I don't care!*

*Ok, well in case you do, it's Aldrin Buzz. Even though you're brainless, I still love you to the moon and back.*

Our texts made me laugh. And this is the way it carried on with him—teasing, loving me and making me laugh until I cried. I recalled our first dinner at a restaurant near the beach. Not a single word was exchanged for a while and then we both broke into a chuckle as we realised how effortlessly the silence had expressed the way we felt about each other.

Just when I was absorbed in his thoughts, another message beeped.

*By the way who was the first?*

*The first what?* I replied, with mild irritation, as I wasn't as adept as he was in general knowledge.

*The first man on the moon, Blondie?* he texted, followed by emoticons expressing both his surprise and disgust.

*No idea, my man with a strong arm!* I responded and then asked him.

*Who was the first woman prime minister in the world?*

I knew which country she represented but couldn't spell her name and hoped that he couldn't either, except he did and his response came in within seconds.

*Okay, clever clogs! Sirimavo Bandaranaike of Sri Lanka who died recently at the age of 84. Ha! And yes I can Neil before you anytime!*

I was aware that they usually all looked good at the start, but I had been in this relationship for the past several months and so far, nothing had gone amiss besides my own angst.

"Hey, Richa!" she called out from the entrance as she sprinted towards me, wearing a pink floral dress. She looked lovely, with the pink dress enhancing her complexion. My eyes trailed her and I noticed she had blow-dried her hair, lost a few inches off her midriff and wore make-up that highlighted her features, making her even more inviting. I caught her whiff of perfume—it was the Jo Malone fragrance. My heart galloped as I realised how much I still loved her and longed to tell her that. But instead, I rapidly regained my composure. After a peck on the cheek and a warm hug, she sat opposite me, leaving behind a trail of perfume on me. "How's Mars and when did you fly in from there? Anyway, I have no right to complain as I too have been inundated with dating," she said, breathlessly, with her customary girly giggle. "But I've missed you and as usual, there are chronicles of my love life to share!" she said, while settling her handbag on the empty chair next to us.

My new bag was already placed there and she made an immediate note of it. "Hey, nice bag and it's the limited edition Hermes! So, who's the old man splurging on you now? Hey, I'm guilty as sin too, Richa. I'm so self-absorbed that I've not had a second to delve into your latest escapade. Once I start with my rant, I have no end, so *please* fill me in about the guy that's brought you this expensive bag? I'm almost offended by it!"

"One is still the number, I'm afraid and the bag was brought by Ravi after we broke up as a tactic to woo me back. I pitilessly rejected him and pitifully retained the bag. I believe I got the better deal since this has more utility than the old bag he was," I stated, blithely and we both broke into a chuckle, except hers seemed a little forced.

"Anyway, I'm impatient to read every verse about your love life that's dressed you in this celestial glow, though I'm sure you've been far from an angel," I responded, breaking into a superficial laughter. I almost abhorred myself for the way lies rolled off my tongue so effortlessly.

"Good on you. A designer bag can often look better on us than a man, except I have both right now. One dresses me up while the other dresses me down!" she chuckled. Then, she added, "I, however refuse to believe, that your days are complete without any pillow talk!"

"I reaffirm most emphatically that no man is warming up my bed. My career as a man-eater has been an unmitigated disaster, so please, bypass me to relay your saucy story!" I insisted humorously, trying to distract her. I was attempting to spare myself from lying, as it had become easier to lie with time. Lies were like a potent peg of neat whisky—the first time you gulped it down, it stung your throat with its pungent edge, but after having it several times, the same drink glided down smoothly, turning most palatable. I noticed she didn't warm up to my attempted humour and was curt as she commented on my countenance.

"I'm also dying to disclose every detail but I seriously can't help commenting on how different your aura is from the one I usually know so well. You're twitchy, Richa, and I noticed it the last few times we met. But I brushed it aside because of my urgency to spill the thrill of being with Raman. I hope you know that you remain my number one and I do notice stuff about you. I have this nagging suspicion that something has come between us but I just can't place my finger on it," she stated. "Let me ask you one more time before I read all my chapters out to you. You appear edgier each time I meet you. Are you okay? I mean really *okay*?" she asked, now with a hint of irritability.

I felt angst, I needed to tell her the truth as the pressure of lying was soon going to sabotage the friendship we had fostered so endearingly over the years. Except, I didn't and instead, I lied again.

"You know me, Shivani! I have my good seasons and bad and currently, I'm learning to keep myself warm instead of depending on someone to be my blanket."

"Perhaps, Ravi's left a vicious void in your life because after you broke up with him, you've made yourself unapproachable. But allow me to offer you my expert advice because I feel like a veteran, thanks to the man in my life," she said, proudly. "Someone will meet you at the most unforeseen hour. He'll tap on your shoulder and voilà, you'll have what you never imagined possible."

"I insist, Shivani, at this juncture of my life, I'm not holding my breath. I need to expend my energy on finding my true vocation in life. Do you recall the time we both engaged our minds in creative visualisation? I know you didn't believe me but I was alone in my vision. After that, I've started visualising myself in a place of success. So, right now, I'm targeting getting my career off the ground and men don't fit into my plans."

"Oh, I wish you all the luck, Richa. What an irony— you've stepped out of your man-devouring phase just when I've driven into it! It's a double-edged sword; I'm learning to love myself through a man and I'm learning the ropes of entrepreneurship that will hopefully draw the confidence to do more with my life too."                    •

"This illicit affair is going to liberate you, Shivani, as I knew it would. Raman is a refuge from your marriage, but he is also your road to finding who you really are. Now, give me a taste of what you're savouring and I want to relish every bite of it!" I said, trying hard to sound cheerful.

"Well, do you have a year because I have so much to tell you. An experience is nothing unless you have good friend to share it with."

She hailed, enthusiastically, "It's incredible because I didn't know there was a 'me' and that I mattered even before meeting him."

I nodded as I marvelled at her newfound confidence. Her energy was buoyant and her eyes revealed new aspirations and promises. "It's my new-found confidence with which I face my Ma these days. She no longer intimidates me and I no longer feel like the lesser one of all my siblings. I know now that I'm not a leftover piece of scrap.

"Raman has taught me to respect my individuality, and now my views are changing. From submissive, I'm becoming strong and hopefully one day, I'll be independent and I wouldn't need Raman's support either. In a sense, he is my saviour who I will perhaps let go of once I progress in my journey. The exposure at Ma's office has permitted me to see outside the folds of marriage and Ma's conditioning. I'm happy, very happy and equally hopeful of life," she said, jovially.

"I'm thrilled for you; you do appear incredibly fulfilled," I remarked.

"So now I'll share the details of what we have accomplished and our future plans to spice it up further. And please, okay, if you genuinely are thrilled for me, then at least try and look it. *Please* return from the land of Socrates and Plato, back to the land of Shivani and Raman. Love stories are far more exciting than philosophies," she commented, hoping to lighten me up.

"I know and I'm sorry. I attribute my aloofness to being away from you for so long. I'm back now, trust me," I said as I adjusted myself to look attentive. I was trying hard to celebrate the changes she had accomplished.

She was the most flawless person I knew, but I also knew that I was going to inadvertently hurt her at some stage. My indulgences with my new beau were not free of consequences. I couldn't expect to sow the wind and not reap the whirlwind and most importantly, I knew illicit goods never prospered. I whispered this time, "Shivani, are we good now?"

"Of course, not! Someone I know has a friend who knows someone who knows a lesbian who knows your secret," she replied with an arched eyebrow.

I immediately felt blood rush to my face, making me more scarlet than the shirt I wore. Did she know about me? And were the people around us staring suspiciously at me because my secret was out? What I tried keeping under wraps all my life had perhaps become hearsay now. Even the waiters must've heard and that's probably why we intrigued them each time we gathered here for our customary coffee and chats. I felt vulnerable with their prying eyes all over us and why on earth hadn't she acknowledged it earlier? Was she expecting me to confess? I felt faint as zillion enquiries sprinted through my mind.

It was a lucid moment when I finally awakened to the stark reality of what had become of me. I was with a man whose wife I adored infinitely more than I did him or any other man in my decaying world, but now I was exposed. My heart was pounding as it did when my actions were out of sync with my intentions. Suspended silence filled the air and then I rescued the moment with a defensive note.

"People talk Shivani, but you can't possibly believe hearsay. Do you in your heart really believe I keep secrets from you? I mean, why would I do that when we are best of friends?" I asked, trying to sound normal.

"Of course not, silly, but your eyes don't know how to pretend! They're narrating a story I'm not entirely familiar with. Ordinarily, we met twice or thrice a week and now that's been reduced to once a month or even lesser. I, too, don't get time out of my new routine and it sounds great admitting it, but all these years, we maintained regularity because you always told me I was an integral part of your life. Recently, chatting on the phone with you is a nightmare too as you sound distant. I can't do this alone; I need you around! Ma will drive me nuts and Sameer isn't even there, except on paper. He's legal, my affair's illegal and everything in between is what makes all the sense and that includes you, my soulmate."

My hand at last reached out to her and after drawing a deep breath, I reassured her, "Shivani, we all have issues; some we express and others we suppress, but just know that I love you. Now look into my eyes and tell me I'm lying."

"I'm sure you're not but just know that if there's anyone on this earth who relates to me, pulls the weight off my shoulders, makes me roll in hysterical laughter, has copious cups of cappuccino loaded with sugar and is incredibly insane; it's you and only you. I've met a melting pot of personalities in this city, but you, Richa, are the single most amazing woman I know. You've understood to the extent of Ma's plot to salvage the union of two slashed spirits. You embrace me more than she ever can or for that matter anyone else I've ever known, including Papa. Even the so-called heavenly father up there must've given up on me, particularly now that I'm indulging myself in an extramarital affair. But frankly, I don't care since He's never been on my guest list and it's not Him I go out for a chat with; it's you! So, do me a favour and call the old Richa that I so deeply love.

"We were both wedged together like clasped hands, so you can imagine how inadequate I feel without her. Ask her to come and join me here in this restaurant at this very moment, *please*," she said with a desperate plea in her voice, sounding every ounce like her husband. It was no big deal, I mused; couples frequently adopted each other's lingos and after a number of years, began sounding like each other.

I had an impulse to open up to her, clasp her face, to kiss her and lock her in my arms, but it wasn't meant to be and I was in a sense, shunning her like I had shunned all my previous friends and lovers. She had triggered anger in me all those times she ridiculed homosexuals, believing them to be inferior.

I sat before her, trying not to be obvious about my feelings for her as what she considered unnatural was so irrepressibly natural to me. Sleeping with her husband seemed like another day at the office now that I had come face-to-face with her and she appeared more beautiful than ever. I could cover my feelings for Sameer, but it was my love for her—though forbidden—that I found hard to contain.

"I love you too, Shivani, and I'm sure you recognise it. I have and will till my final breath, but life doesn't bend to our dreams and desires, so I've chosen a path that works best for me; for now, at least," I said. I needed to concoct a tale to justify the lost expression on my face.

"So here's my story and then we will close the chapter before you relay yours. Deal?" I asked.

"Yes, deal and be honest!" she replied.

"Ravi has been in touch but I'm not considering going back to him. It's been several months, and it's hard to reacquaint with a person that you've left behind. He's been reduced to a mere stranger now, but I suppose, the past is haunting my present. He's always been terribly insecure, so I'm just handling the situation as well as I can. Besides that, there is nothing of substance to report. I swear there's nothing and I'm not suffering from manic depression either, in case you're doubting me," I said, swallowing a lump of guilt and realising that I was, without a grain of doubt, turning into a pathological liar.

"I'm hugely relieved!" she gasped. "I'm concerned because I know you *so* well and know that intentionally or not, you wind up becoming the subject of controversy. Your edginess troubles me because I feel that maybe, just maybe, you're on a track that will make you hit a brick wall again and I aspire better for you. You've had enough thorny experiences and it is time to break these self-destructive patterns. I admire you in myriad ways. You defy the very Indian mindset of 'just adjust' even when the situation is 'unjust.' And you are usually so composed, but here, I can see you drowning into the depths of despair. It's one of your lesser-known sides—to look defeated. No matter what you've done or about to do, I'll never point fingers at you, marginalise or ignore you," she said, breaking into tiny ripples of laughter to lighten my load. "You've established yourself a slut and I love the role you play! In fact, I'm so inspired that I too behave like one when I'm with Raman. He makes me wholly whore!"

"Holy or wholly?" I asked rhetorically, already knowing the answer and finally feeling relaxed. Suddenly, I didn't care what people sitting around us thought or said, if at all they did. Guilt had an overpowering voice and it was never the peoples' opinions that mattered—it was always our own.

"I guess you're right in your observation, it's a kind of withdrawal I feel after each break-up. Life has been thrown into disarray once more, but differently this time. I'm glad and sad in the same breath. I have a talent of drawing chaos into my life. But I promise you, the winds of change are gusting through me. This time, I'm not going to resist it," I announced, almost ominously and yet, with a plea for forgiveness, because I had broken the first rule in our friendship—sleeping with the spouse of the other.

She reassured me she trusted my judgements more than she ever had her own and then she reached out for my hand.

I felt a warm and welcoming sensation of love ride up my every vein, and I clenched my other hand beneath the table with needy tension. I longed to curl her in my fieriest embrace and keep her there for as long as was possible, but I receded to rest my head against the chair and smiled at her.

She moved back too—almost hurriedly—to share the intimate details of her lover. She was dizzy now with rapture as she switched from questioning me to spilling out her wildest reveries. She spoke with an endless stream of emotion and reminded me of the way I was, after my first kiss, during my teens. I remember coming home and innocently sharing the intimate details with my brother, only to be reprimanded later by my mother. The visuals of that frightening moment when she assaulted me verbally and physically imprinted their scars on me, which till date, I failed to recover from. Before that day, I was insanely popular and after, I went into a shell. Childhood scars, it seemed, didn't heal in one lifetime.

In a tell-all tone, her story seemed mercilessly long— filled with raunchy details that evoked feelings of jealousy in me. He was deeply lodged in her chest and so she carried him with her everywhere she went, probably in the same manner I carried Sameer in my very accommodating heart. Her enquiry into my broken story was mercifully short and in the end, I was glad I had met up with her because she was undeniably the loveliest friend I'd ever had.

# 19

"You are the loveliest lady I've ever been associated with and I don't really want to lose you as a friend," Raman said as he held me by my waist.

"What makes you think that you will?" I responded, caressing his face with my lips. He moved back in a business-like manner.

"Well, my lovely but naïve friend, if we carry on the way we are then one of us is surely going to fall for the other. And that will lead to a crash landing and a crushed heart. Between the two of us, you are the one most likely to fall for the trap and I'd much rather you invest in me than in my heart."

"What do you mean by investing in you?" I enquired, puzzled.

"Well, I'm an intelligent man and I'm also patient, particularly when it involves you, so why don't you consider me more than your lover? I am willing to mentor you in ways that you never imagined and the pillow talk doesn't have to disappear till you want it to."

"Are you talking about setting up my very own business?'" I asked, and immediately shrugged in agreement. "Why not? But would that work, considering I've already fallen for you? You know that, don't you, Raman?" I asked.

"Of course I do, you clown. That is precisely why I'm trying to broaden your perspective. I'm not heartless and

I do feel for you too, but my vision differs from yours and somewhere down this track, you are going to fall into a pit. I fear that you will get increasingly attached while I will continue moving upwards in my career. The truth is, my first and only love is my ambition," he said, ardently.

I could see he meant everything he said, including his feelings for me, except not in the same proportion as I did for him. However, I enjoyed being with him and would allow him to bring out the best version of myself. When it was about accomplishing a professional goal, I wanted him to be proud of me.

"As long as we remain close, I will allow you to be my mentor—you anyway have been in bed!" I teased.

"I know!" he said, flatly; he wasn't in the mood to flirt.

"Perfect! You come to office every day in any case, so while you are here, I can train you. Who knows, one day you will be a confident, independent woman who can live life on her own terms."

"Now that's seems pretty far-fetched, all things considered. My friend, Richa, taught me the art of creative visualisation, but I don't know if what I saw has any substance," I said, softly.

"But of course it does. We all have the power to close chapters, open new ones and turn as many pages as we want, until we are on the right one. Except, there is that one vital piece of the puzzle missing in each one of us. It's called self-belief which only comes with working diligently and setting targets for ourselves."

As he spoke, I moved in towards him. His intelligence was a turn on and I was falling in love with the idea of him vesting his interest in me. No one had really done that before and it was a novelty that I was beginning to savour. He held me as he continued to express his thoughts.

"The idea is not to be random. You will need to set out goals."

"Goals?" I enquired as I wrapped my arms around his waist, only to rest my head on his chest. I could inhale his aftershave.

"We are all born predisposed to certain talents while we lack in others."

"For example?" I asked.

"Well, I'm an innate lover whereas you had to take months to learn how to satisfy me," he joked, finally lightening up.

I punched him in the stomach as he continued to laugh.

"You were absolutely useless, but now I give you ten on ten."

"Epic! Thank you, Mr. Architect, I am obliged," I said, sarcastically.

"Precisely! That's my other talent and though I studied it, I had a natural flair in constructing spaces. On the other hand, I can't imagine you drawing a single line on a paper, or planning and executing anything other than a meal, perhaps?"

"How condescending, Mr. Mean, or should I say Mr. Sexist. I cannot decide which is worse! As much as you think I can't, I can actually buy ingredients and rustle up a recipe to perfection. I too was born predisposed to certain attributes and I have an eye for good, nutritious food. I understand which food items have what effect on the human body."

"Mmm! Interesting!" he said as he slid his thumb across his chin, reflectively. "So, do you think you can get specific about what kind of business you'd set up, concerning healthy organic food?"

"What? Business and me? I don't know if I have the ability. I've never gone beyond eating an organic meal and perhaps, stretched myself once or twice by preparing a dish or two for my children. Do you think I could make a career out of it? Seriously?" I asked, finding myself getting nervous at the prospect of becoming an entrepreneur.

"Yes, I believe you can, once you are sure of what you want, besides me. I'm a moving train and you are merely a station, but you already know that."

"Ouch! That was painful. I'm nothing more than a station? I feel like such a transitory pleasure to you. You really could make me feel a little more special, you know," I said, fearing it would show on my face how hurt I really was.

"You are special, but you're not my final destination. You knew that from the beginning. I, too, am not permanent to you, am I?"

"Please, Raman, you know I like you very much. It is probably stronger than just 'like', but I know you don't want to hear it, so I will just go on pretending you're no more than a good friend, who's now a mentor too," I said.

"Look, it's natural to like each other when we're meeting as often as we have been, but when you engage yourself in other more meaningful projects concerning your personal and perhaps, professional growth, then you will be able to take a step back and view us from a new perspective."

"So, you want me to have a professional goal? Anyway, what is the point of me coming to office, it is not like I do much," I said.

"You are gaining more exposure here than you even realise. You're always absorbing whilst observing, so don't give up."

"You've exposed me alright!" I said in jest.

"Very funny, Miss Chef! You're so good at cooking up stories. But seriously, Shivani, we will have our moments of intimacy for as long as you want. I throw the ball in your court, so you're in charge of that aspect. But besides that, I want to help you get focused because I know you're better than just doing nothing."

"Do you consider this to be nothing?" I asked as I moved my hand on his buttocks.

"I love the way you do that," he said, almost breathlessly and then his hand reached mine and we kissed. He continued.

"It's everything and you're everything at this moment but what happens when I leave the station? Then what? Don't you think you'll end up going back to square one? Back to a loveless marriage waiting anxiously for the next man to entertain your jaded mind whilst your husband goes out and fulfils his fantasies?"

As I pulled away and sighed, he paced up to me and held me tight.

"Look, I don't mean to open up a can of worms but that is the truth, isn't it, even though you've chosen not to share your woes with me. The fact that you're so happy being with me is an indication of the extent of your misery in your marriage and you're under no compulsion whatsoever to tell me anything if it makes you uncomfortable. I care too much about you to hurt you," he said.

"Except you will be hurting me inadvertently when your train moves on which inevitably, it will, right? Anyway yes, I understand that and yes, I've chosen not to speak about something. When I do, the pain intensifies and the sourness of the marriage is reaffirmed.

"The truth is when love walks out, the marriage turns into an outfit, dumped in the back of the wardrobe. It's a rotten compulsion to live under the same roof when the doors of our hearts are slammed shut for each other. I was squeezing myself smaller to fit into his expectations of me until one day, I woke up to the realisation that I stopped existing for him a long time back.

"I've always danced to the tune of others, Raman, and in a way, I'm glad you're clear about our stance, even though it will hurt; in fact, it already does because I'm not a woman devoid of emotions," I said, sadly.

"Your husband might have stopped caring, but I won't. I can't love you the way you probably expect me to but I can be your best friend and at the moment, the most desirable lover you'll ever have in your life."

He hugged me, keeping me warm in his masculine embrace. He soothed my old wounds as I cried. I didn't resist the tears as they gushed down my face.

"Help me, Raman. I want to be free but don't know how. I'm not saying that I want you to rescue me by being with me, but do something please. I wasn't watching out and that's when the whole thing happened; a marriage of 20 odd years and estrangement for another few, adding up to many years of somnambulism. Now I can't bear to return to slavery. I will revolt."

"You already have, Mrs. Mehra. I've initiated you into the intensities of passion, Shivani, but there's much more. You will have to excel in a host of activities to stir up your imagination. Life is as flat as your marriage is if it's not excited by curiosity, enthusiasm and energy. I'm willing to introduce you to the refinements of life, starting tomorrow. For the time being, just be okay about not being okay because you soon will be."

"Please don't address me by that name. I hate Mrs. Mehra for allowing herself to lose her identity. I feel dead," I stated as I wiped my tears and looked up to him.

"Death is a state of mind, just like misery and happiness, so are you willing to live the way we are meant to?"

"Where do I begin and how, because I really want to; I do," I insisted.

"Well, will anyone notice if you sneak out of your home to accompany me to Goa?"

"How will that free me? I guess I could always say I'm going there to attend a friend's birthday bash, but I hope this means something substantial," I asked, frowning.

"It is because I have this amazing plan to take you on an adventure of a lifetime. We'll start easy and then, plunge into your oceans of fear. I will make sure you resurface as a new woman. Trust me, I know what I'm doing. Just say yes. Have you ever gone for jet skiing, windsurfing, scuba diving or parasailing? Uh, am I losing you?" he asked, raising his brow and realising I hadn't been so adventurous in my life.

He then stated, "Great! These experiences are going to be life transforming. Just remember, Shivani, whatever you dig your heels into will give you results, so the idea is to keep learning and you'll strike the right note. By the time I'm through with you, you will know exactly who you are and in what capacity you can achieve your goals and it may be nothing to do with organic food."

His enthusiasm was rubbing off on me and I was hopeful of all my fears getting washed away.

# 20

He had washed away the worst part of my insecurities as he brought me to a stunning corner of the country. For me, the sea always invited nostalgia and dipping into it cleared my head of past injuries.

Sameer and I were soaking in Puducherry's vibe and because it was our first vacation together, it was all the more charming. We had an invigorating day on the chunnambar boat that drifted us to Paradise Beach. It was there that we immersed ourselves in the endless bounty of the ocean and the fragrant air. I cautiously dipped my toe, after which I courageously plunged into the ocean of reality. I knew I was capable of drowning given how precarious the situation was, instead, I pushed away the wave of anxiety and threw my legs up to float. I marvelled at the indigo skies, turning smoke grey, with tinges of silver feathery clouds dancing across in swift motion. Sameer caught me from my shoulders and at once, I lost my balance. As I turned around, I wrapped my arms around his neck. Playfully, he kissed my face until he firmly pressed his lips against mine. The water encompassed my skin as he caressed and cuddled me. I felt a drizzle, but was too occupied to care and then seconds later, there was a shower. We stood there motionless in each other's ephemeral embrace.

We were drenched as the unruly monsoon rain penetrated our every pore and the gentle salty breeze pushed against us. We strolled out of the sea to sit on the beach. It was here that Sameer ordered what he claimed to be James Bond's favourite drink. I took a sip of his martini as he continued to throw trivia after trivia at me. No one around us spoke as everyone listened to nature's music. I was in sync with its rhythms as I sensed every cell of my body rising in rejuvenation. I looked across to see Sameer, assuming I'd catch him on his mobile phone, but he wasn't. He was as much in the moment as I was. He had a smile in his eyes as he returned my gaze and we began to chuckle like children. It felt as if in our silence, we had said so much to each other. I was grateful for being asked to come out here with him and I was thankful for having him in my life. We sat now with our bodies curled into each other. After a beautiful day, we returned to the hotel where we showered together and lay naked under the crisp clean cotton sheets, wrapped in each other's arms. I felt intoxicated from the day's experience. He also seemed rested.

"I love you!" he whispered.

My heart galloped as I sensed the onset of real commitment between us and even though I loved him, I was certain that he felt more strongly for me. From a physical attraction, it had transpired to an emotional attachment. My thoughts diverted when he stretched his hand to the drawer beside the bed to remove a tiny box. He locked his eyes on me dreamily as he spoke, "I've something very special for you. Neither of us need a marriage but this ring, my lovely Richa, symbolises my never-ending love and commitment to you," he pulled my hand towards him and taking my finger, placed a diamond-clustered ring on my finger. He was usually so casual that even in a serious moment like this, I couldn't calculate his depth of emotion. But the tension in his eyes as he pulled me close to his body was an indication that he was as crazy about me as I was about his wife. This was what my dreams were made of; a non-committal man and a woman whom I could only express love to in my head. I erased the havoc in my head as I didn't want to spoil this pristine moment with this beautiful man. Desire clung to me callously and the well-intended thought of being loyal to her melted. I was inspired by his mastery of not feeling the guilt of cheating on her.

"Please quieten your busy head, my love. I can almost hear it explode with dialogue," he said.

"Don't you feel…?" I began.

"No, he said, closing his lips onto mine. "Shhhh! Let's not engage in any kind of analysis or you will ruin this perfect moment."

I felt his body turn taut and mine too tightened with anticipation as I recalled Shivani's words. "Go wherever happiness is laid out for you. Everyone deserves to be happy."

I let go.

I slipped into my precarious happiness, brushing aside the contradictions that my life represented. Betrayal was not an easy place to glide into but as passion took over, a dark side rushed to brush away any noble thought I may have entertained to be loyal to the one person I owed it to.

In a strange sense, he stabilised me from speeding into one whirlwind romance to another without enduring satisfaction. I was content for now and wasn't that what it was all about anyway?

The villa we had hired was in the remote corner of the windflower resorts, breathing liberally over the lush gardens.

A statue of Buddha sat amidst a pond, in a pose that exuded tranquillity and equanimity; both that my body defied.

His voice turned coarser as he commanded me to stand against the wall of the room. With expertise, he glided into me while I unruffled the hair on his head. It felt like my first as I experienced the virginal purity of his touch that tensed up my muscles. I closed my eyes to fully appreciate the sensations of his tongue all over me. I was just inches away from unmeasured pleasure and after a few minutes, a gentle climax rippled through me as I wailed in rapture and relief. He gripped my hand hard and walked me back to bed where he began to caress me. He thrust himself into me with greater force than usual and after several moments of sheer passion, he bounced off to lie adjacent to me.

"I hope I've pleasured you like no other considering you've got a list of men to compare me with," he teased me.

"How dare you refer to me as a slut again?" I fumbled.

"I doubt you're a slut! I mean, just look at you," he began with amusement. "You're already dog-tired and we've only just begun. I'm not through with you yet, woman. My all-time favourite position awaits you," he teased as he pounced on me once more.

"Are you kidding me? What are you made of?" I asked with humour in my voice, hoping he would agree to just chill together in bed.

"Aha! But I'm not here to watch TV," he stated as if reading my mind. He then cupped my breast and began fondling it.

"Let's not!" I suggested firmly, while sitting up, "Hey Sameer! I'm really sorry, but I'm feeling tired and I think we should talk and then walk along the sea, or probably eat something."

"Oh, that's convenient! Now that you're satisfied, you want to talk, leaving my thirst unquenched. I thought a woman could have multiple orgasms and still not tire. So it's all a myth, then?" he commented, coquettishly. "I wanted you to sit on me and show me what you're really made of! Never mind, maybe age is creeping in!" he said with disappointment splashed all over his face.

I blew the candle out on my bedside as it was about to melt to the end and I couldn't stand the smell of melted candle.

"I just want to draw the blanket over us and chat, take a nap and then get dressed for dinner," I whispered.

"Is something bothering you again?" he asked, concerned now as he slid his fingers gently down my face. "Let it all out sexy, before I let it all in again!"

"Do you even know what the word serious means, Sameer? You're damn irritating at times. Forget it, I don't want to talk!" I snapped as the innate insecurities awakened in me once again giving rise to my temper tantrums. For a split second, I wanted to trust him with my darkest secret, but I held back, dejected by my own lack of courage. My life was destined to be punctuated by a series of near misses.

"Hey, I'm sorry, but I was just trying to lighten the moment. Why do you always end up being melodramatic? We start well, but end up in hell," he said with a hint of frown appearing on his temples.

"So, you want to chat or nap? It's your call so tell me, please!" he said with his usual boyish style that never failed to amuse me. I turned to him with tenderness and did what I was most well-versed in—I buried my head in his chest.

"It's nothing. Don't get me wrong, I'm moved by your reassurance that you're into this as much as I am. The spectrum of emotions I've experienced after all my break-ups has left me disillusioned. It's been ghastly, but now I'm grateful that I found you, someone who enabled me to bask in true love, if I'm allowed to call it that.

"Sameer, despite my feelings for you, I'm not going to deny my love for Shivani. Before you turned up, I was going in no particular direction and then our friendship was fast forwarded to a relationship and lo and behold, Shivani faded into the background. Except now I realise she hasn't. She's with me every time I'm with you and that is what causes the hurricane. I want to apologise for that but I can't help it because she does play centre stage in my life's field. I'm beginning to realise I will always love her more than I can love you and yet I don't know why I've put my friendship with her at stake. Please don't misunderstand me. It's not that I don't care. I do and my journey with you wasn't launched on a sea of expectations. Neither was it my intention to have a whirlwind romance with you, but I'm going crazy now."

"Hey hey! We are getting ahead of ourselves, aren't we? Everyone aspires to find love in his or her life because without it, it's all so mundane. You're not committing a crime, babe. Love can *never* be a crime and particularly in a situation when two well-intended people have drifted apart and you are the one to rescue me. Trust me, men have the same frailties as women do, but we hardly ever admit them," he reassured me, hugging me tightly.

"Do you think I'm playing you?" he asked, gazing into my eyes protectively and then lowering his voice to a whisper, "That's not what I'm all about. I don't play! I told you before, but I don't think you believed me. There seems to be grave trust issues here, Richa, but I'm patient enough to work with you to erase every insecurity that you have. As far as Shivani is concerned, you haven't broken anything that wasn't already shattered, so please don't feel responsible."

"No, I trust you implicitly, but I don't trust myself to maintain my balance. I want to give it my all, but I need to know that you are my friend first. You need to be a friend who understands my love for Shivani and also comprehend that I'm not anyone's spare part," I said, breathlessly.

"Spare me, my ravishing Richa. You are not the only one who has had love stories with unhappy endings. I too attracted women I knew I could break up with because I couldn't commit to them. The first time I cheated on Shivani was tough because I still loved her. But when I came to know she didn't, I stepped out in search of something enduring. It's not unusual to feel guilt and all that. Through your friendship and love, I'm learning to trust myself to make a commitment and support both of us."

"I'm so sorry for being such a pain in your crack. Someday soon, I want you to talk about your marriage though," I began.

"I will, but not yet. And about being a pain in the crack, I've not been lucky enough to experience that, I'm afraid, but difficult and demanding, umm, let me see. All I want to say on that front is cut the crap and listen hard. I'm so glad you've roped me into your topsy-turvy world because you've given me a chance to know you more. But now, we urgently need to get you back to being normal," he commanded, along with his customary giggle.

His humour was unmatched and he possessed a rare attribute of assuaging a weighty situation. He told me about his relationship with his children and how he had changed his approach from when they were toddlers to now, when they were all grown up. He opened up about his insecurities with the fact that they were growing up fast and that he was unable to keep pace with their ever-expanding knowledge of the world. It also cut deep that his role as a father seemed to be growing less significant as his children were becoming more independent, a struggle most parents experienced. But then again, the transitory nature of child-rearing was a lesson we all had to learn and accept.

"You drive me insane with your irrational behaviour," he started in a tone that was calm and controlled. "And as crazy as it sounds, you've left an imprint on my heart and I have nowhere to go except here," he said, playfully, as he circled his finger around my heart. "It's almost impossible for me to grasp the nuances of loneliness you've dealt with but I'm as passionate about you as you are about me which means that you won't have to bear another loss. Without seeing you, I feel a void. It's not a walk in the park for me to cheat on Shivani either, but I don't suffer from chronic guilt because I have my reasons for not being with Shivani. My work is and always will be my first most cherished companion as it keeps me afloat in every sense of the word, but you've become very important now.

"The ring I gifted you is the litmus test for the way I feel about you. It's not for our engagement or wedding as neither of us want that but it's an unmistakable symbol of my commitment to us. I don't shed out diamond rings like boxes of chocolates, you know. And just so you know, what I'm about to say right now is not an impulsive decision but…"

He drew a deep breath as he rose from the bed and strode steadily up and down the room. I felt myself getting into tiny knots as I pondered over his next sentence.

"But," he repeated, "if you still mistrust me then how about you start residing in my second apartment that's lying vacant and I'll be with you as much as I can, which in any case, I am. The flat is bland-looking with not much of a personality, but we can give it one with a good polish—a face-lift, furniture with character and some accessories for a finishing touch. I'll get the entire thing done as soon as I get the green signal from you. In fact, add your touch to it. I know you will create a real masterpiece and I can assure you that no one from my family goes there, as it is our neglected property."

He offered his place without a hint of hesitation and a big lump of emotion clogged my throat, as he had exceeded all my expectations. A part of me was afraid of the final seal but the impulsive part that didn't think before it acted was thrilled.

"Do you mean bag and baggage and you do realise that it will entail my kids too, right?" I asked with my eyes wide open and my heart racing.

"Absolutely!" he said, "Even though there is no need for speed but since your heart is racing to park itself, it can do so in the comfort of my second home. My first is occupied with your best friend, unless you want me to get rid of her?" he asked with an edge of irritation in his otherwise jovial voice.

"I'm sorry, Sameer and I didn't mean to pressurise you but I'm so frightened of the fragility of relationships in my demented world. Plus, you cheating on your wife makes me feel like a slut," I apologised, embarrassed of my insecurities.

"Correction; you're a seasoned selective slut—SSS! From now on, that will be our code. And can we please stop reminding ourselves of our character flaws? I know both of us are cheating on Shivani but I insist that I'm doing so owing more to my fatal incompatibility with her. I have absolutely no regrets about cheating on her and being with you. One event leads to another and I don't need to go into details but I'm guilt-free, so I suggest you try too. Now let's focus on my proposition," he urged.

"The answer is yes. Of course and I'm delighted. I love you!" I exclaimed. "But just so you know, I usually take your kids out, so we need to be careful on that account. I'll need to find an excuse not to as I don't want the children exchanging notes. I can't seal their lips, so I'll stay over only on weekends when my kids are away with their respective fathers. I'm afraid there will always be some complication. My life didn't begin with 'once upon a time' and isn't going to end with a 'happily ever after.' It was more like 'figure it out now that you're here' to 'well done if you've pulled through but the lessons still aren't over,' I said, reservedly.

He at once clasped me in his arms to seal his unfettered support. He reassured me that he was fine with whatever decision I took since he sincerely valued me. "It's your strength that doubles mine so please continue to be my rock."

"And you're mine, Sameer. I'm so glad you made your way to my heart," I whispered. He kept me fastened in his embrace and pecked my head, pulling my hair back as he caressed it. He did more than hug my body; he hugged my soul.

"It strikes me that you've had an unfair share of heartaches but I'm not willing to let you go through anymore, babe. We all have chapters in our lives that we prefer to tear away. Besides, do we really choose the cards that are dealt out to us? I believe we are being monitored by a higher intelligence up there. He doesn't show himself to us because hey, maybe he's shy, but I believe he keeps an eye on his screwed-up creation. Wow! That was good. I didn't know there's a philosopher in me. Be in love because it brings out the best version of who we are," he said.

"Thank you, Sameer," I said, briefly.

"Seriously, be kind to yourself Richa, because from this moment on, you are mine more than you'll ever know. I may not be yours legally, but I am yours, spiritually, emotionally and physically. Have I left anything out?" he asked with an innocent guise of a young boy; at once switching from serious to blithe and bouncy.

"Huh yes, mentally!" I said, breaking into a wave of chuckle.

"That's the one, babe, mentally too! So now can we get back to what we were doing, please? I'm missing you and want you so badly. The passion that you've been searching for all your life is right here, between the sheets. Here, let me show you! It's waiting for you," he said, returning to the sheets with a mischievous grin.

After making out, I spun towards him and told him without a grain of hesitation, "I love you without reservation and I wish it hadn't taken me so long to respond to the advances you've been making over the last few years. I disregarded our chemistry but now I know we were meant to be because your love has enlivened my senses."

"I knew I was right in doing so but couldn't find a way to tell you since Shivani was in the way. I'm glad your good sense prevailed and you came to meet me that day at the coffee shop. Even you couldn't overlook our unmistakable chemistry. Anyway, I'm relieved you acknowledge that I'm a celebrated genius in the laws of chemistry and physics. And for the life of me, please don't bring my wife up, particularly between the sheets. Three is always a crowd!" he teased before his tone turned husky.

"And before your erratic hormones play up again, let me relate tonight's forecast. Please don't dampen it with your bouts of dull insecurities and unfounded fears. There is going to be torrential showers of alcohol, debauched sex and a depraved night neither of us will ever be able to recall. A night not to remember! We'll begin with dinner and dance and conclude with you getting into your sexiest lingerie and pulling the wine bottle out of the mini-fridge!" he instructed while pecking me several times on my neck, until he finally rested his lips on my forehead.

# 21

My forehead is what she first welcomed with a kiss before enthusiastically drawing me into her arms. She planted her lips on my cheek before settling herself down on her sofa, but this time, she wore a slightly enigmatic expression and I wasn't sure whether she was about to rebuke me or rejoice with me.

Ma's endless endeavours to control my destiny usually left me exhausted but recently, I found myself becoming stronger even if I didn't entirely trust her judgement. The sudden satisfaction on Ma's face coupled with a lingering expression of victory pleased me altogether. All my life, I mistrusted her integrity and hoped for our sake that her intentions towards us were well-meaning and not entirely filled with manipulation. One thing that I had taken from all this was that I would always be my children's director, but never their dictator. She was single-minded in her efforts to gain respect from the world while she was simultaneously losing mine, until my involvement with Raman. My perception of her had turned positive over the past several months.

When I tried to thank her, she wore a flat expression as if she was oblivious to what I was referring to. Her astute ways never did inspire me and I hoped I didn't grow into the same mask of cool indifference.

But she did appear pleased with me, making me feel like I had brought home a trophy. Her plan of getting me into bed with another man seemed to have worked in her favour and she felt victorious as it distracted me from my marital issues while she stood firm in her social and business standing. Now that she had changed the course of my destiny, I began to accept her opinionated nature, allowing her to take it upon herself to play the judge and the jury.

With pride in her eyes and a satisfied smile on her lips, she sat opposite me and rang the bell for her customary five o'clock green tea. Within minutes, the slightly stooped figure of Amma ji walked in to apologise for its delay, owing to the preparation of the snacks to be accompanied with the tea and coffee. On some days, she would accompany Ma to the office, for Ma preferred her green tea over anybody else's. She greeted me with her engaging smile that revealed the love she felt towards me. I sensed that I was still her favourite and this warmed my heart. After her announcement, she turned away to return to her domestic duties.

The sunflowers in the tall crystal vase on the table beside her were vibrant, almost tactile, and because I was oozing with love, I related to every animate and inanimate item in her room. I complimented Ma for her brilliant artwork—of a woman and her baby—hung on the wall behind her desk. She painted most proficiently and I contemplated the image for a while before concluding that the baby was Shiv and the woman was Ma herself. She had sealed him in her embrace most endearingly, against the backdrop of Mumbai's calm summer sea. She had brought it alive with profound maternal emotion. Had I been asked to paint my reality before meeting Raman, I would've dipped my brush in one colour—ebony black. But most recently, it had changed into an array of bright colours. It's incredible how our perception of the world changes in a single heartbeat.

"I painted this several months after Shiv was born. I engaged myself in art classes in the comfort of my home. Most bizarrely, it was your grandma who encouraged me, believing it was bound to add credibility to my profile as her daughter-in-law. She showed my talents off to society and their appreciation added a gloss to my personality. In fact, she was the one who found the art teacher for me. He was exceptional but never exhibited his own paintings because he wasn't able to acknowledge their worth. He convinced himself that he was born to teach and he remained humble throughout his living years and then one day, on the day of my class, your grandma entered my room to break the heart-wrenching news of his demise. I cried like a baby for him, but most of it was for myself. He had become my beacon of light, my respite from the family's constant criticisms that never stopped even after Shiv was born. He was a serious man, perhaps because he had studied his entire life in the school of pain and he had come to me to ease me of mine. There was never any humour in his voice and his seriousness manifested in his mannerism. I missed him immensely and drove to his humble abode to give his wife some money as the source of her livelihood had been withdrawn by the inexplicable hands of fate. A human life with such admirable talent could never be compensated for but I wanted, in my own modest manner, to express to her that I cared and thanked his soul for redeeming mine," she said, pensively in a tone that was resigned and her eyes revealed melancholy I had missed before. She appeared vulnerable and I was awed by her modesty.

"My painting depicts both love and pain in the same vein; love for my child and the pain I experienced all those years trying to conceive a son under the abiding pressure from the family.

"When I finally did, I locked him in my arms, close to my chest. Till date, I keep him close because I haven't been able to cut the umbilical cord and he is, no doubt, a good son. I stored the painting away, firstly because I didn't think it deserved to be showcased and secondly, because it evoked emotions of pain. On analysing each brushstroke, I realised it could've been administered better. If the nuances of each object and person are seen too closely, we are bound to feel disillusioned as nothing is perfect and we must learn to accept even the unacceptable at times. It's important to take the shadows with the light as they both are inseparable," she sighed as she concluded.

"Now that same painting proudly sits against the wall of my living space. Often, when we take steps back, the same situations appear different and we value them more with time," she said, almost enigmatically.

"But do we, Ma?" I asked, emphatically, relating her last statement to my marriage. She tried to be cryptic but now I had the confidence to decode her every word and to then express my own views, so I repeated, "Do we really begin to see things differently?"

Usually, it was safer to agree with Ma, so as to avoid stirring her usual put-downs and agitation but she was composed today and I had never witnessed this side of hers. Every woman had a story and I found myself getting intrigued by hers.

"You must engage in art if you can, Shivani—it's a therapy more fulfilling than the retail one, since this feeds your soul. I've recently invested in two paintings for the new block of our office last month, from the annual Delhi Art Summit. There I stumbled upon these peacocks designed by an artist from New York who was showcasing her works. Stunning, I must say, although I didn't purchase them. What's more, your Vijay mama personally introduced me to the founder and director of the Delhi art fair. She's so young and charming with such admirable entrepreneurial skills. She was just 27 when she conceived the idea of an art fair in India. In fact, the idea was born while she was on a flight back from Mumbai and how beautifully she has executed her ideas into a flourishing business. The winds of change are definitely blowing in women's favour," she said with a voice that was still unruffled.

"I *am* glad for them, Shivani and why mustn't I endorse women shining a little? But at the same time, they must learn to weigh the pros and cons in every situation and be smart enough to know what works in the larger scheme of life."

Disregarding her last statement, I remained focused on her love for art. "That sounds most intriguing, Ma. I'd be honoured to meet such a dynamic woman for inspiration. Incidentally, which pieces of art did you pick up?" I asked appearing most enthusiastic about her encyclopaedic knowledge and wondering in the same vein, if discussing art was the reason she had summoned me here.

"One is Seema Kholi and the other one is Sujata Bajaj. Both are eminent artists. One of them resides in Paris. I hope to visit her someday and in addition, I'd like to visit the Louvre to see the world's art wonders dwelling there. Mona Lisa is one of the obvious ones; I do love her enigmatic smile that speaks volumes about a woman's vault of secrets kept in her soul. Da Vinci was a genius, but geniuses are in each one of us, just waiting to be discovered."

"Do I have a genius in me, Ma? Did you ever consider evoking such beliefs in me as a child because I seriously don't recall," I enquired with a hint of sarcasm in my voice, which she flatly disregarded.

"You ought to plan a trip with me sometime, Shivani. It's an exhaustive education that gives shape to your personality by broadening your worldview. Travelling with the purpose of learning makes it all the more meaningful and it brings people closer. I, more than anyone, understand the struggles women encounter in the path to achieve their professional ambitions while balancing their domestic acts. Your generation is fortunate to have the tools and the exposure to unveil their truth, so minimal time must be expended on transitory pleasures and one must remain etched on honing the latent skills."

"Skills? Was I ever encouraged to be my own person? Have you ever thought that travelling with you could pose further threats to our relationship since you may not like the person that I am now? I'm quite adventurous," I claimed, confidently. I was sure of my confidence after my trip to Goa with Raman. It had relaxed all the inhibitions I had, and I felt bold—ready to take on the world.

"How was your trip?" she asked sharply, probably already aware of every detail.

"It was somewhat awakening, almost spiritual, if I may say, since I unmasked my true nature through engaging in activities that I didn't know I could. I let go of many of my preconceived notions about this and that, allowing myself to just flow. I rode through the sea at daytime and in the evenings, I stood on the brink of it. And do you know what? My epiphany was incredible."

"Which was what?" she asked.

"I realised I was a reflection of the sea, my vastness and depth were equal to it, if not more and I could achieve anything I wanted. Anything," I stressed.

Raman walking into my life had changed my perception towards my marriage. He empowered me to step back and see things differently just as Ma stated several minutes ago. I stood in the very same spot in my garden of life but Ma had changed the angle from where I viewed my life's landscape—it now appeared lusher than I ever imagined. Sameer had already figured out a way of saving the wedlock by being with others, instead. He unfastened the padlock of vows and walked free while still holding on to the marital status. I was a latecomer to this kind of arrangement. Nevertheless, I thoroughly understood now that it took more than two people to sustain a marriage—it took four. But sooner than later, I knew I had to subtract three to live with dignity and liberty.

Instead of my eyes turning downcast as they usually did in her presence, I looked at her directly as she blatantly stared at me. Her smile faded. She had brought order into my chaotic existence and now she ceased to smile while I deliberated on what I had done to rock her boat. She was temperamental and I was never sure what expression to wear on meeting her. Very often, I'd be smiling and her reprimands would change my expression. So far, I hadn't been an entrepreneur—not because I lacked in the necessary resources, but in the one thing that completed an individual—confidence. She proudly spoke of other young women rising in the world, but had never managed to elevate her own daughter to that level.

"The new block is coming up well, by the way, thanks to Raman. He is a fine architect with titanic talent. I recognise the aesthetic ability of a person by his mere conduct and character. He is meticulous and has an eye for detail and invariably after he completes one project, he moves to another. He's not attached to any one of his projects you know; it's purely professional," she said, waiting for a response from me. She had made yet another inscrutable statement that was actually an insinuation. She was cautioning me and I responded to her immediately.

"And so he should be. I don't know if I am, but yes, I am sure that I'm attached to the idea of being liberated."

As always, she flared her nostrils. She was furious, never before had I found my tongue before her, "There is no exact 'how to' in an affair but you are not meant to get attached as that defeats the very purpose of trying to save your marriage. So do tell me you're *not* in love with this man. I'm completely aware of how capable you are of becoming intensely interested as well as extremely emotional, hence, I pose this question to you because...."

"Because you know what's best for me!" I completed with mild mockery in my tone.

Meanwhile, Amma ji entered with green tea and coffee and hot snacks in Ma's favourite silverware. She looked at me again and smiled once she was sure I looked joyful. Amma ji approved of my ensembles and particularly, the way I wore my hair and accessorised my outfit with comely coordination. She insisted that a woman must be groomed at all times, as it was a reflection of her internal state. Perhaps, she had been informed of my activities of late as I imagined Ma confiding in her. I found myself cringing at the thought, as I had never failed to maintain my dignity before her. While I was lost in my thoughts, she was instructed by Ma to come in later to fetch the empty crockery.

As soon as Amma ji left, I looked up at Ma in disbelief, "I know you care and I appreciate it, but I don't think I understand! Didn't you tell me to fall…"

"I told you to have an affair, not to fall in love, child. That is like falling into a trap when you're married. Desire, dear girl, blinds our good judgement and trust me, I am here to protect your heart from breaking," she said, reverting to her usual curt tone.

Why is it that a mother's eyes can see right through her child's soul and know every word, syllable and punctuation of its state? I suddenly felt my stomach tighten as she continued to stare at me, while she guzzled down her tea. "It's unacceptably cold! Ring the bell! They seem to get it wrong more times than they get it right and it's frustrating. Ring the bell, I said," she commanded and I did just that, without delay.

Just like the torrential rain pounding the windows of her room, my heart began pounding as drops of anxiety dampened its walls. The heat of the day had clearly passed, but it had entered the pores of my skin. Even though I was gaining more strength and confidence, I was still wary of her.

She smiled, shouted and was sad—all within minutes. To her credit, the tea was indeed cold and I too wouldn't have tolerated such an unforgivable transgression made by Amma ji. Ma's eyes pierced into me while talking down at Amma ji whom she normally respected.

"I don't tolerate such errors, Amma ji. If I have given an instruction, then I expect it to be carried out. Who knows that better than you? Please rectify the slip immediately." It seemed like she wasn't only talking to Amma ji now. The message, undeniably was directed towards me.

"What's the difference, Ma, between having an affair and falling in love?" I asked, gritting my teeth.

Her voice was even brusquer as she abruptly rose and commanded me to follow her to her study. I momentarily mused on what made her so vicious in her life. Behind her soft façade, there was always a volcanic rage waiting to erupt and it seemed to do so especially with me.

"Close the door and sit here, so no one can eavesdrop. The walls in this apartment have ears, so we need to exercise caution," she said, adjusting her printed pale pink French chiffon sari that mirrored her complexion.

"It's the first time I feel passionate about something; I mean someone. I'm going to hold it back because he's bringing out the best in me in more ways than one. He's motivating me by rendering my life a deeper meaning and a stronger reason to succeed in whatever it is that I'm capable of. I thought that was the purpose—to be happy. Ma, I don't recall the last time I felt this way. I got married at 20 to the man of your choice and this guy is just, well, he's just incredible, Ma," I said, softly while I was aroused at just the mere thought of his touch. But more than that, it was about his care for the growth in my life. A sweeping smile passed my face.

"Ah!" intervened Ma, immediately, towelling dry my saucy preoccupation.

"That's the catch! Whilst he's managed to flatter you, and has gotten you into tiny little knots that feel like love; you are entangling yourself in a dangerous web of lies. Whilst his touch makes you feel lovely about yourself, you mustn't forget that this affair was meant to save your marriage and not destroy it further. So, happy is a good emotion but not at the expense of colossal sadness of another. Balance yourself before you are ruined, the truth is that this kind of happiness is as transient as the skies that alter their moods throughout the day."

"I don't get it Ma, in all of this, who's sad? Sameer is too preoccupied to care and since you claim to be my umbrella, no one will ever get hurt. Wasn't that your promise, except in a different expression? How will Sameer ever know, unless you tell him. But then, what's the point of that? It's our secret, right? And as long as I'm happy, I will endure my marriage. Wasn't the whole point of this exercise to avoid a divorce just so you could save your face in a society that's on the edge waiting for a slip up from us?

"Except Ma, we can't be hypocrites forever, especially when I don't have the desire to be one anymore. Raman has become my abiding light, giving me unshakeable valour. I'm not a prisoner of my struggles anymore, but a voyager learning to weather my storms and to sail ashore," I said, mustering the courage to be myself.

Once again, I sat in the grey zone with her. Gloom had been woven in the very fabric of her being and she couldn't untangle herself now. I felt like her punching bag again, except now I was determined not to be as I was emerging into a woman I was beginning to admire. Her piercing liquid brown eyes narrowed and she moved in towards me.

"Make sure you're not in love with him, young lady. The man doesn't fit your criteria—as a husband and as my son-in-law. Besides, we're not looking for a match for you. The idea was to simply distract you and make you feel good about yourself enough to remain in your marriage. Your infatuation cannot grow into love. His charismatic demeanour was only meant to entertain your jaded mind and to lend you respite from your rusty routine, but now you're walking on a dangerous terrain, Shivani. I want you to be very careful about this. An affair is a collaboration between two people who understand the deal. It's an unwritten contract that benefits both parties without damaging the third party. Broken things can become blessed things if you let me do the mending, but you never cease to interfere in my plan, do you?" she said.

"For once, Ma, you will have to trust me. I'm no longer your baby girl who is still learning to walk. I came in here all hopeful and happy and then you being yourself, switched off all the lights. If I get hurt, it's my problem, but at least let me breathe. If I tell you I'm not in love, I'd be lying and perhaps to keep you happy I should always lie, but I won't anymore, so let me be, for God's sake. Let me grow up!"

The co-workers in office knew about us by now as these things couldn't be hidden, carefully tucked away in some file. She had confidantes in every nook and corner of her life. Since she was the one who had coaxed him to distract my gullible mind, she must've warned him to remain emotionally detached too.

Just then Raman walked in to hand over a catalogue to her. Working in the same office gave our romance an edge. I smiled at him with my eyes as I made an intelligent decision not to be too overt about my feelings for him. I lifted a magazine that was on her table, instead. I appeared expressionless while I felt my breasts swell and the flesh between my legs throb with desire at the mere sight of him.

Ma's voice was even more urgent now, "You may leave now, Raman and I'll see you later regarding this matter.

Thank you for the catalogue." Ma once again pierced through my floral dress as if knowing the mischief my body was getting up to, behind the cover. I felt like a silly schoolgirl who had a crush on her teacher. I was unable to contain my obvious excitement when setting my eyes on him, while he set my body on fire. Raman scanned me, as if, knowing all too well the sensations I was feeling. He exited with a smirk on his face. Ma walked to her green chesterfield chair behind her polished walnut desk and began examining me with her questioning eyes.

My grandma used to read to me from our scriptures about how attachment to the sentient and insentient was the cause of our misery and how craving led to sadness. None of the age-old wisdom made any sense now and the religious teachings were so irrelevant to my life. From cultivating my culinary skills from the *Khanna Sutra* by the Indian master chef Vikas Khanna, I engaged in *Kama Sutra* for skills nowhere suited for the domestic front, but way more pleasurable.

"When are you going to stop playing God in my life, Ma?" I then questioned Ma if she had spoken to Raman about our affair, to which she responded, "I will do anything to protect you, Shivani, but at this point, I haven't discussed anything with him. It's my turn to pose the question and I want the truth, no more dawdling. Do you love him?"

"I don't, Ma! He is merely a messiah. Your pundit ji is great because with all his prayers and heartfelt blessings, he succeeded in bringing God into my life to salvage my marriage. Your prayers are answered and so are mine and that ought to make us both happy," I said almost insolently and then there was a knock on the door and Amma ji walked in.

"Shivani, this time I'll let you go, but remember, I'll be watching you like a hawk and affairs are fine as long as they don't interfere in our duties and responsibilities at home. So, I urge you to be wise about this. Give time to your family— your kids need your attention once they return from school and I hear that most often you're not back in time for them. Don't forget they are your central responsibility and the rest must be on the periphery. You are under the microscope, so a single foolish move and I will catch you out," she concluded.

Amma ji stood before me, waiting to pour piping hot green tea into our cups. She had a dedicated expression as she added sugar to my cup. She didn't glance at me this time as she handed me the cup. I tried squeezing a smile at her but she had decided for whatever reasons not to catch my gaze. I almost always empathised with Amma ji more than I did with Ma. I was kind to my own servants and maids too, except, I didn't share the same bond with them. Maids nowadays were crass and insolent. Amma ji, on the other hand, belonged to a lost generation—she was born to selflessly serve and that too, without any resistance or resentment. God had decided her role and she played it with utmost finesse, without any fuss. Despite all, I still wished she'd smile. Surely, she realised how happy I was?

"I understand your concern, Ma, but like I said, you need to start trusting me. I may or may not be in love, but you needn't worry," I stated, exuding a warm glow of gratification. I wasn't prepared to pull the plug with Raman yet. Both my mind and body were lodged into the relationship. Of course, I loved him despite him and Ma not wanting me to.

Which world did Ma live in anyway?

# 22

"I live in a world that most people rebuff. I'm a fallen angel, Shivani and the less you know about my illicit engagements, the better. I ought to write chronicles on my calamitous love affairs. It could be inspiring for the reader. We all learn from others' mistakes, after all."

My voice was hoarse as I flung myself back into my chair. I was slouched, with the lethargy of having spoken innumerable lies. My cheeks were pallid, eyes tired, and my jawline was drooping in the fear of being beaten at my game of deceit. Colour was drained from my face despite my efforts to appear attractive but as Sameer had stated, sadness always appears in one's appearance. Shivani glowed so intensely that if we were in a dark room, she would light it with her mere presence.

"We couldn't have been more dissimilar; you and I, Shivani, and that is probably the reason we attracted each other in our lives. You admire the traits in me that were latent in yourself and I admire yours, but they don't even remotely exist in me. You are patient and compassionate, which I'm not and I'm sexy and attract every man in town which you totally don't!" I laughed as she too broke into an innocent chuckle. Sameer's light-hearted nature along with his knack to switch from a heavy moment to a lighter one had inspired me. And so far, it had been effective, swiftly melting the air of awkwardness that we had recently been encountering on meeting each other. She seemed settled now.

"Thankfully, you've just refreshed my memory, Richa, and I remember now why I love you so much. I'm calmer and more patient than you, probably because of Ma's rearing but you're definitely the chirpier one who hasn't got me rolling in laughter for a while now. Of late, that particular quality of yours appears to have been switched off. But the serious demeanour doesn't suit your image, so you need to switch yourself back to your light-hearted nature that used to flow so effortlessly. I miss my funny friend terribly, so *please* call her back for me," she said, pleadingly.

Meanwhile, messages beeped on my phone and my muscles tensed up. I dreaded her asking me who it was and brushing her enquiries aside would confirm I was concealing something from her. Her eyes flicked down my phone to catch a glimpse of my messages—for that clue which threatened the friendship between us. I quickly tossed my mobile phone into my bag. I never intended to hurt her and the last thing I wanted was to lose her respect and love. I was able to switch off my phone but not my feelings, as the heart wasn't designed with an on-off switch. I'd hurt many men because of my repressed issues but my friendship with Shivani was meant to last. I was convinced we had been associated in many other incarnations but here, I found myself destroying her soul and with it, the very delicate fabric of trust. All of a sudden, I panicked and felt terribly removed from my scruples.

From sharing everything while growing up together, we were regrettably growing apart. Apprehension gripped me harder and being in her presence started to suffocate me.

Impulsively, I pulled my chair back as I was no longer able to contain the urgent need to leave.

"Hey, I'm so sorry, but I have an appointment with my nutritionist and I must hurry. It completely slipped my mind and I mustn't miss it," I said as I hastily got up from my chair, apologising profusely.

"What? Really?" she asked in a disbelieving tone and a deep frown settled on her brow as she had specifically asked me to chalk out a few hours for her before her rendezvous with Raman at the Taj suite.

"You can either chill here with another cup of cappuccino or you could perhaps inform Raman to meet you earlier. I'm sure he'll be ecstatic about this unexpected turn of events. The positive is you will get more time with him and I can meet you another day. Any other time except now. I'm gravely sorry, but I must leave you, so ciao!" I said dismissively, feeling the heat rush from my skin.

"Hey, that's rude! You promised to stay all afternoon and you're abandoning me in just a few minutes. I *postponed* Raman for *you*, so you can't go! Scrap your appointment with your nutritionist. He can wait till tomorrow. Besides, I can't believe you didn't remember because you never fail to feed your appointments into your phone and the reminders regularly pop up, so what's the real deal?" she retorted, raising her voice a few notches.

"Richa, you're scaring me, so please tell me the truth for God's sake and why is your hand shaking? Are you all right?" she said, concerned.

My mask seemed to be most unconvincing and I couldn't bear for her to unveil it, so I continued to gather my bag while I talked, "Look, I'm sorry, but it's really urgent and this time,

I forgot to feed it in. I'm okay, I promise you, but I can't afford to stay."

I couldn't possibly be blamed for being with a man whose marriage had already collapsed, or could I? She too had found her bliss elsewhere and I was hopeful of her reconciling to my liaison with her husband. I needed to tell her what I mused without fumbling and tumbling all over the place like a bag of raging nerves.

"What, a regular appointment with your nutritionist is urgent?" she enquired suspiciously, ripples of my lies disturbing her calm. "What are you keeping from me, Richa? Where exactly are you going and what are you up to? You used to share everything with me but winds of change have swept across our friendship. I need to know the reason because I will rectify the matter immediately. I want to resume our friendship," she declared, sounding precisely like her Ma.

"Look, Shivani, perhaps I can explain later, but I must run now," I said, unable to make eye contact with her. The complexities of my life couldn't be ironed out in a single moment, so I paced faster before I induced further injury. I loved him, but I loved her more.

"Hey, Richa, I'm not comfortable about this, I sense a deep disturbance in you every time we meet. Your body language has changed. You look as if you've pocketed something that doesn't belong to you and you either repent it or you're trying desperately to amend something you've broken, inadvertently, perhaps. But I hope you know that whatever it is, you don't need to carry the burdens of your woes single-handedly."

"No, it's nothing. Really," I replied, curtly.

"Our equation has altered radically in the past several months and this heightens my anxiety as losing you was something I never imagined," she said with sadness etched deep in her face.

"Look! I need to know if we should even be trusting each other anymore," she pressed. My mind raced with what would happen once she found out.

The icy air between us made it unbearable to remain friends, as we both were evidently disconcerted. It was a tragic transformation from our cappuccino routines to the ridiculous suspicions, from the familiar to the foreign. If we continued this way, we invited the risk of becoming strangers.

I momentarily considered leaning forward to whisper my secret to her and after disclosing it, sprint out of the cafeteria. I looked around to make sure no one was listening, but all eyes seemed to be on us owing to all the shuffling and shambling we were doing. Perhaps, my illicit love affair had by now become national news and maybe Shivani's escapade had been revealed too and they were judging us. There was a distinct possibility of them being acutely aware that whilst being infamously promiscuous, I was an unscrupulous friend who had stabbed her soulmate in the back.

She abruptly rose from her chair and grabbed me from both my shoulders, pressing me back on the chair. "Until you level with me, you are going nowhere," she commanded.

I exhaled and closed my eyes. "I *do* have chronicles to share and I promise I will, but please give me time. I'll reveal it all out before you discover it through the grapevine, but don't hold your breath. I need to muster the entire universe's courage to disclose this particular chapter to you along with my previous chapters that remain untold. In fact, it's the old that led me to the new. Throughout my life, I have never had trouble attracting men. I was a magnet for short-term flings, but the vacuum in me never filled. Now this new friend of mine has come along and I feel somewhat protected and loved. How can happiness ever be wrong, Shivani? Someone close to me told me recently that love is not a crime. I've always been made to feel like a criminal for being in socially unacceptable relationships," I said, breaking down and she leaned into me empathetically. I jolted my head forward with my hands covering my eyes and cried with abject tears. I wailed and wallowed as I was a jumbled mess, but she settled her gaze on me with compassion and concern.

"Hey, Richa, I owe you an apology for being totally out of line there. I've been so immersed in my newfound joy that I suspected your joyless expression was attributed to your break-up with Ravi. I wasn't aware you had secrets you've never revealed to me. In fact, I'm disappointed as I'd given you the golden key that opened every door to my life and I believed it was the same for you too," she said, perplexed as I instantly felt guilt stab me in my chest.

"Whatever it is, stay safe with it and when the trust between us returns, I will be here waiting for you. There's fret painted across your face and I'm genuinely concerned as much as I am hurt you didn't consider me worthy of pouring your heart out. As I said, I'll wait till the end of earth for you to revert to your usual spirited self. I agree with whoever told you that love is not a crime and I can vouch for that. Richa, I believe, you deserve happiness and just remember that I have and will always love you."

The three wound-healing words turned everything around as I felt tranquil and apologised for being impulsive. I drew deep breaths as she clasped her warm hand over mine.

She ordered another cup of cappuccino for me while she conveyed to the waiter that she was in search of a quick sugar fix. What wouldn't I do to make us both bounce back to the way we were. She appeared genuinely concerned as she asked the waiter to pour water in my glass and then urged me to drink it before the cappuccino arrived.

"Phew! And I thought I was hard work!" she chuckled as she sat back to scan me, "You intrigue and irritate me in the same breath. As if your life wasn't exciting enough, now there are more secrets? I'm inspired already!"

When she observed my shallow breaths, she grabbed my other hand and massaged it gently, and most affectionately. My betrayal gnawed at me as I felt my gut churn in disgust. I straightened my spine and took several deep breaths while tears streamed down my face.

She quietly articulated her feelings for me while looking deep into my eyes, "I just want us to be the way we used to be. I miss the old us. I don't know where you've taken this long-haul flight to but *please* return home soon. The weather conditions are favourable and the return flight has a special offer; it's free! So, can I book you?"

We both broke into outrageous laughter, because that is precisely the way life had become—outrageous. Once the air had turned lighter, I sipped on my coffee and admired her beauty. I switched off my mobile phone so as to not get distracted or raise further suspicion and on finding my voice, I began, "As soon as I bounce back, I will disclose all my chapters. Trust me, I miss you and love you much more than you will ever realise. Be patient as I'm riding on low tide and need to figure out how to stay afloat. Anyway, let's turn the floor to you. How's it going with Raman?" I asked, trying hard to manoeuver myself back into the moment.

She wore a faint smile as she began, "Yeah, he's good. But before I speak about him, I need you to know that I look up to you, Richa for all your bold attributes and I *am* genuinely concerned."

"I know, but now I'm here and all yours, so let's be in the present," I said, realising how love made her appear youthful and how it distressed me. Both were love and yet they had a different impact on us. She nodded, unconvincingly and I anticipated her broaching this episode at a different time to clear the mist, but she was wise not to needle me at this moment.

Her perturbed expression eased as she scanned the place with curiosity, "I wonder if Raman's designed this space. It has a sparkle. So, to answer your question, he is just that, the beat to my existence. I'm as emotional about him as I am about any other significant aspect of my life, even though that wasn't supposed to be the deal. The challenge was to *not* be in love with him, but it's too late to take a U-turn, as Mr. Wrong feels so right."

Light was tumbling through the French windows of the café we sat in. Fascinating 18th century art hung over the mantelpiece and a glass bowl filled with potpourri sat proudly. There was another wall of three windows on the other side, dressed in an off-white colour. This place was bric-a-brac and bricolage, where many expatriates hung out for casual afternoons—generally for hot beverages, pastries and toasties.

"You know, I wonder what his house is like because I imagine it to be a reflection of him—a den with his most distinguished characteristics. I'm impressed with the way he gives the space he works on a complete makeover, just like he's given my life one, Richa. Some people come into our lives to rearrange it while others come to destroy us so that we can build ourselves from scratch. So either way, we win in the end.

"I recall the first time I lay my eyes on him. His suit boasted of the precise cuts of an Armani. His flirtatious floral print tie had a personality of its own. He was affable, charming and a breath of fresh air. It was physical at first and now he is my mentor and guide too. I'm convinced I love him because all I seem to do is think of him. He makes a fine teacher."

I listened as her eyes glistened with love and happiness—happiness that we pursued all our lives only to be evaded by it because we all made the mistake of wanting to possess it.

"You will agree then, Shivani that loves blinds us, sometimes to remove us from what is morally correct. We succumb to what we believe is our best choice and more often than not, what we need is at odds with what is possible."

"Yes, Richa, that's true but unfortunately, karma never sleeps. So, if we steal from others for our happiness, we must pay a price. I thank God Raman is single, so I have no feelings of guilt in that regard. He is my moment's strength that will shape my future and of that, I'm sure."

"Shape it how?" I found myself asking.

"Neither of us are in this for the long haul. He has made that abundantly clear and my love for him has not abated because of this claim. On the contrary, it has only made me respect him more. He is my friend till I've set up my own business and I'm thrilled that he believes in me.

"Infidelity was almost a foreign language and after having learnt it, I confirm this to be the finest hour of my life because it's more than I thought possible," she said, biting into her chocolate cake.

"It's most desirable just like Raman, sweetly delicious. Have a bite of my cake since you don't have anything to bite into, do you? Oh wait, you do! But you are not ready to share it just yet," she commented with undertones of sarcasm in her voice.

"Stop being so sarcastic, okay?" I said, lightly. "I'm afraid I wasn't blessed with such an understanding mother." I shared the bite with her and as I ate, I observed her obsession with Raman and realised that her fixation was as great as mine. She then swiftly steered the conversation to a different direction.

"Anyway, I needed to tell you about Raman's brother. He recently came out of the closet with his sexuality and all hell broke loose, as you can imagine. He's gay or more accurately, he's bi-sexual, so his wife is devastated. Catching him with another man in her bedroom caused fireworks. There were hints and whispers before she married him but it was only later that she got the big picture, so in effect, her life has been a nightmare from start to finish. Raman is very disturbed since his brother has two children whom he is deeply attached to. He tried persuading the mother against walking out with them, but now she has. I fail to understand the reasons people marry when they are gay and know very well it will end like a tragic opera. They jeopardise the lives that become dependent on them. They ought to muster courage to come out of the closet, instead of hiding in it. The more the homosexuals come out, the more courage it gives others to do the same."

"I guess it's because courage isn't an attribute that many are gifted with," I responded.

"You know, Richa, Raman reassured his baby brother that had he confided in him about his sexuality before getting married a decade-and-a-half ago, he would've supported him. He insists there's nothing unnatural about being in love with a person of the same gender, but the stigma is deep in our culture's consciousness. You know what I mean? His parents, however, believed that time would change him but it has revealed him, instead."

My heart leapt in my chest and I shrank in my seat while she went on relating Raman's family issues. "Well, thankfully, Raman has softened your perception about homosexuals. Your attitude was unacceptably biased before. Thank God for the love of your life," I said.

"Raman is a great human being who not only believes in gender equality but in standing up against people who criminalise others for not being 'normal', as society would call it.

"He is upset with his brother because of his weak character and wished he could've been proud to be the man he is and not hide behind a web of lies. How exhausting it must be to lie all the time," she commented, looking up at me for my reaction and devouring the last piece of the cake.

"You're right, Raman is a great guy, but if only, there were more freethinkers urging others to express their sexuality without constraint. We live in a hypocritical society, Shivani, and it's still easier for Raman's brother than it is for a homosexual woman. It's challenging for both, but tougher for lesbians to walk out of the closet. I personally feel they're stigmatised and ostracised infinitely more than gay men. You only need to look around at the fashion industry to see how we *all* revere gay fashion designers and yet the homosexual woman on the same platform becomes an object of mockery. Undoubtedly, lies are exhausting and it's the truth that frees us but it's the dysfunctional society with its many biases that coerce homosexuality to remain closeted. As I mentioned earlier, I know lesbians who've fought hard for their rights and in the end, have been defeated. An acquaintance of mine even turned to promiscuity owing to her repressed feelings. We need to reconstruct our beliefs and cure ourselves of narrow-mindedness."

And then I enquired, rhetorically, "What would we both do if our best friend turned out to be homosexual?"

I was relieved that Raman was able to change Shivani's mindset. In a sense, I hoped she'd discover the truth about me and with all the facts laid out before her, she might be sympathetic towards my life choices. I felt tired of sweeping the dark aspects of my life under the carpet, as that did nothing to assuage my turbulence.

# 23

The turbulence of gusty winds thudding against the windows of our room aroused the abiding passion inside. I rolled my gaze towards him and he was already staring at me, sending a warm ripple of excitement through me. His eyes were hungry as I stood before him, unequivocally defenceless. The moment was filled with expectation as he moved towards me to press his lips against mine with irrepressible passion. We then stepped into the bathroom.

"I suspect you want us to freshen up first," he offered with a gentle voice. He turned on the shower and began to ease the straps off my dress, only to let it drop on the floor before he undressed himself. His eyes moved up and down my body, soaking in every inch of my flesh.

"I love you naked. You have a great body and I fantasise about it all the time. In fact, every moment spent with you is imprinted on my mind, only to be relived in my solitary times."

I was proud of my womanliness as he slid his finger lightly down my cheek—the very finger that expertly turned me on with its unerring precision. I gave myself over completely to his steady caresses. His voice turned into a whisper as I shivered with nervous expectation, "I love every millimetre of your body, but mostly, I enjoy touching you down there."

The fuelled heat of our bodies began to inflame me from inside as the fire travelled through my every nerve. I quivered with anticipation as he tingled my lips gently with his thumb and then rubbed them lightly. I relived these moments even when I was at home in my marital bed, without the husband who was meant to accompany me. I was glad in a sense that I had been given the luxury of dreaming alone without anyone to break into the stream of my fantasies.

Raman had changed my view on life. We often exchanged notes on the films we separately watched and he gave his suggestions on the books I ought to have read to develop my imagination. A dose of Raman both detoxified and developed me on many levels but at this moment, he contaminated my thoughts as he thrust into me hard. I wailed in ecstasy and gasped uncontrollably. I closed my eyes to feel the sensation of the flowing water from the showerhead splatter on my face and body. I breathed heavily with my eyes shut and as the gratification mounted, I cried out, "I can't hold any longer!"

He switched off the shower and walked me to the bedroom with a large white towel wrapped around me. He then wiped me sensuously before laying me down on the bed. I allowed my head to plunge back into the pillow anticipating him to take over again.

"I have bought you pink rose oil. I love the smell of roses, just as much as you do and don't fret, it's not over yet," he said, sensing my disappointment at the thought of it ending. "You can easily turn me on again with your sensuous body."

I felt my palms turn damp as he massaged every part of my body whilst he gently rubbed against me. His mobile phone was ringing on the bedside but his eyes did not avert even for a split second as he continued gazing deep into my eyes. "I want to climax with you, babe." I wailed, barely being able to say the words with clarity.

He moved away momentarily to take a matchbox out of one of the drawers and lit the scented candles on either side of the bed. They too emitted a rose fragrance and he turned to look at me with eyes that were tender, but lustful.

"I was just trying to create a warmer ambience," he justified. "You know me, I never stop working even if the space has nothing to do with me," he giggled.

"I give you all the space on my body to work on," I offered, huskily.

I waited tensely to see what his next move was going to be as he moved into me. My pupils dilated and my stomach churned as he plunged into me hard, touching me intimately at the same time. Our bodies slithered into each other while we kissed most vigorously and then we both relaxed.

"I love you," I said most naturally and as soon as the words were spoken, I felt I shouldn't have said them.

"That was exceptional! You're exceptional and you look as stunning as ever," he said, breathlessly. He continued.

"I love making love to you and I love you enough to change the course of your life by lending you everything you need. I want to be the one to arouse you—not just sexually, but mentally as well."

"I know and we've been through this before. When I said those three words, I meant the same; that I love you for your consideration towards me," I immediately responded, regretting my outburst of affection earlier.

"That's not to say I don't love the way you kiss so passionately because even when the fire between us has cooled down, I will come to you just for your inviting lips!" he joked.

"Is that it? That's the only reason you will come to me?"

"Umm? Well, let me think if there's any other attribute in you that will make me gravitate towards you," he teased.

"Go to hell, except come back soon because I'll miss your ass!" I said.

"Whoa! I like your boldness," he said as he continued holding me tight in his arms.

As he sat up, he announced his need to return to office. "Wish I didn't need to but the last thing I want is for you to be the reason for me lagging behind in my work. I want you to be my inspiration to move forward," he said and I nodded, affirmatively as I looked forward to a nap. He rose and buttoning his shirt, he said, "Baby, we need to draft out a business plan for you. First thing in the morning, we will run over the model and discuss further points that need to be executed. I'll throw out the inessentials of theory so as not to bore you. Let us focus only on the rudiments of setting a shop." He then walked to the door, turned his head and blew me a kiss before exiting.

"Thank you, again!" I yelled as he closed the door behind him.

Usually after his departure, I remained physically aroused but this time, I was more aroused emotionally. I didn't know the extent to which he would actually be able to assist me in developing my own business but I did know that he made me feel significant by merely projecting a keen interest in my evolution. Each time I showed my keenness to learn, I saw the respect he had for me in his fluid eyes. That man believed in me and that made my heart pound with rapture.

I recalled Ma's advice that I practised detaching myself since after a while, the attachment would inevitably leave an enduring ache. Richa too, had demonstrated to me—through her endless experiences—the lingering hurt of a broken relationship, cautioning me to be comfortably detached, except I wasn't. I was falling more in love with Raman for the faith he had in me and even though I was arriving at a juncture where my focus of being with him was becoming clearer, I was not emotionally aloof.

I tried defying the very fabric of being a woman by ensuring my heart remained untouched, while being physically and mentally gratified. The eyes had eyelids to shut out what we shouldn't see, but the heart couldn't be shut to feelings we shouldn't have. Nevertheless, I managed to balance the scales better by focusing on my children and other activities I had been introduced to through Raman. If Ma sensed my emotional attachment, I'd be reprimanded like a defiant schoolgirl who'd broken the rules.

I snapped out of my daydreaming as Ma's number flashed fervently on my mobile phone. I answered it in a vigilant voice so she wouldn't sense my dreamy state of being. She surprisingly enquired about my well-being in a lenient, almost loving tone before asking me to visit her later in office. She sounded unusually calm and her typical sternness seemed to have thawed, turning me suspicious of her intent. I reassured her I'd be there after a couple of hours and on immediately ending the call, my head collapsed back on the soft pillow. My body exhaled as if to release the probable qualms Ma intended to callously cripple me for.

# 24

As crippling disquiet seized me, I could barely hear myself breathe. I had never held a high moral ground but this was the lowest I had ever stooped.

What was never at odds though was the extent I prized her as my best friend. Soldiering towards her to disclose the truth, I desperately anticipated her understanding and forgiveness, as she had a humane heart. A part of me imagined she'd ease my conscience by admitting she already suspected it and she'd justify my sleeping with her husband as a mere result of a behavioural pattern to conceal a deep scar. Being in a joyful space with Raman and the formation of her business would hopefully turn her tolerant to my disloyalty. A guilty conscience had its own slimy way of easing itself.

Sameer sent me frantic messages to reassure me how much he cherished me, despite the recent ripples of angst between us.

*I'm down on my knees with gratitude for having you in my life but if you are trying to call it a day because you love me too much then let me seek a solution.*

*Sameer, I can't talk right now; I'm busy.* I typed, brashly.
*But kindly reassure me that the emptiness of your response is not owing to an absence of emotion? Please?* He pleaded.

*Sameer!* I responded, irritatedly.

*I feel my ship is sinking but you can rescue me to the shore if only you ease the storm.* He suggested. I didn't respond.

*Thanks for being the voice of optimism.*

I still didn't respond.

*Okay, one trivia! Who quoted this—'Don't waste your love on somebody who doesn't value it?'* he asked.

*You!*

I responded, speedily, as I was expecting her any second and didn't want her to catch me with an irate expression. Sameer had been a gem and because of him, I had begun viewing my life in a new light. He had been a lover, a friend and a counsellor—all blended in one superpower tonic.

*It's nice to know you're also feeling unanchored without me. And thank you for being monosyllabic because it makes me feel sooooo loved! Have a nice day doing whatever it is that you are!*

He ended the one-sided conversation with an angry emoticon.

I had finally decided that my mask of caution, after being with him for well over a year, needed unveiling to both him and Shivani. The web of lies and deceit I had woven needed unravelling.

I owed her my truth more than him and it wasn't exactly her blessings that I expected but I hoped I would gain her reassurance. Admitting the truth didn't feel so earth-shattering anymore and the second I would unload myself, I'd no longer be plagued by self-reproach.

Her footsteps were almost inaudible, as the dominating voices in my head had silenced the external noise. I often failed to hear Sameer's steps into the apartment too as the sound was deafened by the incessant stream of questions spinning like an unstoppable wheel in my head, that too, at lightning speed. He'd always break into my stream of thoughts in a seductive tone.

"Hey, prisoner of the mind, I'm here to lend expression to the lover's angst in you. The physical is always a good place to start, so shall we?"

I prayed that while undressing the cloak of truth to her, I'd be able to endure her reaction. Would the expression be resentment or most optimistically, compassion? Or would she mindlessly yell at me for being a damaged soul with a demented head? In a few moments from now, there would be either calm, chaos, compromise or catastrophe.

She came and sat opposite me, staring vacantly into my eyes as if she needed an introduction. Her vibe was alien and that transformed mine. She rushed to order our customary cappuccino—less enthusiastically than usual—while I deliberated on a glass of wine. But reading her expression, I realised I needed to stay in control of my senses, as ironical as that sounded. I hoped that in my madness, there was some kind of reasoning and order.

"Hi!" she said, icily. "I'm not going to sugarcoat my words. You have turned into a virtual stranger and I've reconsidered our stance as friends because I can neither relate to you or trust you. Your voice when you speak to me carries lies just like your face and I refuse to allow my intelligence to be insulted by you or anyone else anymore. I've taken a firm grip on my life and my purpose is more than just looking good."

"Whoa! I'm proud of you and I'm glad that you've arrived to this space. Well done and no, I'm not lying. You know that we are both to blame for not staying close. Affairs tend to consume us and that is precisely what's happened with you," I responded, confidently.

"Don't!" she commanded, raising her hand.

"I've tried to interpret your behaviour in the most optimistic manner. But my mind reminds me that I'm more intelligent than to just buy your self-pitying stories subsequent to your never-ending break-ups. They are then followed by the crap you give me about being so positive in life that you move from one romantic space to another in a heartbeat. You cannot spin any more yarns as your tales just don't add up. They're on the verge of jeopardising my faith in you. I needed to meet you face-to-face for this very reason and most importantly, to inform you that you've exhausted my patience. Therefore, I can't trust you anymore with mine," she said, most blandly.

Her face was strained and she sent broad ripples of shame through my veins. My optimism evaporated and along with it, my intentions of revealing myself. Given her disturbed expression, I couldn't confess so I ordered wine instead.

She clearly wasn't in an amicable mood and neither was the weather, as the unexpected rain carried on, making the temperature drop in the same manner her trust had. I believed I had gone too far with my fabrications.

I was determined to reveal a fraction of the truth, if not the whole as a desperate attempt to bridge the growing gap between us. Good sense prevailed as I turned the table on her.

"Shivani, your imagination has been stretched too far. Besides my chapters shared with you, I have nothing of substance to report to you and I too could point my finger at you for not giving me the attention you used to."

"What? What in God's name are you talking about? Are you going to blame your aloofness on Raman? Does that sound fair to you?" she seemed livid.

What I was witnessing today was Shivani's strength of character and I was taken aback. In less than a year, she had turned from subdued to strong and I was convinced that her meek phase was over.

"There's been a paradigm shift in your personality and I applaud you and Raman for that."

"Raman and I are not an item, so please don't place us together in one sentence. Things have changed as they were meant to for both our benefits.

"He is a very practical and intelligent man whose love for me was unconventional. He's taught me the greatest lesson of all—if you sacrifice too much of yourself for others, there is nothing left of you."

She then stated very sharply, "Relationships, Richa, are like glass. Sometimes it is better to leave them broken than hurting yourself in mending them."

I skipped a heartbeat and began perspiring as she uttered those words ominously.

"No!" I exclaimed. "No, Shivani! You're overreacting," I gasped and moved in towards her. "It's my mother. It was her death anniversary a few weeks back and I just began to relive my memories of her. I've been preoccupied, I admit, but you've been no less for crying out loud, so there really is nothing to be suspicious of. But anyway, it was the memory of my teenage years that was a taboo phase and by disclosing its chapters to you, Shivani, I want to release myself from the shackles I was imprisoned in. I'm honestly ashamed for not getting myself to unveil the truth to you, my best friend, in all these years that we've known each other."

"And where does your mother figure in? You've always been most independent and self-reliant," she remarked with a deep frown and a bemused expression. "I'm utterly confused because you are fiercely liberated, not likely to be influenced by anyone. You've always abided by your own rules, so I don't get it," she commented.

I revealed the real picture of my childhood with its shocking shades, carefully concealing my hidden homosexuality and the fact that I was sleeping with her husband. The courage to spill the entire jar of beans failed me and besides, the relief on her face was priceless. It was enough to ease my conscience. I recounted Ma's dominance over me as a child, including all the physical and mental abuse.

"She took preposterous measures, compelling me to marry the men I later abandoned. I was constantly deprived of her affection, as she didn't consider me worthy. She created differences in the way she raised my brother and me. He was the apple of her eye while I was an eyesore and she never shied away from relating her regret of not giving birth to two sons instead."

As I recounted the truth about my mother, Shivani slid back in her chair, still wearing a frown. She was visibly disturbed on learning about the injustice I had been subjected to.

"You met me in the prime of my life—footloose and fancy-free. My rejection was characterised by a desperate need to be the centre of attention. I had a distorted self-image and was dependent on the approval of others. I reached a chapter in my life where I projected happiness in the hope that I'd eventually attract it," I gazed up at the ceiling thoughtfully before returning my gaze on her.

"I *don't* blame my mother for my destiny anymore because I realised I needed to take responsibility for everything I do and have done. I've forgiven her because she was a single parent and terribly afraid of losing me to perhaps something she didn't believe in or was not familiar with.

They were different times; more closed and conservative—not that woman emancipation is a reality today, because it isn't. Be it the 18th century or the 21st, women are still enclosed in a capsule of societal norms. We are still struggling to shine our light and be the most honest version of ourselves in the most hypocritical patriarchal society. It is constantly trying to curb our evolution at every juncture of our lives, hence, my mother had no choice but to hurt and hate me as she too was gender-biased," I concluded, empathetically. Her face softened and she heaved a deep sigh before turning to me in a soft tone.

"I still don't grasp why your mother detested you. I understand Ma's resentment towards me because I was the fourth girl which meant heavy doses of dowry to be given out, but there's only one of you."

She exhaled deeply before continuing, "Listen, I don't know your mother's reasons for hurting you, but I do know that from our current stance, we have the choice to either look back and stand still or move forward. So, I advise you to not compromise anymore. Stop seeking external validation. Stand tall, Richa, for who you are, because it's more than sufficient. Don't be starved for shallow attention—not even the briefest nod. Basking in the glory of the spotlight will only lead you into the darkness of insecurities once you're no longer wanted and there will come a time when heads will turn away."

She sipped on her coffee, but she was reflective before she spoke again.

"I'm sorry for being harsh, but that's because I know you deserve better than settling for these transient pleasures. They go as easy as they come and if you're honest to yourself, it'll all be fine. I speak from experience. I have done it. It's my goals that I'm in love with now, and they keep my creative juices flowing. All my life I've been homebound, and then Raman encouraged me to become who I am. Accept and love yourself first, the right people and situations will arise on their own. Courage and conviction are prerequisites to a life of success and happiness."

"I agree, Shivani, I really do," I stated with genuine admiration for her.

"But there's still a piece missing in your story because that really isn't a valid reason for being so distant from me," she claimed.

"I was involved with yet another married man," I responded, hastily, speaking as though Sameer was already out of my life. "And that's the reason I've stayed clear of you because honestly, I dreaded your reaction. It was my predictable pattern that surfaced when I couldn't tolerate tedium, so I jumped recklessly into another non-committal affair. I'm sorry for being such a loser, but now I've cut the cord," I said, swallowing a lump of guilt before continuing, "I wasn't choosing my men with a fine toothcomb and neither could the same comb tidy up my fundamental flaws, as I was dangerously entangled, I said, genuinely dishevelled.

"But like Raman, that friend taught me to let go of painful memories because they prevent us from giving and receiving pure love. The change in you is inspiring me to change too," I said with a sincere smile.

She suddenly threw back her shoulders and her body relaxed. She forced a flippant smile before it turned natural. She nodded her head in disbelief.

"There are umpteen ways to connect nowadays with all the click and ticks, but if you disconnect from me on all fronts, what message am I to get besides that you no longer wish to stay in touch? And do you think I'm concerned about your flavour of the month, as unsavoury as he may have been? When have I ever judged you for your meaningless escapades? Seriously, Richa, your affairs are of no consequence to me as they are as transient as my next breath and frankly, I don't see how a man in your life can change *our* equation. It has never happened before, so why now, considering we both know that they just come and go; both literally and sexually! I'm still perplexed but if that *is* your real reason then get over it because I'll say it again, *I don't care*. You're my favourite person in the entire cosmos but you drive me nuts with all your incomprehensible secrets. I love you and my only concern is that you shouldn't get hurt," she concluded, finally becoming normal with me.

'Even as a lesbian and a slut who has slept with your husband?' I thought to myself.

"You don't need to talk about him if you're not comfortable, but let's please try and rescue this friendship," she pleaded.

"He's of no consequence now!" I said with conviction. "I'm heading in a new direction, but I need to admit," I began truthfully, "that it was because of the big burly and brainy man who was as humorous as he was academic that this realisation to be true to myself prevailed."

I moved to grip her hand, "I'm sorry for not trusting your judgement and I thank you for your warmth and understanding. I promise not to be aloof ever again. Now tell me, are you through with Raman?"

"No! Not at all!" she exclaimed. "He is still in my life, but our equation has changed slightly. He also helps me achieve my goals now. Life is meant to begin at 40, Richa but all I experienced before him were more complications. He's not my 'prince charming' though I admit I fell in love initially. But now, he is my best friend."

Then she continued.

"So, it's because of this sugar daddy that you've stopped taking my children out too. You do know right, that they miss bowling with you? But only because they know they'll beat the living daylights out of you," she said, breaking into a chortle to revive the cheerful mood that we were accustomed to.

"Have I?" I responded, absent-mindedly. "I suppose that's because this man was possessive and wanted me around all the time. That's enough about my fragmented love stories. Maybe years down the line, I'll reflect back and transfer my wisdom on to my children to save them from making the same mistakes."

"We all need to make our own mistakes to learn from them. I advise my children, Richa, but I can't live their destinies and neither can I alter them. It's the individual's journey, but children do learn through observation. We are their visual aids—they watch our every word and action and subconsciously learn from us as they go along. Hence, it's of paramount importance to be their role model.

"To an extent, the reins are in our hands, so you don't need to indulge in relationships with married men that are habit-forming. Weed out the negative and only then will you be able to break your ties with such men," Shivani said.

As she spoke, she turned reflective again as though she wasn't entirely convinced of my story.

"You sound like Ma who gives me only small pieces of the puzzle. The English language is pretty straightforward, so why twist and turn it to make it enigmatic?" she added.

"I'm sorry for confusing you, but I've been raised with a limited vocabulary—men and break-ups. Today, I find myself rescuing my wailing daughter and wounded son from the abandonment of their respective fathers who take them out on some weekends, but not all. Besides instability, their fathers' erratic behaviour instils insecurities in my children and more so recently, because they're all grown up and have an opinion of their own. Their fathers travel on business and regrettably call me to excuse themselves. Imagine Shivani, growing up with a single parent who has her own irresolvable issues. I hope all their childhood experiences won't spill over into their own liaisons. We're living in a precarious world and more women are increasingly raising their kids single-handed. I intend to protect my children as best I can, Shivani, and no matter what, I will always support them. Anyway, we've met after a long time and I don't wish to dig out old muck anymore. I'm just glad we've come back together, I really am. You are the caffeine to my morning and the sugar to my cappuccino!" I said, concealing the reality yet again.

"Except there is *still* a mood between us that isn't the way it was and all said and done, you *do* sound different and we need to piece it all into place sooner than later. After that, I can go back to being the sugar to your cappuccino and whatever else I am to you," she said, sarcastically.

She was no longer a babe in the woods, but I still longed to lock her in my embrace. She drank the remaining remnants of her coffee with a flat expression and with her eyes in her cup. She turned notably pensive and I stared at her with feelings of remorse gnawing my body like a deadly disease.

The rain had stopped but the sun hid behind a grey cloud just like the brightest spark in my life—my friendship and my love for her—had been eclipsed in the silhouette of lies and deceit. Deep in my heart, I knew she wasn't persuaded.

"Well," she began, "I guess as long as we can redeem our friendship, I'm okay about not knowing everything. But do remember what Raman has taught me, Richa—unless we spill out our entire story, we deprive ourselves of experiencing empathy and moving from isolation to connection."

# 25

After years of isolation, Ma and I were finally making a connection. The radiant topaz sun streamed into her office as I sat reflecting on my life. It had taken many sharp turns in the past several months—from wanting to 'uncouple' to falling into an affair and sleeping with a stranger, to my best friend turning into one.

I avoided Richa like a plague and I wasn't ready to confront her. As for Sameer, I hadn't exchanged a glance with him for the longest time. I wasn't sure if it was out of guilt, resentment or lack of love that two people deliberately avoided each other, but no words or actions could bridge our irreparable gap. Our marriage had been relegated to a mere habit; a disturbing one at that.

On the other hand, it felt like a million years I had made any contact with her. Ever since one of our mutual friends disclosed her most unpalatable secret to me, I loathed both of them and yet there was an element of fear that prevented me from confronting them both, as I believed myself to be no better—hoarding my own skeletons. The common friend had very ungraciously described the exact location and the nature of activities she had found them engaging in—and that too, in our customary café. It was betrayal of the worst sort. I had completely lost faith in Richa and I feared that she had probably revealed my affair to Sameer to ease her position.

There was a tone I had been acquainted with over the years that I had known her. In the past several months, we were out of sync with one another and throughout, she had worn a strained smile. I should've figured her out myself because her vibe was alienating and her body language, most restrained. She had clenched life's darkest secret in her fist. On recollecting our times together, she had avoided my gaze but I still hadn't caught on to the fact that she had embezzled from me. Sameer wasn't my most prized possession, but he was someone she shouldn't have stolen from me.

As for Raman, I had ascertained the ability to be in a relationship with him without feeling the void of his absence, hence, redeeming my marital status that was so sacrosanct to Ma. By redeeming, I meant I managed to preserve its fragments without finding it abominable. That was more than I had bargained for, at least for the time being.

I no longer wanted a future with Raman. I had finally detached myself emotionally from him. But I did indeed want him as my best friend and it no longer cut deep to be the woman who acknowledged being sexually excited, and being emotionally anesthetized. Professionally, I was already excelling, which in turn had raised my self-esteem.

She pressed her soft pink lips on the centre of my forehead as she usually did, but now it was the prolonged physical contact that was most enduring. She gripped my shoulder as she customarily did, but this time, I felt her emotion. And then, she gracefully stepped back onto the sofa. She wore a plain pink sari that was elegantly accessorised with diamond and ruby earrings. She was dressed for an occasion, but then, that was ordinarily her style. I scanned her from head to toe and felt a tingle of pride to see that beauty had not lost its grip on her.

She spoke in an inaudible tone at first, "I've called you here for a particular purpose. It's intimate and I don't want to guard it anymore, so I'm going to make a confession to you, my darling beta, Shivani." I pondered over it as I wore an intense expression of concern and enquiry.

I thought hard about what it could be and then I suspected that perhaps, my neglect towards my husband was glaringly obvious to her and she now wanted me to cut all ties with Raman to work on my marriage. I was done with her manipulations, so I wasn't going to remain quiet and recessive.

"What is it now, Ma? I do hope it's not about dictating my love or work life because I have no ears for it, so with all due respect, I have no more than five minutes," I said, firmly.

The dark side of Ma was profoundly disturbing and I was done with holding my tongue while she juddered hers. I had decided I would no longer edit my sentences while speaking to her.

I looked at her, inquisitively, as she adjusted the drape of her sari and twisted the ring on her finger, nervously. She wasn't her usual sprightly self and I sensed undertones of angst.

Amma ji entered and placed a pot of green tea and a separate pot of coffee—my favourite—before us as she gave me her customary smile and left us alone in a tense atmosphere.

I poured Ma a cup while she sat in an uncomfortable silence and realised my mistake a second later on picking up her cup, and taking a sip from it. I had given her coffee instead of green tea and I broke into laughter. Her face remained stunned. Normally, I would shrink and shrivel for making such a small but significant transgression, significant still, because I ought to have known Ma's undisputed likes and dislikes. Having spent considerable amounts of time together in recent months, I shouldn't have made such a faux pas. Tea is tea and coffee is coffee. A friend is a friend until she sleeps with your husband and then she becomes a serious slut. A husband too is a husband until he unforgivingly sleeps with your best friend. It's all black and white, simple and straightforward until rules are bent owing to bent minds that long for more than the ordinary. Some people can't deal with the monotony of everyday life, so they break rules that eventually break hearts, but they still don't bat an eyelid. All said and done, it was all about the sex anyway and when the blazing fire extinguished, ashes of tedium remained with pieces of broken hearts.

To rectify the matter, in an absent-minded state, I poured tea into her cup which was already filled with coffee.

"Let it be, Shivani, I don't mix coffee with tea," she confirmed, calmly, raising an eyebrow, good-humouredly. She broke into a subtle chortle and I sat back aghast as I had hardly ever seen her lighten up, particularly in my company.

"I do request you to be calm because I haven't called you here to discuss either your work or love life. Anyway, let me just call for an empty cup first," she said, about to ring the bell. But I offered her my empty cup as I wasn't in the mood for coffee anymore.

"Before I proceed, tell me how is it all going with you?" she enquired.

Her question triggered a stream of thoughts in my mind. I wanted to say, 'It's all going good, except Richa is bedding my estranged husband. Only I can't tell you because I dread to hear that you told me so!

'And then, you will remind me of her instability and drama. What is more, you ask? I'm still sleeping with my architect despite having decided that he will be no more than my mentor, but hey, he's my friend with benefits now. So, that isn't such a horror story now, is it? I can endure sleeping with him considering he's raised my self-esteem that you had crushed from the word go to which I say thank you now because if you hadn't, I wouldn't be able to acknowledge the greatness of one individual against another. I've learnt through contrasts. So to answer your question, I've actually gone from strength to strength and my confidence is touching the seven skies. Thank you for giving birth to me. And above all, I'm proud to be a woman and that too, a seasoned one who has learned to stand tall against those who are condescending towards my gender. After all, here I am standing before you without an apology for being me.'

But instead, I decided to first hear her out.

"Yes, Ma, I think I am," I said with calm confidence. "I think I was tangled before I met Raman and I was upset with you for always dressing my life. I guess I was nothing but a coat of paint for you that enhanced your image in front of your friends and acquaintances. I remained under the lock and key of your conditioning and I looked up to you as you looked down on me, but I'm grateful to you today."

She appeared somewhat bewildered as she heard me out, perhaps because she never actually listened when I spoke.

"Beta!" she began, after adjusting her diamond earring and straightening her hair. "I know what a marriage is and so I completely empathise with you as I too have walked a path parallel to yours. Not to say it's bad as there are many examples of good ones too, but in a deeper sense, you and I share the same destiny—a fate that barely resonates with our innate character."

My head was distracted by the immaculate design of her glistening earrings, and I suddenly began deliberating on where she was taking this. In Ma's eyes, there was a reflection of a tale never told, a secret locked in her soul. Her tone was unusually gentle; almost meek, but I kept my defences up.

"I too had an affair," she said in a whisper and I moved closer to her to confirm I hadn't misheard. "Indeed, Shivani, you heard me right." She established, as she saw my jaw drop till my knees. "I loved him very much and probably still do, but then, that's the fundamental difference between your generation and mine. We understood love in a way that you don't and for the generation after you, I am afraid love will be further dismantled. We knew what it meant to feel tipsy over someone whereas you know what it means to feel the high of wanting to bed someone; you mistake a little passion for love!" she said, smiling sheepishly.

"But I'm not judging you—not anymore, anyway. I don't want you to hate me any longer, Shivani. I have loved you immensely, but just wasn't allowed to express it. I wasn't meant to, beta. You were my fourth daughter, so I was meant to resent your birth and reject you like worn-out clothes. What was required of me was complete submission and I suppressed my love for you just like for the man I truly loved and I want to disclose that to you today, so please listen without a trace of judgement," she pleaded and I nodded in agreement.

"Firstly, about you and I. I know how you've felt towards me because eyes don't lie, Shivani. You always felt that I passed you a life sentence of sacrifice but by doing that, I had sentenced myself to resentment, anger and guilt towards myself. I realised I evoked in you a lack of self-belief and low morale, but now I understand that you've inherited the individualistic nature of mine and I know you better than you believe I do. Undoubtedly, you're like your Papa but you have inherited my stubbornness. The only difference is that in my time, I wasn't able to define it as unreservedly as you do now. The climate for women has changed and I *am* happy for your generation. I no longer wish to imprison you in the shackles of my conditioning."

I was beginning to feel at home with her and felt my facial expression alter from insolence to intrigue.

"Loving someone deeply doesn't mean you need to relinquish power and control over your own lives. It means a healthy flow of communication to stay together and to raise good children, but in my time, your grandmother didn't know how to delegate and make decisions. She imposed her age-old opinions on me. She believed that your birth was a curse and so I banished you from my heart."

I heard it in her voice and it was, for the first time, a bottomless pitch of self-reproach.

"I was coiled in animosity towards my marriage for many years as the underlying expectations based on gender were very evident. They rattled me inside but I didn't express myself due to the domineering personalities looming over me. They were adamant to redefine my personality by giving it a complete makeover, just to fit in their views. Your Papa unrelentingly sided with his mother on every stance, and so, I felt dejected and neglected at every junction of my marriage.

"Destiny expressed its empathy by opening a gateway for me, a way to feel love for the very first time and even though he and I never married, we were undeniably, soulmates. I'm not going to glorify or vilify my marriage to your Papa, but to put it mildly, I never loved him like that. Your Papa and I married to bring together our family enterprises just like you did and then the daily responsibilities and duties dominated our days, pushing aside the chances of love ever developing between us. The only communication we had was restricted to children or work, so love never entered our space."

Without a hint of judgment, I listened. And this time, with compassion and almost admiration for the fact that she too had a heart and was capable of dropping her defences. She appeared vulnerable and old as she pensively recounted her love story to me. It brought a faint smile to my lips, making my eyes flicker with the realisation that she had switched from being my mother to a friend. She too emitted a vague smile and eased back in her sofa with eyes that revealed love—was it for me or for the man she missed?

"He was simply as handsome as he was simple. But above all, he was a man with a magnanimous heart and gentlemanly mannerism—perhaps, a rare attribute in a man today. He wasn't in a hurry, always mild-mannered, patient and tolerant. We wrote letters to each other. That's right! They were written in italics on imported paper that had an embossed flower on it in gold and I have preserved all the stationery," she said, excitedly.

"I brought my letter pads from London those days, but he never travelled outside Mumbai. He wasn't wealthy, you see, and yet he had a heart that was richer than an Indian maharaja's. He looked debonair in his black suit and a plain navy blue tie that he wore to work every day. It was his uniform," she recalled, fondly, while visualising him. "He worked closely with your Papa and your grandfather and when I fell for him, I too joined the family business. It was a convenient love affair. It's destiny that brings two people together and we were meant to be," she said, cheerfully, with eyes gleaming at the mere thought of him. A glow brighter than usual settled on her face. Her eyes were laughing as she spoke of her prince. I listened with interest as my fascination and respect for her grew in the last few hours.

"Oh, and let me remind you, young lady. I may be vulnerable but I am still in a position of strength," she laughed. It was genuinely from her gut and I gladly joined in, her tale of love was finally bonding us, melting the resentment of the yesteryear.

And it was then that it happened.

She cried—audibly and overtly, without an ounce of reservation, releasing years of pent up hatred towards others and herself for not expressing her desires. The sea of love she innately felt for me as a mother was stagnated by the overruling authority of beliefs towards the female gender. She wasn't meant to love me and so she didn't. She turned hard and closed over the years instead, particularly, once the elders of the family passed on and she held the bate in her hand, but that had never been her true nature.

I broke down inconsolably as floods of suppressed tears opened the chasms of pain I felt on being the undesirable rag in her neatly set wardrobe.

"Shivani, my love, woman to woman, every woman has her share of fantasies and romantic notions, but we are conditioned to behave in a constricted manner; to be monogamists, when in truth, women are just as much polygamists as men. We are conditioned to nurture and be tamed while the man hunts, but there is an innate desire in every woman to explore her sexuality. The only difference is that a man is overt about it and a woman, covert. A man likes to flaunt and boast about his escapades while a woman keeps her desires hidden in the deepest vaults of her heart.

"In my time, a bride was expected to be a blank page for her new family to write their script on. She had very little authority to edit it and so she followed it in letter and spirit. Her silence was her gift to them and they cherished it more than her.

"If a marriage had cracks or was broken, we were expected to fix it and not throw it all away like your generation. Women found ways out without really having to make an exit. I found mine and I don't regret it as Chetan ji saved my marriage and me. I wouldn't be where I am today if it wasn't for where I had been with him yesterday. He believed in me in a way that your Papa didn't. He inspired me to find my feet at work whereas your Papa and grandma insisted my feet were chained, preventing me to cross the boundaries of domesticity and duties as a wife, mother and daughter-in-law," she said, while turning reflective the next second.

"Oh, Shivani, he was one in a million and I don't think they make them like him anymore. He was part of an extinct breed. The love you find nowadays is more mechanical as you either send out heart emoticons or create a fantasy in chat rooms without any real intimacy. You send out a hugging emoticon to replace a physical hug. Face-to-face love has its challenges, but that's what builds our character whereas Facebook love only builds our contacts and that too, automated ones!"

I smiled at Ma and her analogies. She seemed so refreshingly relatable as she poured out her unrelenting stream of emotions. I found myself becoming one with her as my eyes were still wet and my heart had irrevocably softened towards her. I never hated her as she commented, but I had begrudged my upbringing without her maternal love. I finally poured some coffee in the cup Amma ji had replenished and sipped on. I then reached for her hand to clasp in mine; it was wrapped in fine lines, although her nails were well-manicured.

"Ma!" I whispered, as there was a recess in her recollection. "Try and remember everything because I want to get to know you." Tears rolled down both our cheeks, but she dried only mine with her dainty fingers.

"I have definite gaps in my memory and I'm unable to recall names and events. I don't clearly recall the advice my mother-in-law had offered me when I had expressed my abiding anxiety about your father's cold indifference towards me. She had said I needed to bear it with a grin. Divorce wasn't endemic back then and it was strictly a stigma. The entire family of the divorcee would be looked down and frowned upon, like they had committed a crime. I'm grateful for my failing memory or else I'd have to hire some assassins to go and kill your grandmother in heaven, or more likely, hell, where she must be throwing her weight around," she broke into laughter and paused as if reflecting on it all, once more.

I raised my brow as an insinuation of her own dominance over people, particularly over me and she realised immediately and smiled.

"I know!" she said, quietly, "Believe you me, I do know!"

"Anyway, why dissect the past or the people in it? I am the moment that has passed and you are the present that will rise into the future. Live it like there's no tomorrow because when this moment passes and you look back, you will have something greater to hold on to, apart from the bitterness of your marriage. Unless you have something to look forward to, you will slide into decrepitude. I certainly would have if Chetan ji hadn't walked into my life to rescue me from my falling self-esteem. Youth fades fast, Shivani, and what remains is grey hair. What disappears rapidly is verve and vitality, filling you with regret if you don't keep the flame of passion burning. Our life lessons don't always come as gently as the tickle of a feather, but remember, what destroys us eventually defines us."

It was invigorating listening to Ma and her timeless perspective on love and life. The secret she had kept neatly tucked away in the closet of her meomry was disclosed to me. She didn't consider it appropriate to disclose any of this to my siblings, but now that my life situation resembled her past, her hidden treasures opened up. I felt a pang of pride for being the one Ma considered worthy of sharing a slice of her life with. 'Chetan ji', I mused.

"So, Ma, can I dare to ask you about my…?"

"Relax, Shivani, I *am* the same controlling mother of yours, but now you know I have a compassionate heart. I know that the world isn't the same place as the one I've left behind but it is hard to move with the times. The words 'sacrifice' and 'tolerance' don't even exist in your dictionaries. You play with sentiments like they are for free. Oh, I'm not condemning you or your generation, since it is yours that has brought about progress. There are acceptable and unacceptable elements in every era and as for your marriage that you were about to ask me regarding…" she stated before descending into complete silence.

Ma, who kept her cards close to her chest, was in a mood to chat and she relayed how my affair was the same story, played again. I too had fallen in love, with immense passion. But over a certain period, my passion spilled over in my work. She was incorrect in claiming our generation to be frivolous in matters of the heart. At least, I wasn't and if Raman had not changed my perspective on my ambitions and achievements, I would still be smitten.

For a split second, I wondered if Papa knew about her affair but I continued listening to her. I was genuinely feeling glad that Ma had experienced a rare kind of love in her life.

"The last time I let go of my stone cold soberness, I fell in love and got terribly hurt. My reserves emptied once he left and I began to look at the future without him filling my days. The skies appeared gloomy and the sun never revealed its face again, or so it seemed. It was hard for me to keep passion alive when my hope was fading fast. My sternness and sobriety became a shield but not a day went by when I didn't wallow in my memories.

"In the end though, love has left a memory that no one can ever steal from me. But to accompany it, there is pain that not even time can heal. There is no perfect recipe for making a marriage work, so you need to create your own. Courage, compassion and compromise are the three main ingredients and then it is wisdom that needs to be kneaded in. Of course, there will always be periods of tension and conflict, but when the tension is not vented out, the marriage isn't a good one," I warmed up to Ma, understanding her better than ever. Diplomacy was never a part of her vocabulary and even now, she said it the way it was.

"Ma, I have used all the basic ingredients but it still remains rotten and ugly with absolutely no flavour left."

"I know," she said, concisely.

I couldn't believe we were finally humming to the same tune. It felt good to come home to each other. Life had magnanimously given us a second chance and I was eternally grateful for having a mother who loved me with all her heart. I felt a lump of emotion stuck in my throat as I continued to listen to her as she walked me through her journey. I nodded and smiled as she continued, "You know, my love, life's jigsaw puzzle—with its tiny pieces—can be tiresome. Its complexity can drive you nuts while you try to assemble it together. God isn't always fair, you know, and some mysteries remain unresolved till another time; perhaps another life," she commented, sadly.

I asked her to relate her story from the beginning in a gentle voice and the choicest words. I had to break those internal walls she had built against the world with calm persistence. I insisted we bonded further with a fresh round of green tea and coffee and something warm to eat. She agreed at once and rang the bell.

"I was the quintessential good-natured wife who never voiced her grievances and your father had abandoned me, emotionally, until Shiv was born. Then too, he only returned to me partially, because the rest of his time was invested in work and the apple of his eye. My values were different from yours, as they didn't permit me to cross my boundaries, so I had an affair with my heart and soul. It was all in my head whilst yours was all in the bed!" she said, staring at me gleefully.

"I'm proud to report that no one, including your father, suspected me of having an affair as there was no physical evidence besides the letters, which I burned later. Thank heavens, we had no mobile phones back then. I still feel the love that neither time nor memory could wilt."

So she never slept with him?

"Ma you never…?" I began.

"No, I never slept with him," she said, completing my sentence to avoid awkwardness between us.

Ma inched towards me on the sofa and her hand, already entwined in mine, tightened its grip. The lump in my throat got bigger as I felt the unconditional love between us, and this time, without allowing the tears to stream down our faces, we both cried inwardly. The eyes didn't lie and hers revealed pure maternal love. I forgave her but as a mother, I promised myself to be in tune with my daughter's struggles and do my best to keep her warm from the cold world.

"I renounce my control and release myself from the web of my past. I'm tired and I'm admittedly old, though I say this through gritted teeth," she sneered while she tightened her grip around my waist and I realised how genuinely weary life had turned her. She continued to pour out chapters of her tale while I listened with utmost intrigue and empathy.

"But I am satisfied that I've experienced what true love is and with absolute truth, I love you too, my daughter."

I noticed her eyes turning wet again.

"I'm sorry, Shivani," she struggled as she broke down.

Without reassuring her that I condoned her upbringing, I rubbed her hand, awaiting words of comfort for my future.

"I'm at that age and stage of my life where I finally have the right to choose my destiny. Looking back, I've learnt that I was swallowed up only because I allowed it to happen. The real enemy is not men or our in-laws, but it is us who tend to denigrate ourselves."

I was intrigued and asked her, "Ma, where are you going with this? What is the point in holding on to regrets? Today, you are strong and you still have so much to look forward to. As far as my life is concerned, I don't see the light with Sameer and it's not as though I haven't given it my all."

"I know you have," she uttered. She then continued.

"I steered you to have an affair with Raman so that you could experience life on the other side of your marriage and you did that. It wasn't the best of solutions, but it was the only way out I knew of. Then, I wanted you to build your trust in him to allow him to guide you towards your emancipation. I knew that once your confidence grew in constructing your business and earning your own income, you'd feel liberated. Only then would you be free to make your own choices. Those choices can be translated to holding on to your marriage while you chalk out your own terms and conditions or..."

"Or?" I asked, assertively, rising from the sofa and standing over her. I felt stronger and more courageous than ever.

"Look, Shivani, I am not going to write the future chapters of your life. But I will say this much, you don't have to be your grandmother or mother unless you want to be. If there's anything you should inherit from the women in your family, it's strength and resilience. The only person you're destined to be is the person you decide to be and you've proved over the past few months that you are truly worthy of deciding for yourself. You have achieved so much because of your determination. I say with regret that I've been blind to your needs, but Raman has successfully opened your eyes to your capabilities.

"I wasn't sure if you were capable of walking alone and sometimes, marriages begin to appear better once you have a fresh perspective but…"

"But," she repeated, "the decision to preserve it or pack it away is for you to make and if you're anyway not standing by your husband as the comrade of his soul, then my dear girl, it is time to take your call."

I shrugged my shoulders, almost insolently.

"Just like that? Are you sure and why now?" I said.

"You're a fine, young and a beautiful woman with admirable intelligence to rewrite your script. My confession has set me free and I hope someday you can forgive me for robbing you of my love but it's important that you know one thing. All these years I was engaged in a fight, but it was never with you. I am sure today, because, I know you're strong and ready to spread your wings in whichever direction you deem fit. Besides, times are changing, so it is time to move into a fulfilling space. Why be in a marriage which you don't even consider true enough to stay loyal to?" she said in a contrite voice, still teary-eyed.

In her eyes, I spotted a lifetime of regret and pain that she had camouflaged just to appear happy to those who didn't care either way. She betrayed my father, me and her son-in-law—her favourite though he might have been. She still plotted against him to prevent me from breaking the tie with him, perhaps to protect us all. My lifetime of anger towards her receded as I found out that the woman I had deemed capable of loving only herself had given her heart to another man. But now I knew that it had never been closed for me.

Forgiveness was necessary to set me free, but it was reigniting the love I had for Sameer that was difficult at this stage. If I were to give him a second chance, it would clearly be on my terms and if not, then at least the exit option was available. Either way, I was the winner and I would walk with my head held high—no more compromises and only choices that encouraged my liberation and evolution as a woman.

"I really believed that one day we would both die with our hearts bursting with resentment towards each other. I'm angry with you, Ma, of course I am, but you've redeemed yourself today."

I kissed her on her forehead—usually her gesture—and then I excused myself for the day. I stepped down to walk along the silvery sea while the sky smiled serenely down at me. I recalled Richa's love for the sea. My heart couldn't have found a safer retreat as the waves curled towards me to embrace me in its care. I inhaled gratitude and felt my entire being smile as the storm of protest receded to make room for a wave of acceptance.

As I felt the love, I empathised with her and was grateful for being able to express myself before her with such liberty. I marvelled at the love she felt for Chetan ji, far greater than my transient love for Raman.

'Raman was here just for a reason and a season', I mused as I looked at the sleepy sea. Its reflection on the water shone soothingly as I walked on, waiting for my destiny to unfold.

# 26

My destiny was about to unfold as he walked through the door with a small package in his hand. He usually got me flowers but since I whined about it becoming a tedious habit, he stopped. No woman in the world complained to her man about receiving flowers, but this was another tactic to antagonise him. My pattern had reared its hideous head as love's landscape had turned from light spring to a dark winter.

He said he loved me as he usually did and in return, I gave him a lukewarm response. He then handed me the gift, hoping to draw a smile on my otherwise unreadable face. I unwrapped it to find an emerald ring. He took in his hand, extending my finger to slip it on. He emerged oblivious to my indifference at first, but the joy on his face faded as soon as he sensed my ungratefulness. He reached his breaking point and leapt out of his skin.

"For God's sake, Richa. I've rearranged my entire world to accommodate our love and the transition has been far from smooth. But again, all hell breaks loose. I fail to understand why you're sabotaging what we've built at the risk of losing everything—my reputation, my wife and my world with my children. You gave me a taste of love that's turned sour by your recurrent tantrums. Seriously, Richa, I'm frazzled and I have to admit, the spell you cast on me initially is weakening by the minute. Your regular rage scares me," he said, throwing his hands up and down with anger.

He wore his rage like a misfit shirt and his face turned crimson as he paced before me. The mask was falling off as I stared admiringly at Frida Kahlo's original painting hung on the wall behind, while he strolled. Kahlo had been ahead of her times; fiercely independent and determined, despite her on-going health issues and here I was, unable to be true to myself in a world where morality was fast changing. He noticed me staring at her portrait and his voice softened, "You know, Richa, you're a hypocrite and I'm sorry now that I misread your character as being strong, independent and balanced. Do you know what Frida's most famous quote was? She said, 'I paint myself because I am so often alone and because I am the subject I know best.' She was a woman's woman who knew who she was and what she wanted."

"Good for her!" I retorted, "But why are you comparing me to a dead artist?"

"Because you're glaring at her while I struggle here in agony!" he shouted back.

"Well, I hate comparisons, so don't do it again," I yelled, turning to switch on the espresso machine in the kitchen.

"Stop evading me and answer my questions," he demanded, following me. "Seriously, Richa, have you ever been alone long enough to know who are you and what you most want, besides melodrama? Our greatest ally is the courage to be who we are, Richa and I'm convinced you score zero on that front."

"Well, many thanks. But can I please have my coffee in peace?"

"You're just allergic to any sensible advice, aren't you?" he asked, visibly enraged.

"No! No!" I repeated, frantically. "You misunderstood me. I'm allergic to you!" I yelled, instantly regretting my words.

"Ouch!" he exclaimed, receding against the wall.

"So, I'm right to be scared of you. The sky falls on me every time I walk into my apartment. While parking my car, I get palpations, unsure of the mood I'm going to find you in. You've killed the joy of being together and it's at the flick of a switch that your emotions rise and fall. You scream, suspect and accuse me of not loving you enough. Even the flowers have turned into a meaningless gift for you! I bought you an expensive ring and your expression is that of grave ingratitude. And now because you're *allergic* to me, I don't even know what to say to you."

I nodded my head aggressively, "No! I didn't mean to say that...I mean..."

"Gosh, Richa," he continued, disregarding my last statement. "You're an atom bomb—windows quiver, walls vibrate, sparks fly." He exploded and even in his angry state, he was beautifully boyish. "I love you but I'm glad I don't need to deal with your manic highs and melancholic lows. I'm not shallow, so I wasn't ever seeking an easy relationship, but there has to be some consistency," he sounded sad as he concluded the last sentence.

"I'm sorry, Sameer, I really am. I'm not allergic to you. I'm so stupid for saying that. My agenda wasn't to hurt you or your wife, my best friend. I, too, am exhausted by my tumultuous temperament. It's *all* my fault that our romance has turned tempestuous and I can't deal with it any longer. I'm screwed up beyond redemption, but you are the one who has given me the courage to be myself and for that, I will not apologise. I know you love me with every fibre of your soul but I can't love you the way you love me, Sameer."

"Of course, you can't, Richa. I got the same response from you several months ago. You showed weakness when you said you didn't mean to fall in love with me, but you insisted on wanting more. Do you even remember any of it?" he asked, glaring at me.

"You locked me in this waiting game where I sat and wondered if the sun was ever going to rise. I still foolishly try to capture your attention, but you're constantly texting someone and that infuriates me to no extent. I could not have imagined you being unfaithful to me, but my guess is that now you are!" he continued.

"Sameer, before the ugliness thickens, we need to call it quits. I'm sorry for hurting you with all my tantrums but we need an ending right now. Trust me, I'm doing us both a favour," I said, calmly.

"Stop dressing betrayal as a favour," he remarked as he sat himself down at the kitchen table, looking profoundly perturbed. I joined him in strained silence.

"Ordinarily babe, I'd tell you to leave immediately, but I'm willing to wait for you to confess your disloyalty," his hand reached out expectantly to invite me back into his life, but I sat before him—icy. He took his hand back, lowered his eyelids and spoke in a whisper, "I'm convinced now that you are in the corridor again, Richa, so for your sake, I pray that you know which room you are going in. But where on earth am I expected to go considering I love you and factually have no marriage except legally?" he enquired.

"I'm sorry that it has to be over without real evidence of what's gone amiss. I tried my utmost to hold us together," he said, pensively as he continued quietly. "Before, the mere thought of you brought a warm smile on my face, in anticipation of an evening of dinner, wine and lovemaking and now it's whine, whine, and only whine. *Please* come back to your old self and perhaps we can work things out. Richa, don't throw it all away. Maybe we are just one small adjustment away from being happy together and if it means legitimising this, I will find a way—for us."

"I'm sorry, but it's more complicated than that," I stated briefly.

"We all embody complications, Richa, but you take the cake!" he said with sadness I had never seen in him before. "But I still want to help you disentangle your webs. If only you give me a second chance," he pleaded.

Stress lines had formed around his forehead and his mouth was down sided. I had caused him more misery than I cared to admit and it was time to rectify matters.

"I don't know what to say, except *it is* time to take a drastic decision. I'm not seeing any man and that's just it. It's not about men!" I said, somewhat nonchalantly, hoping he'd understand. But instead, he seized my arm aggressively and said, "When I'm nice, I'm nice but when I'm nasty, Richa, my love can quickly turn into hate. Tell me the truth and don't let my efforts look futile. I've invested everything into this and I'm not going to take lies from you. You're so arrogantly trying to end it without a shred of remorse. How dare you be disloyal to me and what have I not given you that this man has?"

How horrible and harrowing relationships can sometimes turn between men and women. By the end of it, I knew I had to stand up for myself even if it meant standing out like a sore thumb. I was no longer going to forsake my own happiness by living an oversized lie that reduced my self-worth. Constantly trying to prove my worth was a result of not knowing my value. I had made enough mistakes by masking my truth and I knew that no matter what I had done, I deserved to feel good about myself now.

"Sameer, let go of my arm!" I said, stepping back. "I do love you and why shouldn't I? You're an amazing guy. I've invested my time and emotions into this and that too, at the cost of losing my best friend. But now life has put me on the spot and I'm doing what's right for *myself*," I justified. "You need to calm down and not take this as a brush off, but instead as an awakening for both of us. Every relationship teaches us something about ourselves in the end, so please don't get aggressive about this."

I looked at him, empathetically, knowing that someday he'd be a blur in my memory. Time had taught me the transient nature of people. The ones I had considered my heartbeat became people I no longer recognised or related to. They were out of context, but the lessons they had taught me always remained as a reminder.

"I've lied to myself for the sake of pleasing others and I've underplayed my intelligence and suppressed my natural tendencies. In the end, my relationship with you has rendered me courage to live my truth. You said, love can never be a crime and those very words finally set me free; though not free of the guilt of lying to my best friend who probably will never forgive me for betraying her. But you are too magnanimous not to, perhaps not today but someday, Sameer," I said, softly.

He stared at me, confused, and then trying hard to ease into his relaxed self, he said, "I don't know how I've freed you after you were 'imprisoned', so please speak to me in English, Hindi or Punjabi. Anything but Portuguese!" he said. Sameer's tone changed from anger to helplessness. He had been good to me, ticking all the boxes a woman seeks, but I didn't want it anymore.

"You're amazing and I know this sounds clichéd before someone is about to break up, but we'll remain friends. This is heart-wrenching and more so, because you're a good guy with pure intentions. With my previous men, it was much easier to break up. But the quicker we end this, the better it is."

"End what? This conversation?" he asked, hoping the whole thing was a joke. The nature of our relationship had changed over the past several weeks, but now I was calm.

"I went into each relationship for all its romantic notions, but more importantly, believing I'd learn something about the other person. But with you Sameer, I actually ended up learning about myself. The stamp of approval from others is just a notion."

He froze in his seat, his face in his hands. He sat like that for a few moments—motionless. He rose with a strained expression making him look tired and older than his years. Sadness added years to our face in the same way happiness took them away.

He stared at me sorrowfully—like a schoolboy who was about to lose a match—and said, "Don't break down walls needlessly, Richa. You are calm about calling it a day, but I'm not ready to watch you walk away. I've jeopardised everything to be with you."

"You truly are exceptional, Sameer, but I'm setting the final seal on this. I can't entirely explain the reason for sprinting away. Believe me, our relationship is under assault because of *me*. It's nothing to do with you, as you've been most caring, kind and encouraging."

I wasn't ready to reveal myself to him but he knew from my expression that it was irrevocably over. I was hurting his ego perhaps a tad more than his heart, but either ways, he saw that I had relaxed my grip on him.

He looked so defenceless that I hurried to where he stood and wrapped my arms around him. We were enfolded in each other's arms for a while and he rested his head on my shoulder. After a few moments, I pulled myself away from him.

"Now, I want to redeem myself by recovering Shivani's trust and a shred of my integrity. You may ultimately leave her, unless you get distracted again, but I can't be the one to rescue or destroy your marriage. Listen to your instincts in the same tone as good sense prevailed in me to salvage my truth. Please don't let any of this hurt your pride because Sameer, out of all your presents, you've bestowed on me the most priceless one—the gift of truth. It's been better than anything that was ornately wrapped," I stated, bravely, gazing into his eyes. He needed the same reassurance I did—that I was invaluable irrespective of my sexuality. We contributed significantly by our goodness, not our sexual preferences.

"Someday, you will know my reason for leaving, as this city's gossip never sleeps!" I said, decisively.

"You're so skilled at brushing off your men like specks of dust. All your men have been on the rebound and I suppose,

I was too. But I won't let the good times slip away from my memory so carelessly and if ever you change your mind, you know where I am and you better have a darn good reason for leaving me," he said, good-humouredly with hope set in his eyes.

"Sameer!" I whispered, "I'm quitting us because there's dignity in my bones. I just need you to let go of the aspersions and to accept my decision with grace. *Please*," I pleaded.

"Okay. So, now that we're through, will you tell my wife about us?" he asked, remorsefully.

"No, I won't. Though she already suspects it, but I've not confirmed it to her and she's…."

"She's having an affair and even though I'm not supposed to know about it, her aura has changed since she's been out and about? Yes, I know," he said. "No one can fool anyone forever, Richa."

I looked at him, aghast. "I had no idea you knew, but she also needed to distract herself from your rejection. If you still love the mother of your children, then navigate her back into your arms. We all make mistakes, but given a chance, we can redeem ourselves. Being with the same person for years can make you take each other for granted. But after treading on them, we usually arrive at the realisation that the place we were in was no better or worse. Do you want her back?" I asked.

"And again be a rebound in her life?" he questioned.

"A rebound?" I asked, puzzled.

"I don't want to get into details but she put a dent in our marriage before I did. In one of the Christmas Eve parties we threw, she got too drunk and made a fool out of both herself and me. I found her flirting with one of my friends, and that too, in front of all our guests. Everyone was staring, and as for me, I was heartbroken. I never knew she detested me so much. Anyway, at that moment, it was over for me and since then, I philandered too. I never exchanged a word again with my friend and hardly talked to her either," he said, sadly.

My mouth was agape and suddenly I felt emptiness in the pit of my stomach.

My best friend had lied to me.

I had turned into many unanticipated corners but this had to be the most trying one.

Four hours later, a raw cold voice called me and asked me to meet her at the Atrium lounge in Bandra.

# 27

A raw cold wind blew outside. Richa's complexion was as pale as Mumbai's landscape at this time of the year except unlike her, Mumbai was lit with Christmas trimmings. Observing her now, it felt like her beauty had been passing through. She never took it for granted and yet, it had clearly pulled its plug from her life. Tell-tale signs of age appeared on her neck and brow.

I had never believed I'd meet her face-to-face. I assumed I would simply wait till her image paled into insignificance, but today, I wanted to watch her remove her mask of deception in front of me.

"Skip the prologue, Richa, and tell me how you plotted getting my husband into bed. Spare me the seductive tactics you employed and focus on what prompted you to do something so stupid. Were you seriously expecting a happy ending to this soap opera?" I yelled without punctuation.

"Of all the men in this city that you've had and probably are yet to have, could you not spare Sameer?" I asked, acridly as she gave me her nervous monosyllabic replies. Her eyes were lowered to the floor. Clearly, not having the nerve to refute me, she permitted me to vent. It was my prerogative to malign her with immeasurable vigour as she, my best friend, had stabbed me in the back. All along, I had confided in her and she had taken advantage of my vulnerability.

"Sorry to be the bearer of bad news, but I absolutely abhor you. The mere sight of you nauseates me and after today, I'm breaking all ties with you. Your liaison with my husband is a sign of a disordered mind. Sleeping with anything with pots of money is an instinct for you, but choosing Sameer is repulsive," I remarked, implacably.

I was seething with rage and she was visibly disturbed, but I couldn't blame her enough. Her lame excuse of her behavioural patterns wasn't good enough. If she was aware of her compulsive disorders, then why in God's name didn't she seek treatment instead of causing collateral damage in people's lives?

She looked like she was about to collapse, but she remained dry-eyed and sat slouched with her head lowered. She failed in her attempt to hold herself together and appeared sorry, but I wasn't transferring my compassion to her.

"It was sheer stupidity to go for a temporary relationship over a permanent friendship. I hope you live with this blame and shame for as long as your heart beats. I won't make a meal of this meeting, as you don't deserve even a morsel of my time. I'm ashamed to admit that you're the woman I loved and whom I believed to be different, but you turned out to be a shambolic slut. Even though I wasn't warming up his bed anymore, it was none of your business to rectify matters on that front!" I yelled, obscenely.

The waiter walked up to our table and asked us if we'd like our usual cappuccino with toasties. I looked at him, actually talking to her, "No coffee today, and from now on, I won't be taking sugar either. I don't want to be reminded of someone I don't care to be acquainted with," I said, bitterly.

What was worse than her knowing about my affair was that she was using that to feel better about sleeping with Sameer. I knew Richa well and the guilt she felt was probably melting down each time she reminded herself of my relationship with Raman. We both had our justifications for engaging in activities that we weren't supposed to. The human mind had a remarkable mechanism that gave it permission to behave in an illegitimate manner and then ease its conscience by convincing itself that it was justifiable.

I regretted having shared the tears and tantrums of my marriage with her. She listened to my grumbles and then presented him a sympathetic ear before offering him her carefully crafted body and her twisted mind. I momentarily paused to ponder if they were in love, but then wasn't it easy to give someone your heart outside your marriage anyway?

By the end of it, I was sure Sameer wouldn't forsake me for Richa because he was aware that she had the reputation of a dark horse and wouldn't make the sacrifices I had made as a wife. She was perfect as any man's mistress, nothing more. It infuriated me that she tried taking my place, particularly after knowing that mine was so precarious.

"I don't need a crystal ball to predict that you won't ever forgive me. Karma will play out and we'll all pay for our lack of judgement. Be it you, me, Sameer or Raman, no one is flawless," she said, sharply with measured meanness and at this point, I saw that she could barely breathe as the strain settled on her exhausted face. He hair had limpness instead of their customary bounce and her eyes were sallow. But she appeared angry and that didn't add up.

"What are you getting so angry about? Isn't it me who needs to point fingers at you?" I said.

"Look, Shivani, I don't want to dig out your dead liaisons but you must stop casting mean aspersions. I, for one, have changed and so have you and we are in a space that allows us to make our own choices. Whatever I say won't redeem our characters but it will give clarity on our road ahead," she said, frustrated but firmly, as she gave me a piercing glare.

"I was a broken spirit and I'm not trying to redeem myself from all my unforgiveable transgressions. But it's important for you to know that I broke off with him for someone I deeply love and always have."

"So, now you want my blessings?" I asked, sarcastically.

"Of course not, but you and I both know that even you are not guilt free."

"Ah! So you're going to shoot me with the Raman ammunition just so that you can ease your guilt. I knew this was your tactic to make yourself feel better for bedding my husband. Only broken spirits cheat and all three of us have, but you seemed to have plotted against me. I won't forgive you, I just can't. I'm not so noble and no matter how hard you try, you can never salvage our friendship. Sameer and I may or may not work, depending on my decision. But you and I end here. I'm clear about that," I stated, confidently.

"Raman's been the architect of your inner dignity and he's built your self-confidence to live life on your own terms, finally. And as enraged as you may be, you will view my life from a fairer perspective once you have the complete picture," she said, calmer than before.

"What's that got to do with anything? If you were so desperate to get laid, you should've contacted one of your thousands of exes who would have gladly obliged you," I yelled with anger bursting out of my skin and as more venom spilled out of me, the more strained her expression became as she slouched back on her chair, crestfallen. She averted her gaze as she continued to internalise my slander. She was mute now, but with a self-assuredness I had never observed in her. I expected her to break down heart-wrenchingly but she sat without a speck of sadness.

"You have done enough disservice to yourself by sleeping around indiscriminately—I beg your pardon—I mean discriminately, with loaded married men who desperately need validation from bimbos like yourself. I hoped to God you had turned over a new leaf but I suppose, you're doomed, just like our friendship," I kept yelling.

Her lips quivered as she assembled her pride and gathered her body to sit straight, to boldly glance at me. I didn't see hurt in her eyes as she spoke with a plain voice.

"For what it's worth, Shivani, I'm remorseful and that's the reason I'm here. As I see it, both our worlds needed to cave in before we could rebuild it with dignity. I apologise profusely, but I'm sure now that I needed to blow out a few fires first before arriving at my truth. It was through him I met myself, so I won't apologise for my awakening to you, Sameer or my deceased mother. I've travelled exponentially and in the end, Sameer was a phase I needed," she stated in a poised tone.

"A phase? Acne or eczema is a phase, not sleeping with your best friend's husband, so cut the cryptic crap. I never imagined you to kill my trust and as women, we were intimate with each other, even while you were with him. How deceptive can one be, Richa? Now, I'm convinced you have a pathological disorder," I cried with a deep disdain in my tone.

Our squabbling continued as the tone of our voices raised and lowered intermittently.

"I don't know if Sameer and you slept together by accident or by design, but I don't care. You are excluded from my life and I'll make sure Sameer too is," I said in a profoundly hurt tone, before rising from my seat and glaring at her.

"I *am* sorry, Shivani, it's complicated and I can't convey the nuances of my impulsive decision to sleep with your husband," she said, apologising again.

"I'm rapidly running out of patience, so goodbye and *please*, don't ever get in touch. Ma was right, you're an accident waiting to happen. But I defended you every time. She warned me about your unscrupulous character, always stating that you are bad news. That's the obnoxious truth."

# 28

The truth, irrespective of how obnoxious, needed to be told. I braced myself for an icy response and the voice at the back of my head cautioned me, making me resist contacting her. The last time we met, there had been a sharp gust of frosty air as she had left and following that, there was no mention of her.

I presumed she had her own personal war to triumph over and so, I stayed away. Understandably, she refused to take my call, so after a considerable punctuation, I emailed her, writing about my feelings towards her and apologised profusely for hurting her. I didn't expect her to grasp my sensibilities, but I sent it anyway.

"Each time I looked in the mirror, the verdict was always the same, guilty. I looked thrice my age. From five feet seven inches tall, I'd been reduced to nothing. Something vital was taken away from me in my very first marriage and since then, I fed that emptiness with men who failed to satiate it.

"Since my teenage phase, my mother insisted that I behaved *normal*, particularly after I proclaimed my sexuality to her. She reacted in the most abnormal way—by violently threatening to abandon me and disown me from the family inheritance.

Words like 'You'll be *cured* once you get married' rolled off my mother's tongue and she acted like homosexuality was a disease I'd contracted. Through religion and regular doses of homeopathic medicine, my mother convinced herself that I had indeed been *cured*.

Papa passed away before my teens and being the eldest, my mother instilled in me the need to act *responsibly*. Raising my brother and me, single-handed, brought with it pressures that often made her physically sick. I felt deep sympathy for her but at the same time I tried to dismiss my own natural instincts. I was 16 and had nowhere to go, the only option I had was to please her. I eventually began dating men and even married at a young age to prove that I was *normal*.

My mother's firm dismissal of my real nature compelled me to overstay in a marriage that was over at its onset and subsequent to its breakdown, she implored me to remarry for the sake of monetary support for my son. I was caught in a vicious cycle, and when I was pregnant with my daughter, I understood that I couldn't ever be a typical wife. My second marriage became a copy-and-paste scenario and it ended like my first, falling flat on its face. Life was far from a fairy tale with many desperate beginnings and dejected endings. I married the wrong gender twice, but my mom urged me to save face than to face the truth that would've liberated us both.

Before my second marriage, I decided to do something for myself and explored a bit on my own. That was when I met Rachel, an American, who became my friend first and later my lover. She accepted my son as her own. She was also most companionable and sat well with my life as naturally as breathing, but mom's suspicions reared its hideous head. One night, out of nowhere, when I was staying with her for a while due to lack of funds, she sneaked into my bedroom to check my mobile phone.

I had made a decision to remain honest to myself, but when I got caught with Rachel, she threw me out of the house. She ruthlessly remarked that I was a *criminal* and needing locking up in a cage.

She handed me a life sentence of resentment, shame and guilt. She repeatedly called me *abnormal* and I was treated like an *outcaste*. Her reaction was outrageous, imprinting permanent scars on my psyche. I had no one of my own, so a week later, I returned with the promise of no longer being *irresponsible*.

I pledged on being a decisive mother to my son and a reliable daughter to her, enabling her at the same time to keep up appearances. I had been gripped by the fear of emotional and financial abandonment. Bizarrely, she embraced my promiscuity and yet, she refused to accept my loyalty to the one woman I deeply loved.

Post my second divorce, I had sufficient alimony to support my children along with an apartment that afforded me an independent lifestyle. Although, I had freedom from my mother's dominance, I was under the lock and key of her conditioning.

Each time my heart melted for a girl, I would hear my mom's voice. I took extreme measures to keep my calm, except subconsciously, I became impoverished. I feared getting caught by her and because I was forcing my sexuality, I became non-committal. I, consequently, gravitated towards wealthy, unavailable men who maintained a safe emotional distance from me. They were *always* married and *always* wealthy. Sexuality can sometimes be fluid, so sleeping with men was relatively easier, especially since it meant not giving them my soul. My inner turmoil was often vented out on my men who tolerated me in exchange for the sex and I, for the lifestyle they provided me.

Wrong relationships became an addiction and I found myself in one toxic relationship after another. None of the men were in line with my expectations and they couldn't be, since the man of my dreams, was not a man at all. In the end, I found excuses to fire them out of my life. I needed someone to blame and it was usually them.

My routine was commonplace, dreary and banal, but I let things ride until you walked into my life. I was attracted to you instantly and initially, it was because you resembled Rachel—the woman I had given my heart to and had never forgotten. She had been expelled from my life with ruthless force, but had remained in my soul. I felt an affinity and instantly wanted to curl you in my embrace, before I engulfed you in my soul. You irradiated strength of spirit and there was a sense of nobility in the way you endured the sadness in your marriage. Hence, I was drawn to you for more reasons than physical. Love is always deeper than that and I began suspecting my feelings when I longed to be with you, always. I wanted you, but you were married and very evidently *straight*. I ensured meeting you every other day and in a darker sense, I was glad your marriage was failing as it kept my heart beating. But when you met Raman and began having a rollicking time, a deep sense of insecurity emerged. I often sat in my kitchen with a mug of coffee, pining for you—I was hurting.

I missed you and in a sense, Sameer distracted me. In all this, there were many complex threads that compelled me to act against accepted ethics. I was driven by my subconscious, Sameer was nothing more to me than a pattern I was ensnared in. But it didn't seem that wrong at that time because he became a friend first. We were so comfortable with each other that I even thought my mom's prayers had been answered. But later, I realised it was another pattern, but he did help in finally bringing me home to myself. It was Sameer who taught me that love wasn't a crime.

We are all here to salvage each other. Just as your Ma protected you, Sameer rescued me, Raman liberated you and ultimately, we all awakened each other. But you must be given the complete picture, before you judge me. The day I met Sameer for coffee, I did bring up the subject of divorce as you had advised me to and he agreed there was nothing to hold on to anymore, but owing to family obligations, he was riding it out.

He said he would take the lion's share of the business and personal assets to leave you high and dry. He'd also fight tooth and nail for the custody of the children, since they were minors. I advised him to be just and judicious and not hurt you since you meant the world to me. He then said he'd do anything to save face from society, even if it meant holding on to a collapsed marriage. He would always gaze in my direction with intense interest and later relayed that our friendship lifted his misery. The truth is he was never on my 'to do' list, but before long, my friendship with him transformed into an illicit affair.

We were reasonably happy until one day I went to the gym and lo and behold, I met my old flame there, Jasmine. She and I secretly went on a date in my early days of seeing Sameer and it was when I met her again that it transformed into a torrid affair. She doted on my children as much as I loved her daughter. My fluttering mind arrived at a place of tranquillity and she became the wind behind my soul. After having been on both sides of the pond, I realised Jasmine was a far more natural fit than Sameer or any man. I felt it was time to pull myself out of the grey zone that women of *my kind* are stuck in and Jasmine prepared me to move into the next phase of life—to live with astonishing clarity. She too had her challenges as a lesbian in her past and now walked through life with pride. She was strong and convinced me  we could never be wrong in doing the right thing. I love her, Shivani, without any regret and reservation.

Criminalising me for my sexuality was absolutely wrong and I'm now ready to stand tall before those who had me on my knees. I was fond of men but they didn't float my boat like women did and for this, my mom treated me with continuous contempt. It was hard, Shivani, to be scrutinised by hidden cameras all my life. You always commented on how beautiful I was, but on the contrary, I always felt ugly because of the way my mom had made me feel.

There is no justification for me lying to you. With increasing nonchalance, I lied, giving little thought to the consequences. My relationship with Sameer seems so microscopically minute now compared to the love I have for you. Jasmine is my partner and the love of my life. In fact, it was her who prompted me to write to you.

Society's attitude towards women like me has not altered radically, so taking a courageous stance was a challenge. Shivani, my life is no longer obscure, as I have set the final seal on my sexual preference. Now, I've come to the end of the rope and I'm going to hold on. I *am* adamant to return to life that finally feels *normal* and I've no *shame* in feeling this way as I'm convinced I'm not a *criminal*. My past blunders have given me a chance to reinvent myself; bringing to light that I must come out with the truth to liberate myself because homosexuals, too, are people of God. I don't hear her condemning voice lurking in the shadows of my life anymore. I have taken an oath to myself to always be happy, honest and free from the phantoms of my past so that I can accept who I am, without reservations.

I don't need societal validation. I'm on my own side now and I'm proud to report that I hold the reins of my life. I know somewhere in your enraged heart, you too will be proud of me as you can't possibly stop caring.

With great pride, I break to you that I'm working as a wellness consultant as beauty and health have always been my forte and next year, Jasmine and I fly to Thailand to engage in therapies to enhance our knowledge. She shares my interest and we will collaborate to build our own business.

With all my faults, I hope you can find it in your heart to forgive me, it takes a strong person to say sorry and even a stronger one to forgive. Love lives on a hope that is ridiculous at times, but never frivolous. I don't want to fight for a spot in your life, but I do hope you will understand the worth of this friendship and make space for me, no matter how small.

I believed this was going to be a story with no ending, but now I know it will be a happy one because I have liberated myself and nothing else matters. I hastened towards this moment of truth because I couldn't risk losing you, so I couldn't afford the luxury of waiting anymore. I was afraid that if you left for good, what would remain of my life? You will understand my anxiety stemmed from my state of delirium, and now that the truth stands before you, I hope you can see me in a new light and pardon me for my past transgressions.

Just to conclude about Sameer, I feel you need to look at him with honest eyes and decide if he needs to walk with you in your twilight years. Sometimes the things we substantially lose in a relationship can't be found and so it's wiser to let it go and seek something greater for ourselves. In that context, it takes a strong person to walk away. Becoming friends with the father of your children once you legally separate from him also becomes a possibility as you come to a place of harmony.

He told me his masculine pride was hurt when he discovered your affair, but more importantly, it awakened him to his very own mistakes that led you astray. The mess in our lives is relevant as it is up to us to what we want to retain and remove. I'm inordinately proud of you for stepping out of your comfort zone with Raman and for him mentoring you in finding yourself. Just remember that in the end, it's about being true to yourself. If you do walk back into your marriage, you will again lose your dignity as even Sameer signed off from his ties with you a long time ago.

I cannot clean my slate but I'm proud I've awakened from my somnambulist state. There is no rush for your response, as I don't expect an instant one, anyway, but, I will be waiting with bated breath. I hope to God that it's not too ridiculous to warrant a response from you after all I have said and done.

I can't phrase it better, Shivani, but I do miss you and for what it's worth, I love you very much and by losing you, I don't want to add another heart-wrenching failure to my list. I miss your pale brown eyes that light up at the mere mention of dessert and an overload of sugar in our cappuccino. I was wondering if I deserved to have your company one more time, even if it's the last. I promise to keep it platonic!

I know I was wrong and out of character, but I *am* sitting on the edge of my seat awaiting a reaction from you. A slap would also be fine as I know I deserve it."

Pacing towards my apartment window I noticed my reflection. People always complimented on how beautiful I was and on seeing my reflection today, I believed them for the first time.

I stared out admirably at the sea. I mused on the complex personality of the city that resembled my own. Dawn was breaking over the seafront and my blurry eyes followed people walking besides the sea. Each was trying to iron out the wrinkles in their lives caused by their behaviour and karmic patterns. Each one of us was ensnared either in worry or fear and that is how, we were held captive.

Jasmine, my newfound joie de vivre, wrapped her arms around my waist as she rested her head on my back. I rested my hands on hers as I slanted my head and exhaled. I was home.

I had blossomed and was glad to have finally woken up as the gloom looming over me had dispelled.

# 29

I woke up with a sense of gloom looming over me. The harsh winds receded, but there was an enduring chill that permeated me. A downpour dampened my spirits.

"Stop thinking!" he commanded as if he was following the whirlwind of thoughts in my head. "Concentrate on me. Remember, I'm the architect of your happiness and I'm here to fill you up in a way that no one else ever has," he said in a voice that should've built my appetite for him, but it didn't.

After settling my head back on the pillow, I informed him of an art show being held in the city. I wanted to spend the evening with him as an expression of my gratitude and with his copious knowledge, the evening was likely to turn into a stimulating one. Besides, I needed something creative to elevate my spirits that had been crushed by my loved ones— my husband and my best friend.

Relationships had turned unreliable in these precarious times and trust was as delicate as the cloud in the sky. The weather forecast on my smartphone claimed a clear dry day, but it wasn't. They didn't get it right and I no longer relied on them, just as I wouldn't rely on those making a claim about speaking the truth. I verified everything and until I was convinced, I didn't commit to anything or anyone. Life had smartened me up and in that respect, I was grateful for the hard knocks that toughened me.

"Shivani, I don't enjoy art shows and I sincerely hope that you can accept that. I was never known for my memory, but perhaps you can stimulate it by reminding me what else excites you. It needs to be indoor, under covers and private," he teased, hoping to arouse me.

I nodded nonchalantly because today I needed more than the confines of a bedroom. "You know, I'm enchanted by your ingenuity and your instinctive ways of pleasing me in bed and motivating me in office. I need to talk, but not between the sheets!"

"What is it?" he asked dropping his husky tone and adopting an earnest one. "Alright. Since I've entered your world to support you in every way possible, how about we go downstairs to the coffee shop?"

"Yes! Yes!" I replied, anxiously. "Let's go. I just need to get out of here."

A deep angst filled me as the realisation about the dynamics of my marriage altering dawned upon me. On the other hand, the intimacy between Raman and me had thawed and our friendship had been redefined. I shared my soul's story with him now because I knew he was my greatest guide.

"You're intensely troubled, Shivani, so shoot! Tell me what's wrong," he commanded as he held my hand across the table.

"My path crossed Sameer's in the garden where he was teaching our children golf strokes which he does regularly."

"Oops! So is that a felony?" he asked, raising a brow.

"I really need you to be serious, Raman. I'm very disturbed and I need to share this with you."

"I'm all ears."

"I'm in touch with a lawyer and I've filed for divorce. I want the complete custody of our children and I want a fair alimony," I stated, impassively.

"Woa! The woman has finally flexed her muscles. Bravo!"

"I yielded to him at every turn to let him win but the table has turned and it's him who will be giving in to me now. I'm not speaking from a place of ego, but self-respect. I just know my worth now and I'm so ready to spread my wings."

"Shivani, the cold war between you and Sameer will be over once you both amicably separate, but then why do you look so anxious? Isn't relief the emotion you're meant to be feeling?" he asked.

I shared my concern about my children and relayed the episodes between Sameer and Richa, along with her email that entailed her revelations and confessions. Raman was visibly baffled.

"Did Richa tell you that? It's kind of bewildering and it doesn't add up."

"She slept with my husband and knowing her, she probably made a shit load of money from him," I said.

"Look, if you read too much into this, you're bound to find things that don't even exist. The mind concocts stories that can ultimately destroy the soul, so please don't ponder on the negative," he commented. "Sometimes we need to see things for what they are. Why speculate about their affair? And why would you even care?" he asked.

"She slept with my husband. I just can't get over it."

"Did I just speak to you in Mandarin? You need to get over the past and plan ahead. You've filed for divorce, so he's not your husband unless you want him to be."

Raman's voice faded into the background as my mind wandered back to Richa's email. I was in state of shock and I wished she hadn't slept with Sameer. My heart ached as I reflected on her betrayal and I fleetingly mused on the pet name he must've had for her, given his love for abbreviations. Mine in the early days was R&B, raunchy and beautiful. I felt enraged at her audacity to betray her best friend.

I dismissed them both from my head as I focused on ending one chapter, only to begin a fresh one with renewed hope. I snapped myself out of my reverie, back to Raman. We discussed my plans of separation like it was a project and he spoke at length about the pitfalls and gains of starting over. He explained the importance of breaking the news to the children first since they were my prime concern.

The level of excitement I suddenly felt on moving on outmoded my fury towards Richa. My enquiry into their affair descended into disinterest. I wasn't engrossed in either of them anymore as I looked to my future, without them taking the lead this time. Even Raman's friendship would support me till a certain point and then, I would need to loosen the grip on my dependency.

"For the coming months and perhaps years, you won't be able to afford the luxury of wavering from your goals. You have started your business, but it's not going to be a joy ride. Believe in yourself. You're amazing. If I simply ran into you, then believe me, I would've fallen for you," he said in his customary charismatic tone.

"I'm not flattering you because I really don't need to. Besides, once your career takes off well, we won't need to meet as much. You won't need me anymore."

He read my mind, again.

"It's not that I'm ungrateful or as if I want all or nothing but…" I began.

"But nothing, Shivani!" he said as his tone softened, "I already know where you're taking this and I'm fine with it because it's been an incredible experience knowing you and in the end, that's precisely what life is—an accumulation of experiences that encourage us to evolve and to finally arrive home to our own truth. So, there are no hard feelings between us as I was never attached and as far as desires are concerned, their nature is to soften over time. But what needs to be sustained is what we learn from our relationships. In your case, your children and perhaps your friendship with Richa are very important to you. Don't lose interest in them, Shivani, because once lost, they can never be recovered. I know you're rightfully angry, but perhaps it would be wise to take into account the struggles she must've encountered as well.

"You're now a strong and independent woman and I've watched you evolve. I deliberately held back from falling in love with you but I know you fell for me for a while there," he said, light-heartedly as he switched from being a lover to a concerned friend. "I hope I haven't hurt you as that was never my intention, but I was never in love with you. I'm in love with my work and that's precisely what sustains me. I suggest you too build a meaningful life for yourself.

"And most importantly, never burn the bridges that you've built over the years for your children. It's not fair on them. And with time, they would know which relationships are worth keeping. Don't ever take their dad away from them. It's a crime to do so," he said, remorseful. His eyes were wet.

I gazed at him warmly at the realisation that he had been deprived of his fatherhood.

"When?"

"A long time ago and my son is a teenager now, but we are not in touch. His mother took him away and since then, I've dug my head into building spaces for people because I myself couldn't keep my own home from collapsing," he said with tears in his eyes.

"Anyway, you have all the resources you need, so capitalise on that. Now that you're in a position of strength you need to start afresh with your Ma. Just love her, it's that simple," he concluded and I placed my hand on his.

"Life is as complicated as we make it, Shivani. That is the reason we both need to step down. I'm just a call away whenever you need a friend—in bed or otherwise," he said in a humorous tone.

"You're a clown and I love you. I mean, now, as a friend," I said.

And as I said it, I saw the look in his eyes. It spoke volumes about the way he actually felt for me. I skipped a heartbeat as I realised the intensity of his gaze.

"Don't worry, my feelings are in check," he said with a flickering smile on his lips and then he rose from his chair to sit next to me. "I want to feel your warmth one last time," he said as he inched towards me to clasp me in his warm embrace. "I learnt very early in life the most invaluable truth of all, we have a responsibility to our loved ones, but more importantly, we owe it to ourselves. I would never sabotage your chance to find yourself and in the same breath, I will live by our most beautiful memories," he said, summoning a smile and yet, the pain was more palpable than his embrace.

Listening to him, I realised I had become attached to him and it had taken courage to step back and view my life's situation from a practical stance. I began respecting Ma on many accounts but especially for awakening each one of us to our truths. I was still sad for not being able to share my life with the one friend that mattered the most to me. She had receded into the past but wasn't out of context as she often sprung to mind, mostly out of anger, but also between moments over coffee and snacks. Raman had clearly fallen for me and so had I. He was fiercely ambitious and he taught me to be the same and I could allow nothing to come in the way of my goals now, especially a relationship.

The pleasure of the last several months spent with Raman paled into insignificance as she parked herself in the centre of my brain. She wasn't out of the woods just yet and why in God's name should she be? She slept with my husband when all the while, she yearned to sleep with me. What a chaotic and confused mind she had! And the only place she found refuge was in my husband's bed? I couldn't believe it.

These thoughts prompted me to revert to her email for the umpteenth time. It was heart-wrenching to an objective reader, but since I played centre stage in her story, it was as distasteful as the sushi rolls I attempted to make for my children the other week. They said I hadn't prepared them properly. The damage, it seemed, was irrevocable, as I never did try my hand at anything remotely different. The impact of their repulsion illustrated the importance of letting go and never trying again. If only life was that simple. Perhaps, the memory of them teaching me to let go of things that left a bad taste reared its head for a reason.

The rain spattered severely against the window and didn't appear to be easing off anytime soon. I felt tired and closed my eyes as I wallowed in self-pity and then I re-read her email, dialled her number and instantly decided not to allow it to ring through. The lesson of forgiveness was, after all, the hardest one and in my case, there were two individuals my soul needed to absolve.

If Richa and I were meant to be, then it was solely my call as she had made her move already. I felt depressed thinking of her and how desperately I wanted her back in my life. The love-hate relationship tipped the scales against me so that I could arrive at an educated decision. I assumed the best in her and sought her positive intentions despite the pain she had caused. We were both walking in our truth and purpose after having stepped out of the matrix.

The greatest realisation for me was that no one could 'make me' feel less about myself because I knew my worth and had learned to respect myself despite my mistakes.

# 30

She was worth every ounce of my energy and I respected the fact she was willing to give our friendship another chance despite my mistakes.

We had both come a long way and in a deeper sense, we were both woven together.

"I punched your number several times, only to disconnect it. I even read your email over and over again. I haven't deleted it as I do not intend to delete you from my life."

I smiled, relieved.

"Certain people can't be erased from our minds, but that doesn't mean I'm noble enough to forgive those who've hurt me," she added.

"I'm sorry," I said, closing my eyes—but my heart was open to her.

"My anger hasn't abated but I need to forgive you because I know it's not good for me to hold on to so much bitterness. Your every misjudgement has caused harm to our friendship. I want to start afresh. It will be easy because I anyway feel like I don't know you anymore than you know the new version of me."

"Don't we know each other well enough?" I enquired.

"The truth is I was acquainted with a different version of you, the one that was hiding away her real self in all her secrets. So, in that light, I'll be meeting you for the very first time."

I nodded as I responded, "Yes, that can't be denied. So, are we meeting today for our very first cappuccino together? I would love to see the new you. Oh, also, are you still with Raman?"

"No, but he fell for me and as flattering as that may have been, he encouraged me to move on and I understood his love for his work. We will always remain good friends. And who knows better than you that relationships are our greatest teachers because it's through them that we discover the most about ourselves."

I was keen to meet my new confident friend whom I had loved very much and even though Jasmine had taken centre stage in my world now, I needed to see Shivani, even if it meant for the last time.

"Understanding the reasons you behaved the way you did doesn't necessarily mean I'm in agreement with it, but I do empathise with you in some ways. The commonality we share is our mothers," she said.

"But, Shivani, I empathise with our mothers now as I've understood that only hurt people hurt others. I think I'm beginning to forgive her. Time has done that to me," I said in a calm voice.

"Yes, you're right. I have also discovered a side of Ma that I never knew existed. I know it mustn't have been easy to admit the disturbing disclosures you made in your email so for that you have my undying respect, Richa. And yes, I am ready for that cappuccino, except I want pizza first. I'm done with watching what I eat all the time because all these years I didn't realise it's not about what we eat, but what eats us. I'm so much lighter letting go of my marital blues," she joked.

"Are you divorced?" I found myself asking, as if on impulse.

"I've quit the one and only career I knew all my life—my marriage. I'm now the managing director of my ever-growing business in wellness and organic lifestyle," she announced, proudly.

"Oh my! And do I have the liberty of asking you what exactly it was that you visualised that day, Shivani? The time we were in our customary café and I had asked you to close your eyes to envision your ideal life," I finally asked what had been bothering me for months.

"Well, I saw that I was travelling for work, Business Class, if I may add," and as she said that, I heard her giggle for the first time since our conversation had started and I felt a sigh of relief, being reacquainted with her light-hearted nature. "And I'm a successful entrepreneur working ardently towards receiving an award—that is precisely what I visualised that day, Richa."

"One more thing I've learnt is that homosexuality isn't a disability. I remember how I reacted that day when you were talking about your friend and I realised it was people like me who sentenced you to a life of self-denial. I've lived in self-denial too but now the skies above have opened up and we're free to breathe our own air."

"It's not your fault. I don't blame you one bit. Anyway, now that we are past that, it's time for a fresh start. Pizza it is then," I said.

"See you in an hour at the café. Order their signature pizza," she laughed.

At the café, we met with a fresh pair of eyes. As we sat and ordered the pizza, we chatted more until it arrived. We laughed as we shared our gains, losses and it was then that she held my hand across the table and told me how much she loved me.

"Thank you, Richa, for your candid confession and the courage you showed. For this, you are a true woman. I am warmed by your love and as I said, love is love, be it heterosexual or homosexual. And by the way, you are glowing," Shivani said.

"I guess, love is a rich and powerful anti-oxidant. Jasmine makes me…"

Before I could complete her sentence, Jasmine walked in, looking as dashing as ever. I skipped a heartbeat as my gaze settled on her and Shivani turned her head to follow my eyes.

Jasmine kissed me on my lips, extended her hand to greet Shivani and sat next to me—in our customary café.

# EPILOGUE

Ma had once stated, "Shivani, we are all products of time so no one should judge the other, no matter how deplorable or intolerable their behaviour seems. And of course, we perceive the other only through our limited understanding."

Between Richa, Sameer, Ma and me, we were all able to reform ourselves and on shining our light, our past paled into insignificance.

In the end, we're remembered only for the good we do. People forget injuries once kindness takes over. Richa's *being* preceded her *doing* because in the end, it is who we are that matters—she, with her unrelenting courage, tore through concrete to come out of the closet.

Eventually, I realised, it wasn't straight people who reduced homosexuals, men who curbed women, or the rich who oppressed the poor. It was the individuals' own character and lack of courage to be one with their truth that restricted them. I was deeply unfulfilled, so I blamed Ma and Sameer for my unhappiness. Richa's mom, on the other hand, damaged her daughter's morale, compelling her to believe she was 'God's unloved child.' Richa was a caring individual with a heart of gold and yet, she was classified as a criminal.

All this while, I admired Richa to be a seeker while I was hiding behind my Ma's shadow, but along the journey, I realised that by hiding behind Raman, I began seeking my own truth. Richa was the one who came out of her hiding, eventually, to seek her light. All her life she was expected to place a round peg into a square hole and by the end of it, she felt frustrated and isolated.

In our lives, we have limited time but the rewards can be limitless, provided we are encouraged to unleash our potential.

I, with Raman's support went on to win an entrepreneur award and my children applauded my success as I walked tall.

I couldn't condone Richa for sleeping with Sameer, it was a tough one to absolve, but I embraced her for her courage and encouraged her to accept her individuality. All in all, I was proud of my friend for standing up and believing in herself. We can never be what others are but we can certainly be the best versions of ourselves. We weren't born to emulate others, but were meant to be inspired by them. As Raman said, it is important for every individual to bring out their unique attributes and to hone their skills. The truth of who we are is beyond definition, tradition and image and perhaps, I needed to rise above all three to accept and love Richa the way nature intended. I learnt the lesson of self-love that enabled me to find my balance. In the end, all of Richa's affairs had led her to have the most meaningful affair—with herself—and eventually, a lasting marriage with Jasmine that took place in Vegas.

I was beside her throughout.

*Our deepest fear is not that we are inadequate. Our deepest fear is that we are powerful beyond measure. It is our light, not our darkness, that most frightens us. We ask ourselves, who am I to be brilliant, gorgeous, talented and fabulous?*

*Actually, who are you not to be?*

*You are a child of God. Your playing small doesn't serve the world. There's nothing enlightened about shrinking so that other people won't feel insecure around you. We were born to make and manifest the glory of God that is within us. It's not just in some of us; it's in everyone. And as we let our own light shine, we unconsciously give other people permission to do the same. As we are liberated from our own fear, our presence automatically liberates others.*

Marianne Williamson

# ACKNOWLEDGEMENTS

The wind beneath my wings and the unmistakable reason for sailing through rain and shine are my daughters who are my best friends and mentors.

Thank you, Anishka, for your unfettered support and Sonakshi, for your guidance. I wouldn't have been able to write this without your insights and ideas;

Ajay Mago, my publisher, and Dipa Chaudhuri, editor-in-chief at Om Books International, you have been my encouragement throughout, with all my projects—from *Turning the Page* to *Delhi Anything Goes* to this one, which has been held in high esteem;

The women who encouraged me to write this work of fiction. I appreciate you for sharing your struggles with me.

My late father once told me, "I'm still waiting for you to write your book," and that was when I didn't know I could! So thank you, Dad, and cheers to you up there;

My mother, my greatest guide and guard except in the end, the roles were reversed and I became your mother—nursing and nurturing you whilst you filled my soul and taught me unconditional love. I salute to the maternal love that knows no bounds when it comes to giving and loving. You live through me and in the end, I saw heaven in your eyes. I know you fill the thoughts in me as I write;

My brothers Rajan, Ajay, Sanjay and Sanjeev, each with your own merits, you all have inspired me;

Rittu and Selena, you have stood by me all the way;

Kajal and Amit, you both give reasons to laugh without reason and I love you for your cheerful spirit. My life is dull without you;

My Guruji, you are and will always be my greatest saviour—my mother, father and best friend, all rolled in one;

The last, but certainly not the least, Aparna Kumar, my editor, I couldn't have brought this book to a fantastic evolution had it not been for your inputs, so thank you ever so much.

I believe in this book because of you all.